ARCHIE & FRIENDS ALL-STARS

Archie's HAUNTED HOUSE

CO-CEO: JONATHAN GOLDWATER

CO-CEO: NANCY SILBERKLEIT

PRESIDENT: MIKE PELLERITO

CO-PRESIDENT/EDITOR-IN-CHIEF: VICTOR GORELICK

DIRECTOR OF CIRCULATION: BILL HORAN

D0951803

ARCHIE & FRIENDS ALL STARS, Volume [...] Haunted House. Printed in USA. Published by Archie Comic Publications, Inc., 325 Fayette Avenue, Mamaroneck, New York 10543-2318. Archie characters created by John L. Goldwater; the likenesses of the original Archie characters were created by Bob Montana. The individual characters' names and likenesses are the exclusive trademarks of Archie Comic Publications, Inc. All stories previously published and copyrighted by Archie Comic Publications, Inc. (or its predecessors) in magazine form in 1995-2009. This compilation copyright © 2010 Archie Comic Publications, Inc. All rights reserved. Nothing may be reprinted in whole or part without written permission from Archie Comic Publications, Inc.

ISBN: 978-1-879794-52-8

COVER ARTIST: FERNANDO RUIZ

COVER COLORIST: TITO PEÑA

WRITERS:
FERNANDO RUIZ, BATTON LASH, DAN PARENT, GEORGE GLADIR

ARTISTS:
FERNANDO RUIZ, STAN GOLDBERG, DAN PARENT, MARK MCKENNA, HENRY SCARPELLI, RICH KOSLOWSKI, JACK MORELLI, BILL YOSHIDA, GLENN WHITMORE, BARRY GROSSMAN, DIGIKORE STUDIOS

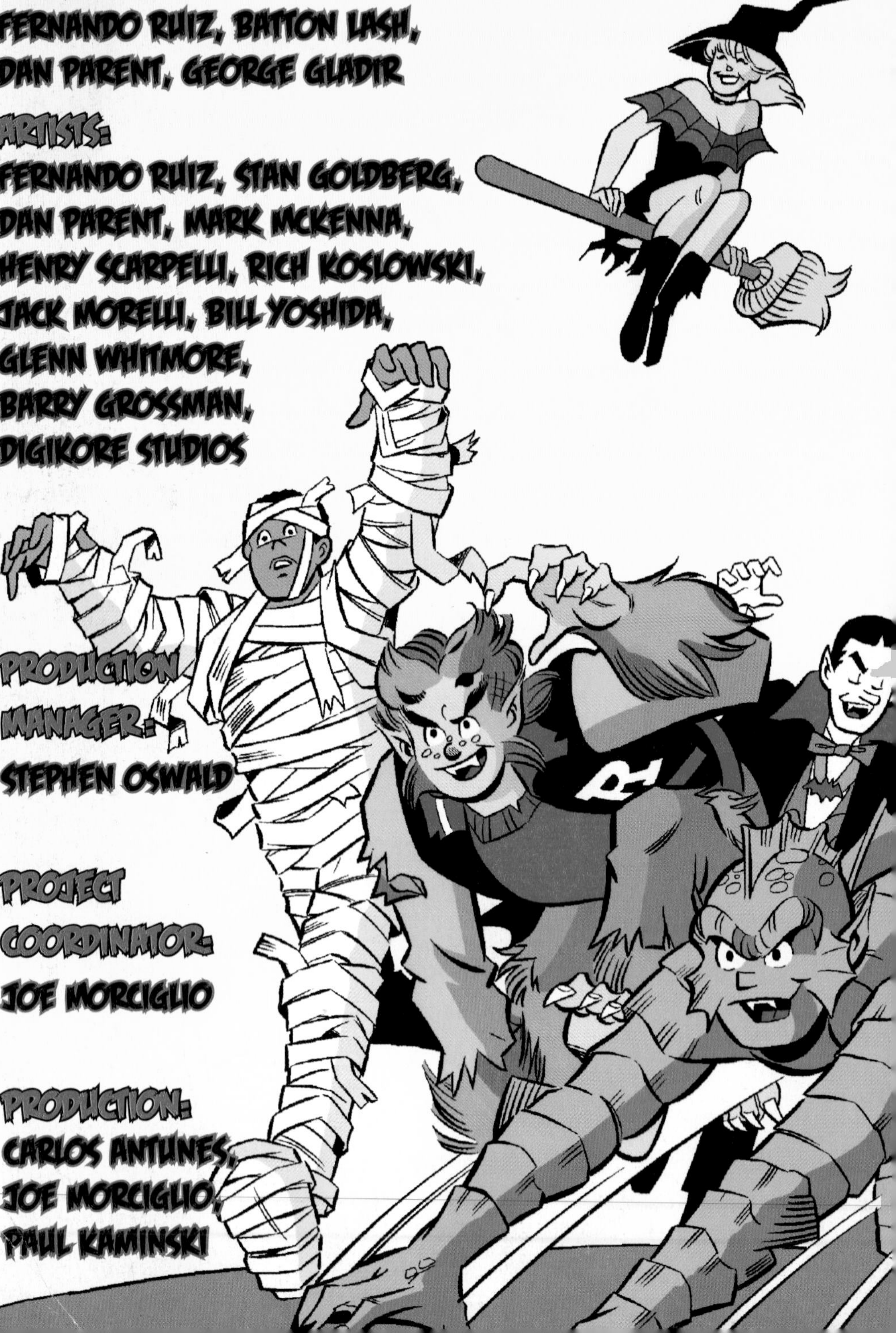

PRODUCTION MANAGER:
STEPHEN OSWALD

PROJECT COORDINATOR:
JOE MORCIGLIO

PRODUCTION:
CARLOS ANTUNES, JOE MORCIGLIO, PAUL KAMINSKI

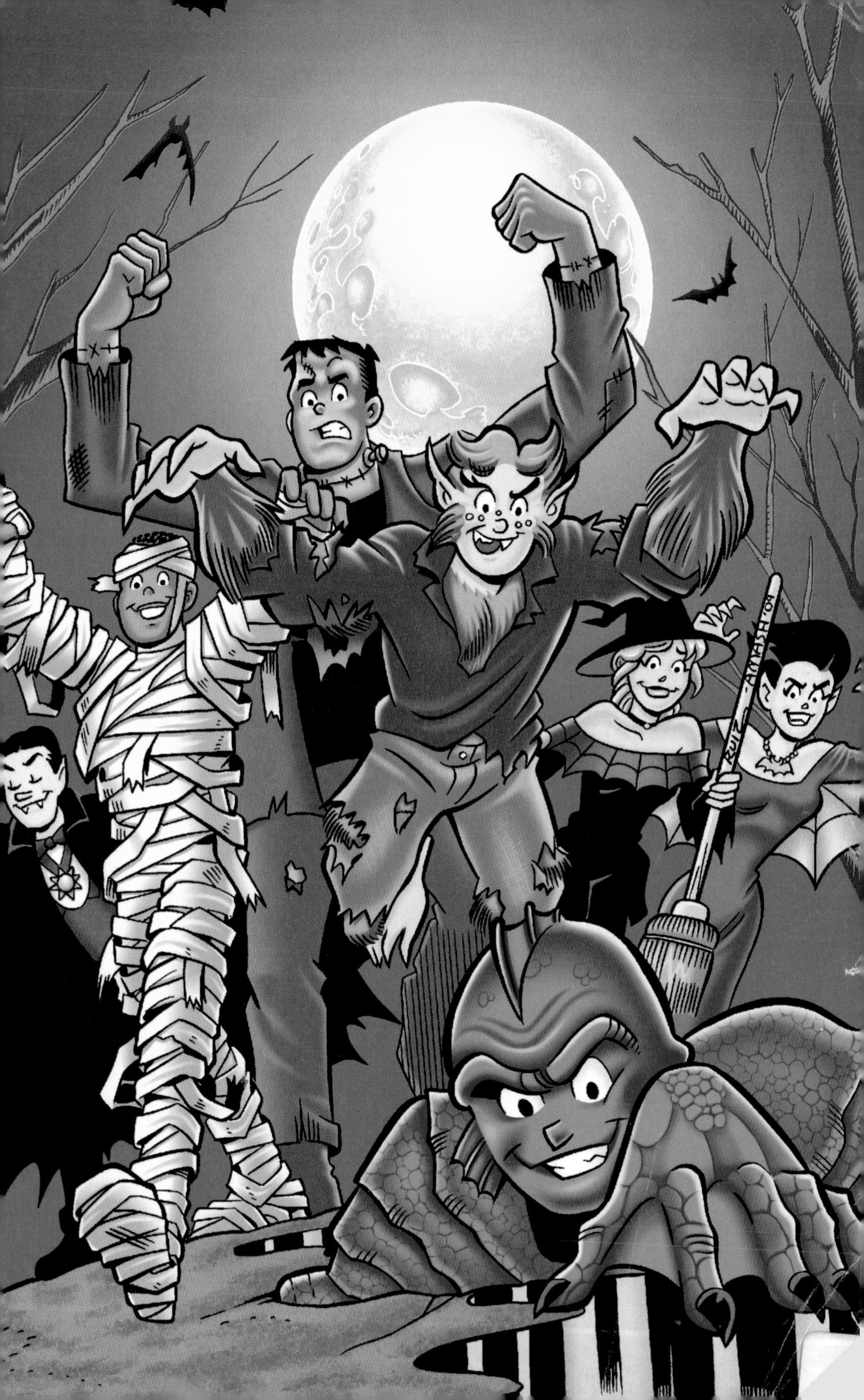

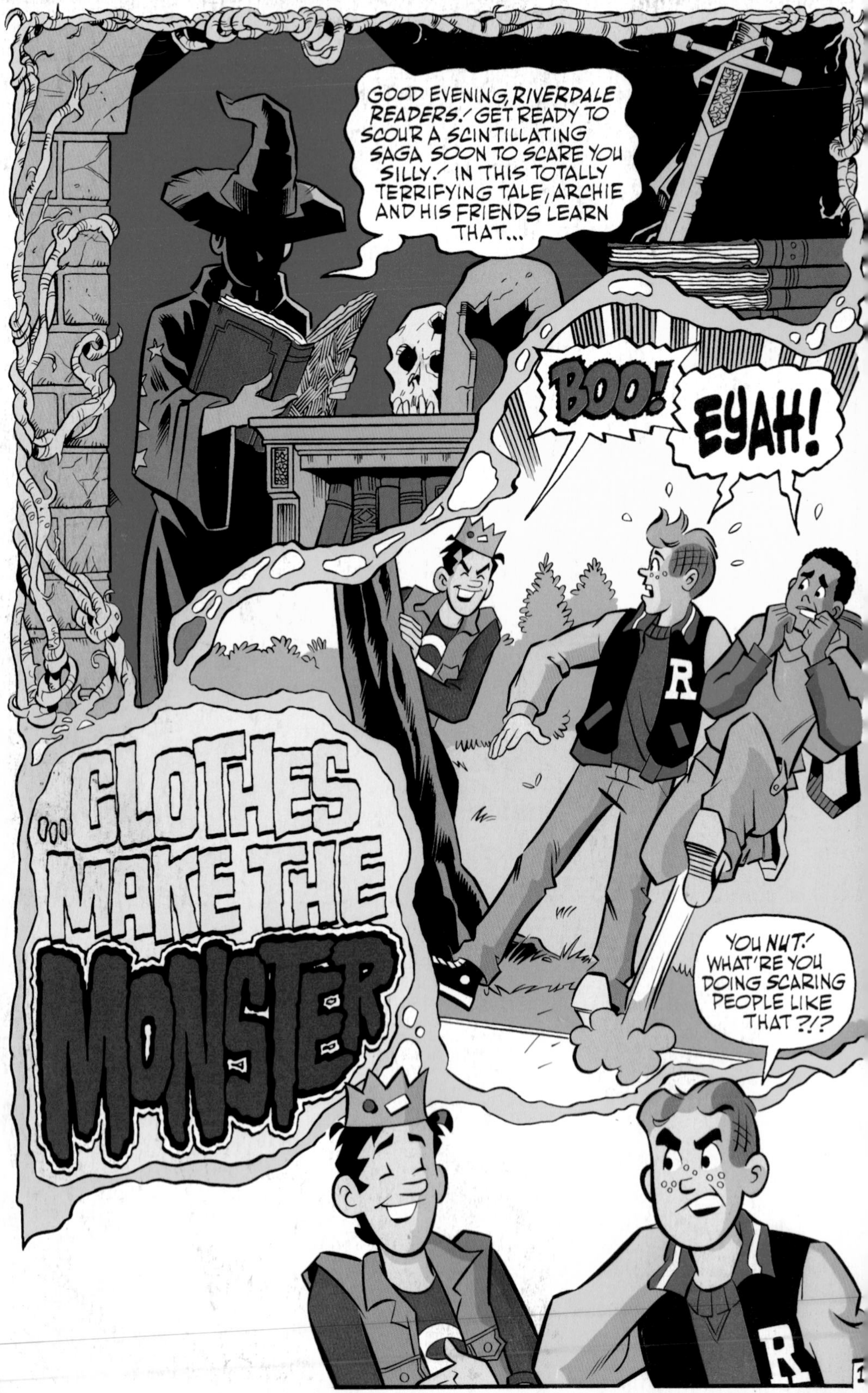
GOOD EVENING, RIVERDALE READERS! GET READY TO SCOUR A SCINTILLATING SAGA SOON TO SCARE YOU SILLY! IN THIS TOTALLY TERRIFYING TALE, ARCHIE AND HIS FRIENDS LEARN THAT...
BOO!
EYAH!
...CLOTHES MAKE THE MONSTER
YOU NUT! WHAT'RE YOU DOING SCARING PEOPLE LIKE THAT?!?
1

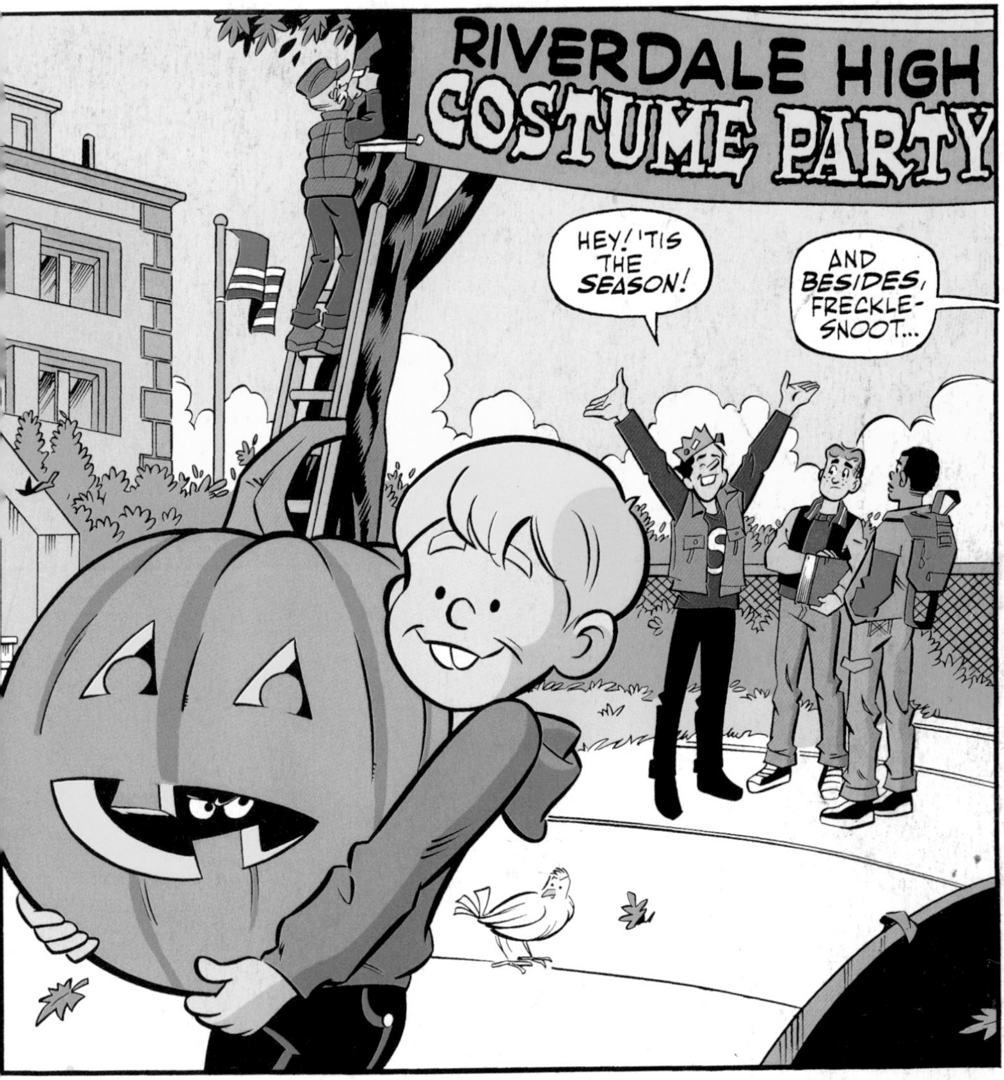
RIVERDALE HIGH
COSTUME PARTY
HEY! 'TIS THE SEASON!
AND BESIDES, FRECKLE-SNOOT...

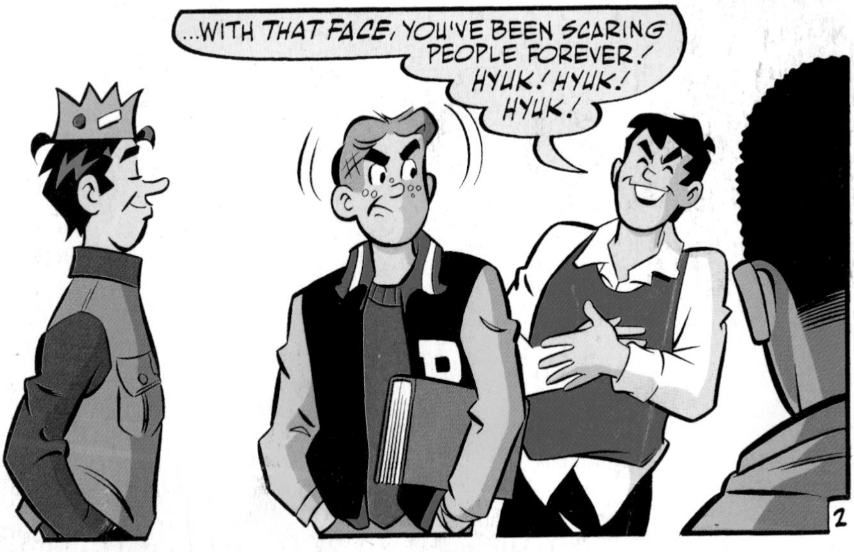
...WITH THAT FACE, YOU'VE BEEN SCARING PEOPLE FOREVER! HYUK! HYUK! HYUK!
2

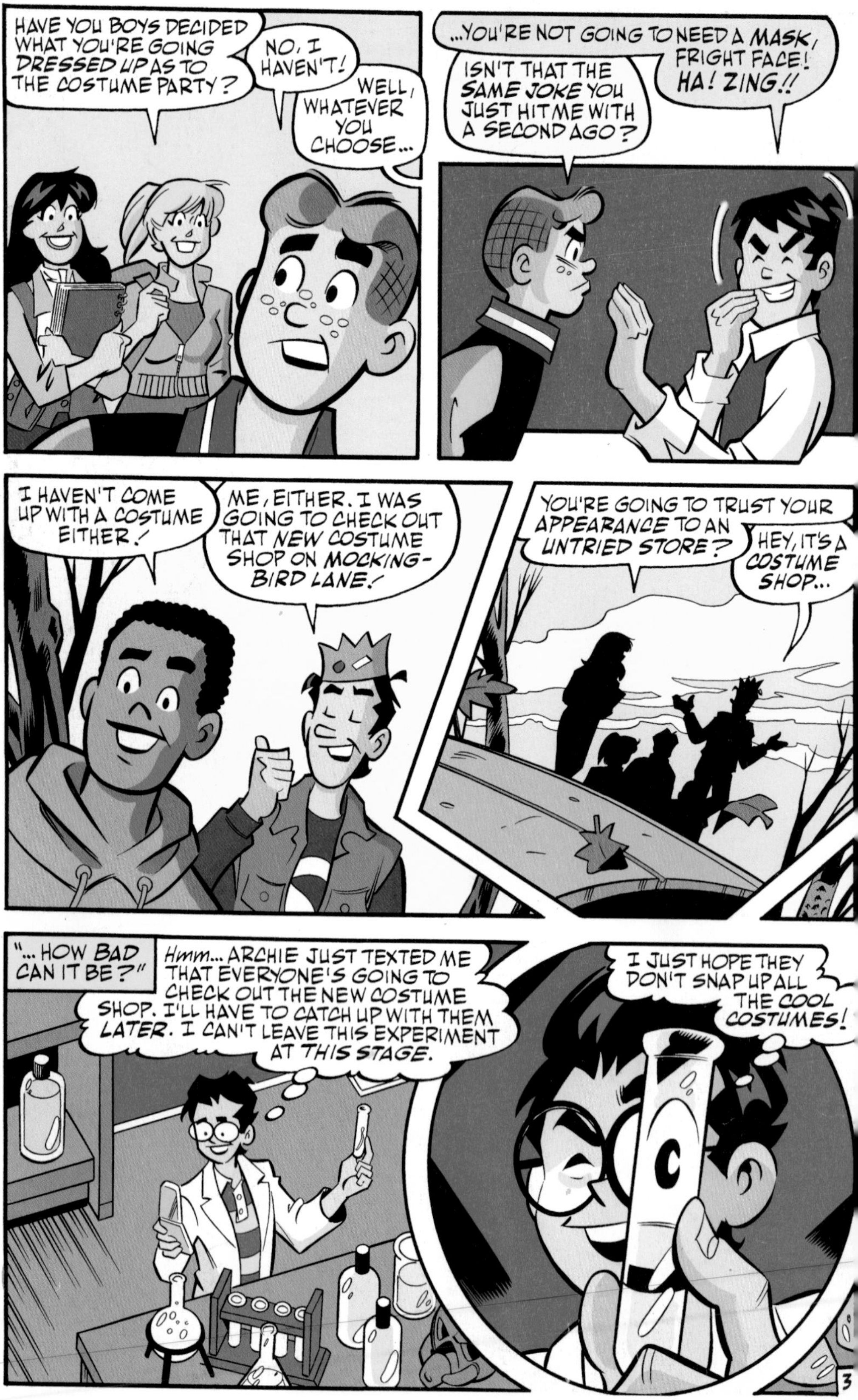
HAVE YOU BOYS DECIDED WHAT YOU'RE GOING DRESSED UP AS TO THE COSTUME PARTY?
NO, I HAVEN'T!
WELL, WHATEVER YOU CHOOSE...
...YOU'RE NOT GOING TO NEED A MASK, FRIGHT FACE! HA! ZING!!
ISN'T THAT THE SAME JOKE YOU JUST HIT ME WITH A SECOND AGO?
I HAVEN'T COME UP WITH A COSTUME EITHER!
ME, EITHER. I WAS GOING TO CHECK OUT THAT NEW COSTUME SHOP ON MOCKING-BIRD LANE!
YOU'RE GOING TO TRUST YOUR APPEARANCE TO AN UNTRIED STORE?
HEY, IT'S A COSTUME SHOP...
"... HOW BAD CAN IT BE?"
Hmm... ARCHIE JUST TEXTED ME THAT EVERYONE'S GOING TO CHECK OUT THE NEW COSTUME SHOP. I'LL HAVE TO CATCH UP WITH THEM LATER. I CAN'T LEAVE THIS EXPERIMENT AT THIS STAGE.
I JUST HOPE THEY DON'T SNAP UP ALL THE COOL COSTUMES!
3

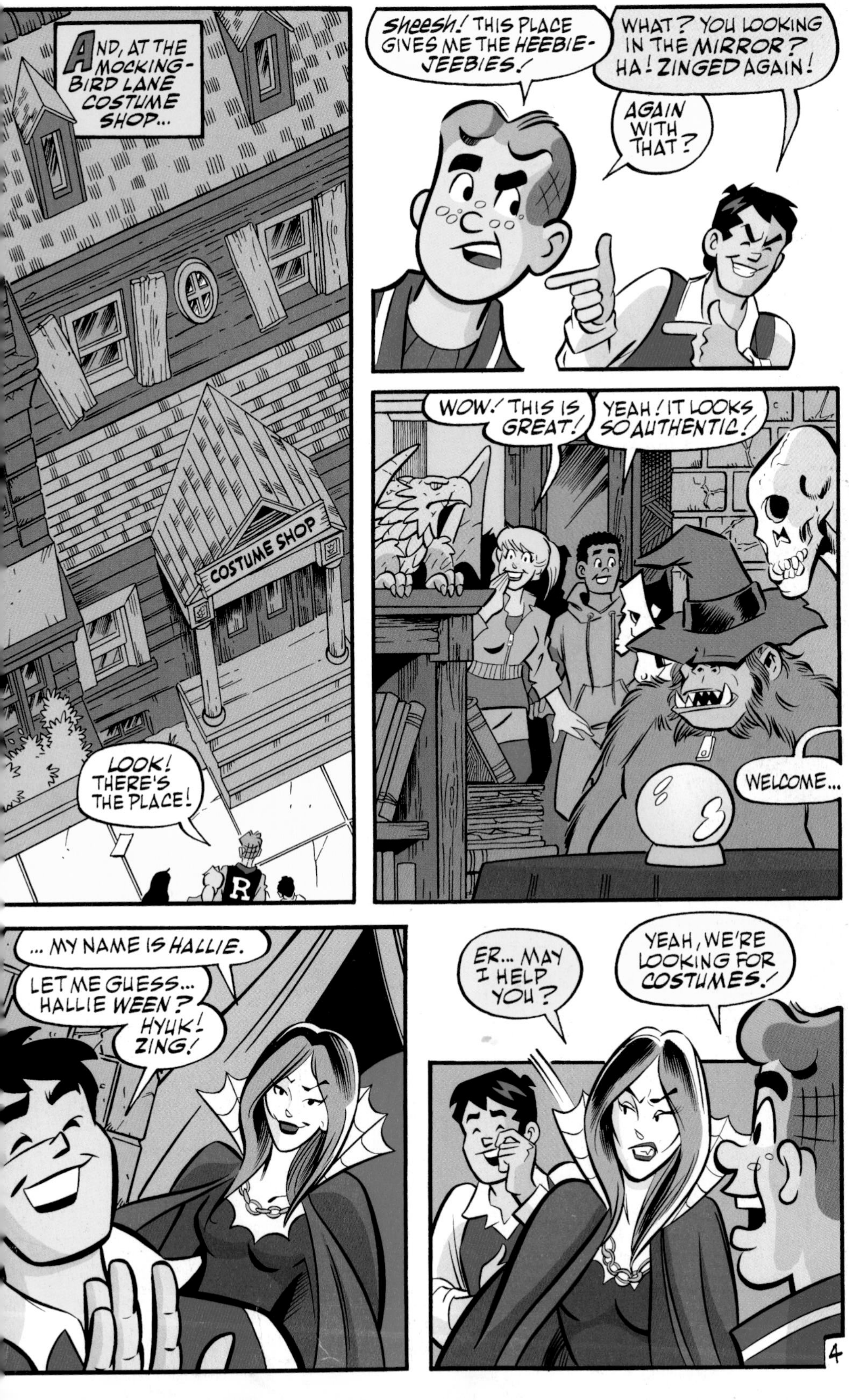
AND, AT THE MOCKING-BIRD LANE COSTUME SHOP...
COSTUME SHOP
LOOK! THERE'S THE PLACE!
SHEESH! THIS PLACE GIVES ME THE HEEBIE-JEEBIES!
WHAT? YOU LOOKING IN THE MIRROR? HA! ZINGED AGAIN!
AGAIN WITH THAT?
WOW! THIS IS GREAT!
YEAH! IT LOOKS SO AUTHENTIC!
WELCOME...
... MY NAME IS HALLIE.
LET ME GUESS... HALLIE WEEN?
HYUK! ZING!
ER... MAY I HELP YOU?
YEAH, WE'RE LOOKING FOR COSTUMES!
4

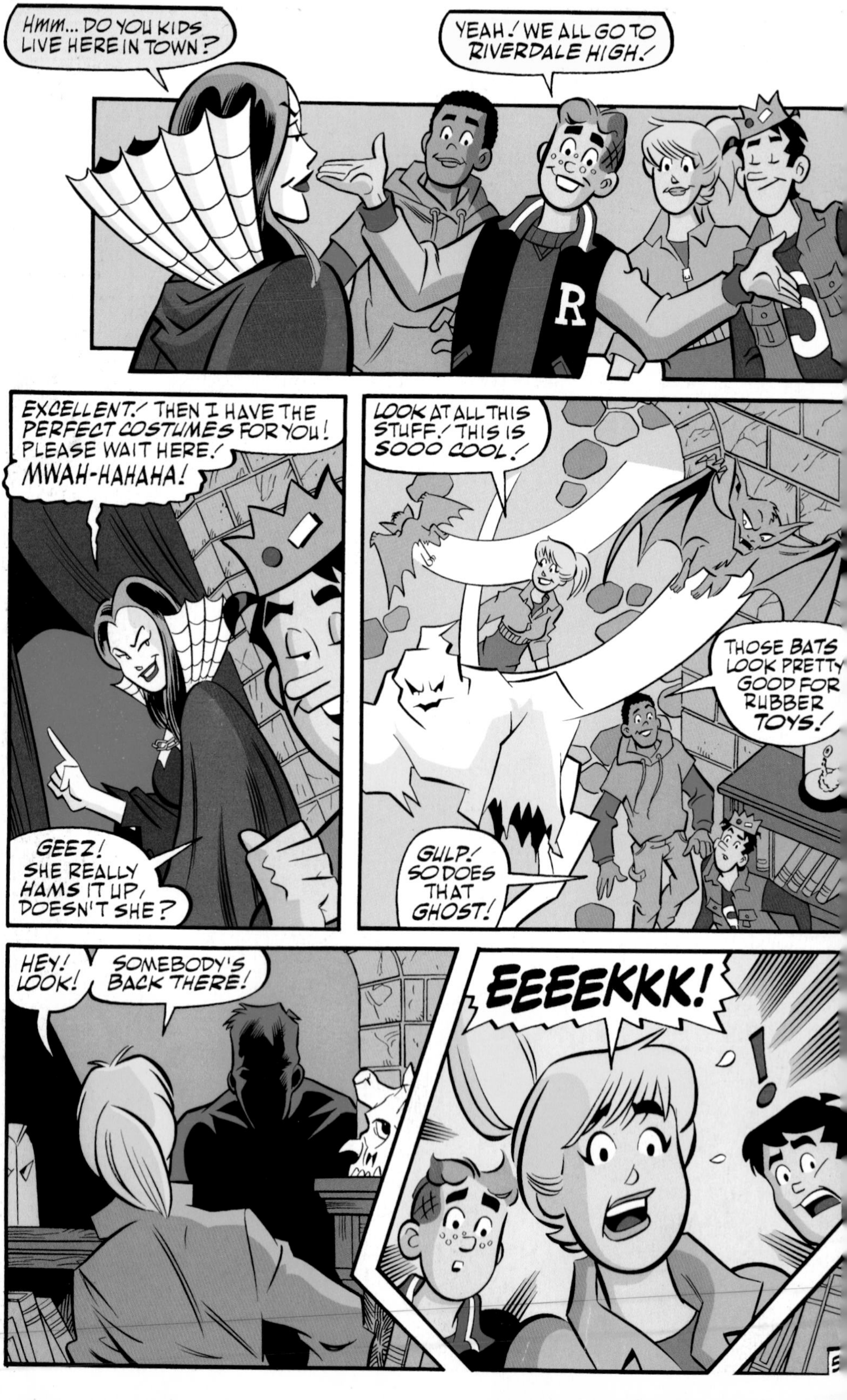
HMM... DO YOU KIDS LIVE HERE IN TOWN?
YEAH! WE ALL GO TO RIVERDALE HIGH!
EXCELLENT! THEN I HAVE THE PERFECT COSTUMES FOR YOU! PLEASE WAIT HERE!
MWAH-HAHAHA!
GEEZ! SHE REALLY HAMS IT UP, DOESN'T SHE?
LOOK AT ALL THIS STUFF! THIS IS SOOO COOL!
THOSE BATS LOOK PRETTY GOOD FOR RUBBER TOYS!
GULP! SO DOES THAT GHOST!
HEY! LOOK!
SOMEBODY'S BACK THERE!
EEEEKKK!
!

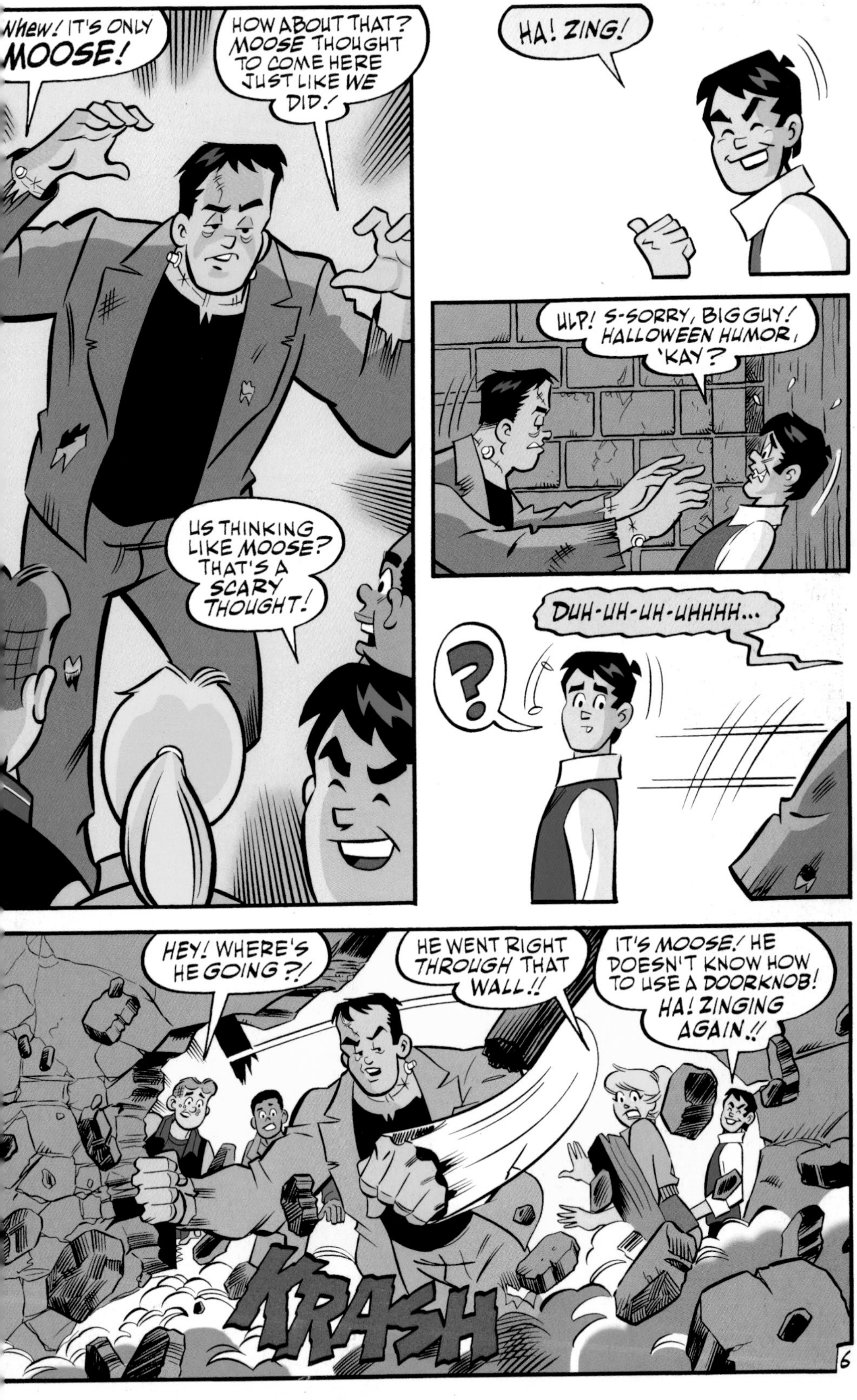
WHEW! IT'S ONLY MOOSE!
HOW ABOUT THAT? MOOSE THOUGHT TO COME HERE JUST LIKE WE DID!
US THINKING LIKE MOOSE? THAT'S A SCARY THOUGHT!
HA! ZING!
ULP! S-SORRY, BIG GUY! HALLOWEEN HUMOR, 'KAY?
?
DUH-UH-UH-UHHHH...
HEY! WHERE'S HE GOING?!
HE WENT RIGHT THROUGH THAT WALL!!
IT'S MOOSE! HE DOESN'T KNOW HOW TO USE A DOORKNOB! HA! ZINGING AGAIN!!
KRASH
6

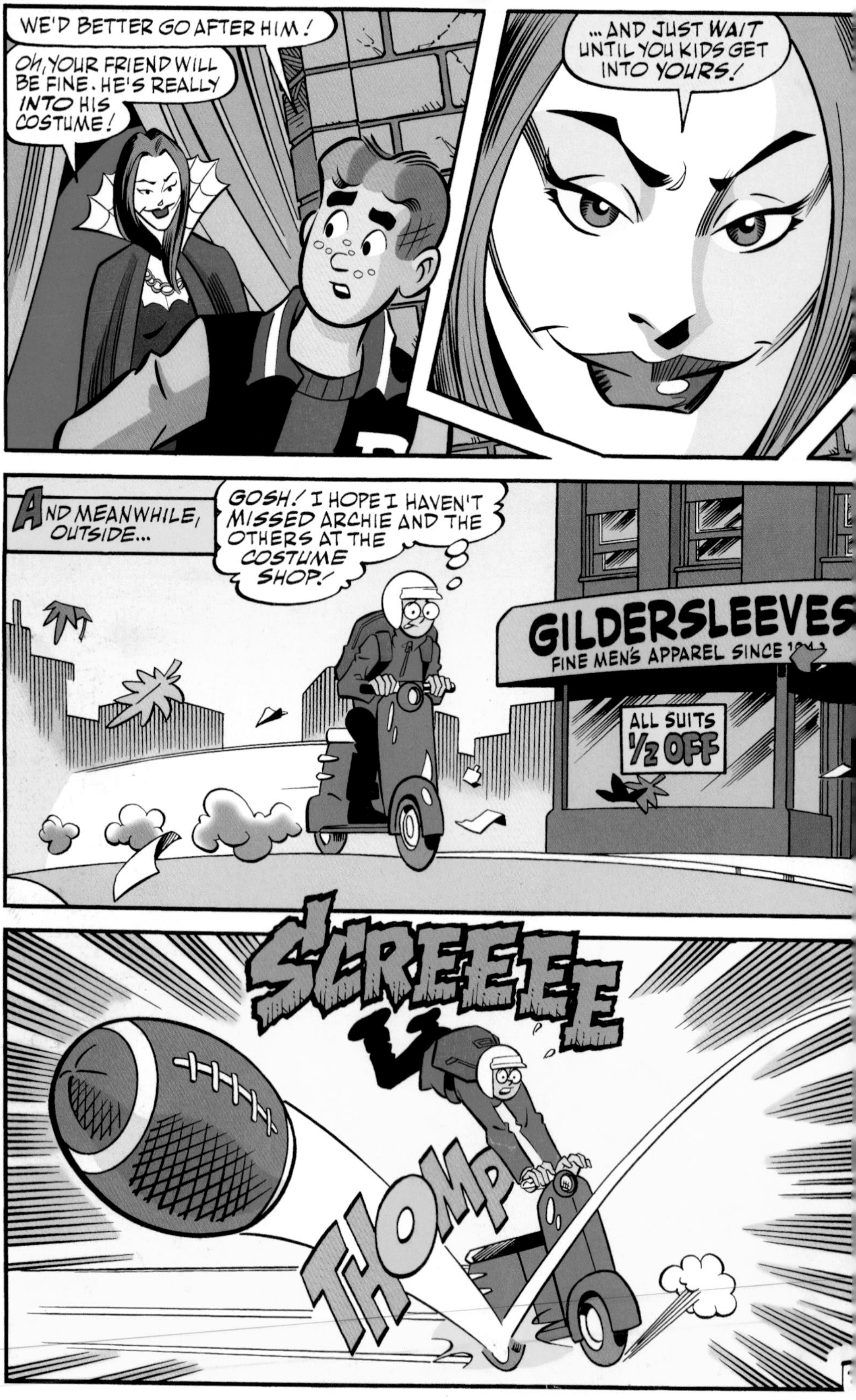
WE'D BETTER GO AFTER HIM!
Oh, YOUR FRIEND WILL BE FINE. HE'S REALLY INTO HIS COSTUME!
...AND JUST WAIT UNTIL YOU KIDS GET INTO YOURS!
AND MEANWHILE, OUTSIDE...
GOSH! I HOPE I HAVEN'T MISSED ARCHIE AND THE OTHERS AT THE COSTUME SHOP!
GILDERSLEEVES
FINE MEN'S APPAREL SINCE
ALL SUITS 1/2 OFF
SCREEEEE
THOMP

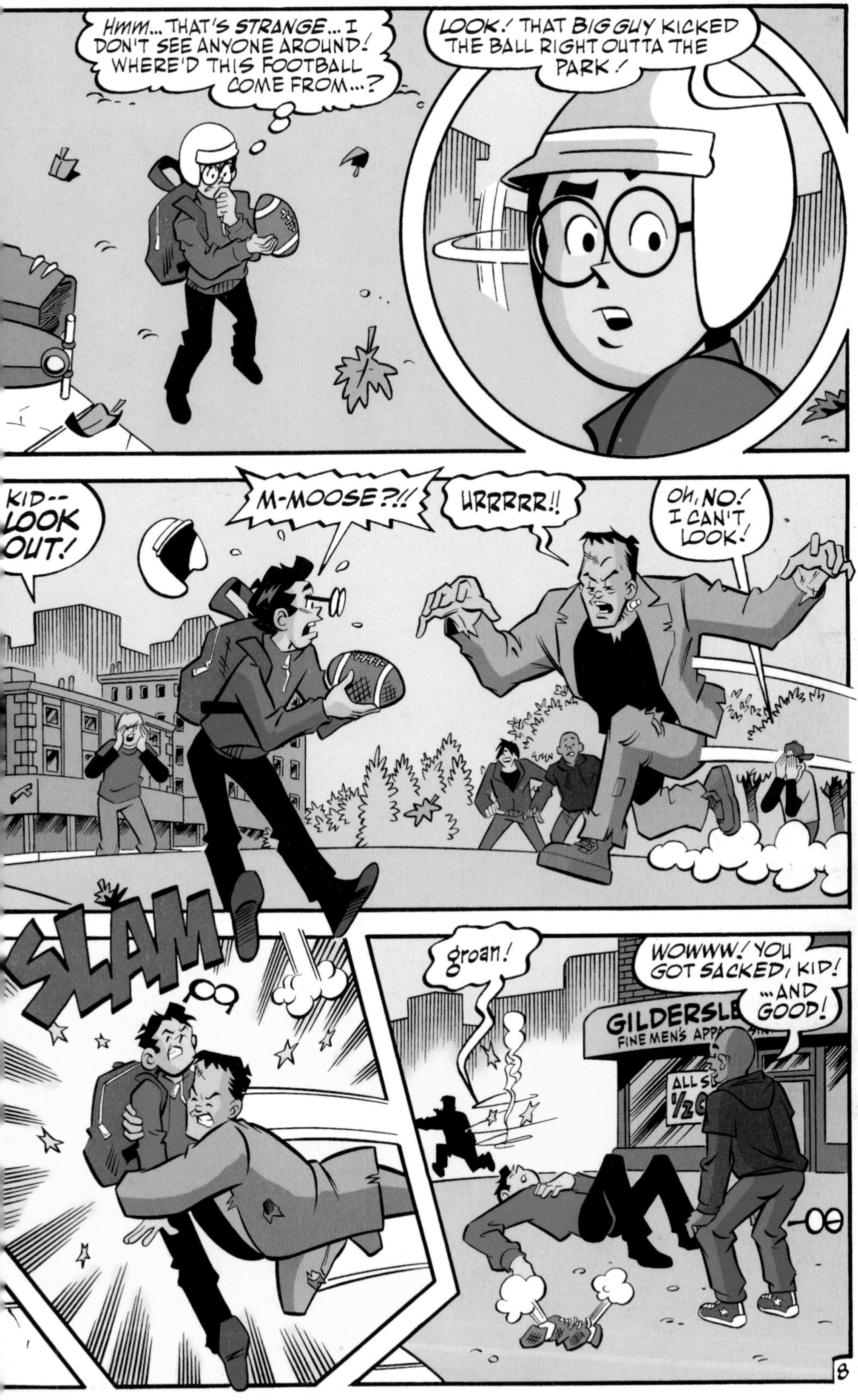
HMM... THAT'S STRANGE... I DON'T SEE ANYONE AROUND! WHERE'D THIS FOOTBALL COME FROM...?
LOOK! THAT BIG GUY KICKED THE BALL RIGHT OUTTA THE PARK!
KID-- LOOK OUT!
M-MOOSE?!!
URRRRR!!
OH, NO! I CAN'T LOOK!
SLAM
groan!
WOWWW! YOU GOT SACKED, KID! ...AND GOOD!
FINE MEN'S APPA

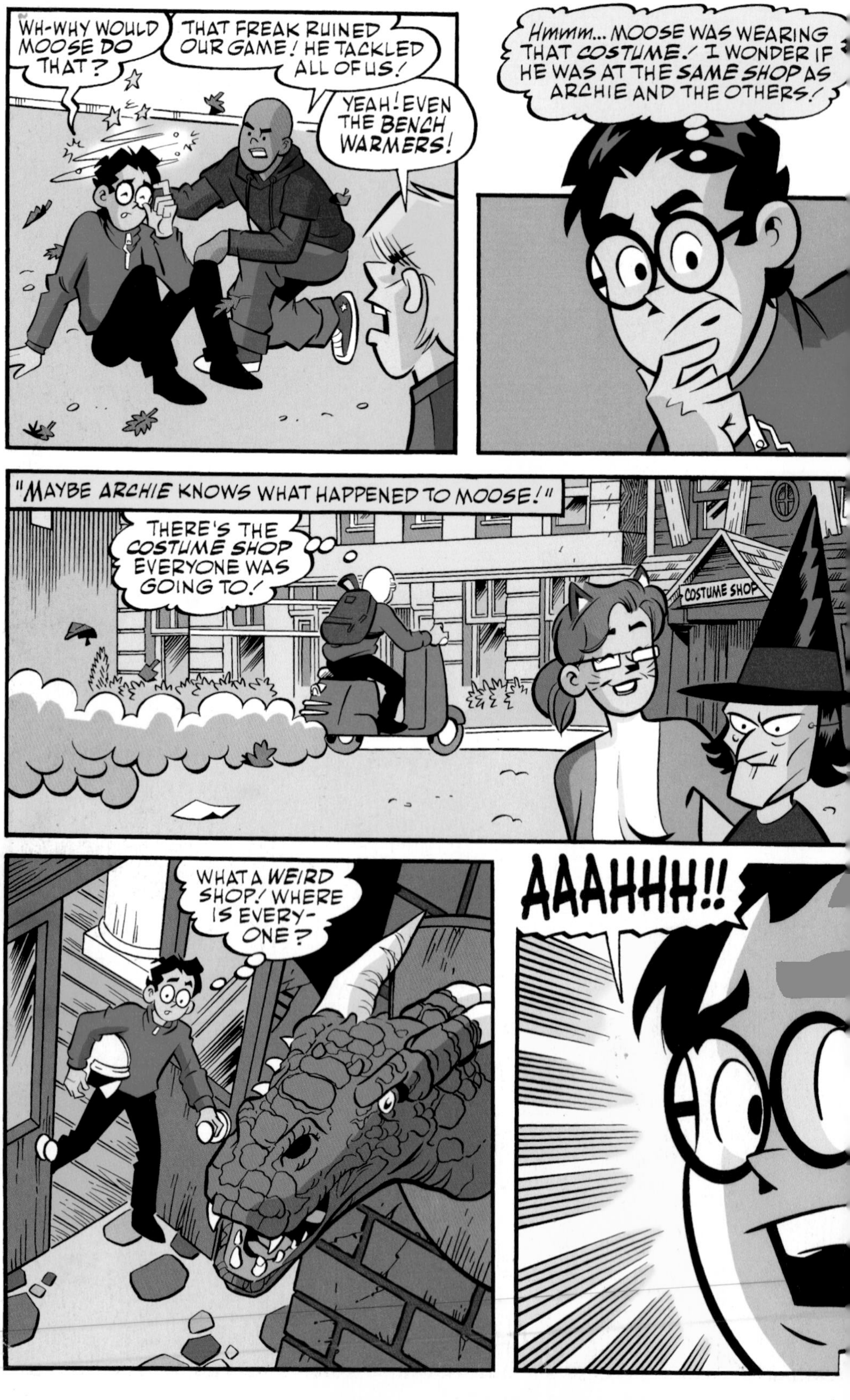
WH-WHY WOULD MOOSE DO THAT?
THAT FREAK RUINED OUR GAME! HE TACKLED ALL OF US!
YEAH! EVEN THE BENCH WARMERS!
Hmmm... MOOSE WAS WEARING THAT COSTUME! I WONDER IF HE WAS AT THE SAME SHOP AS ARCHIE AND THE OTHERS!
"MAYBE ARCHIE KNOWS WHAT HAPPENED TO MOOSE!"
THERE'S THE COSTUME SHOP EVERYONE WAS GOING TO!
COSTUME SHOP
WHAT A WEIRD SHOP! WHERE IS EVERY-ONE?
AAAHHH!!

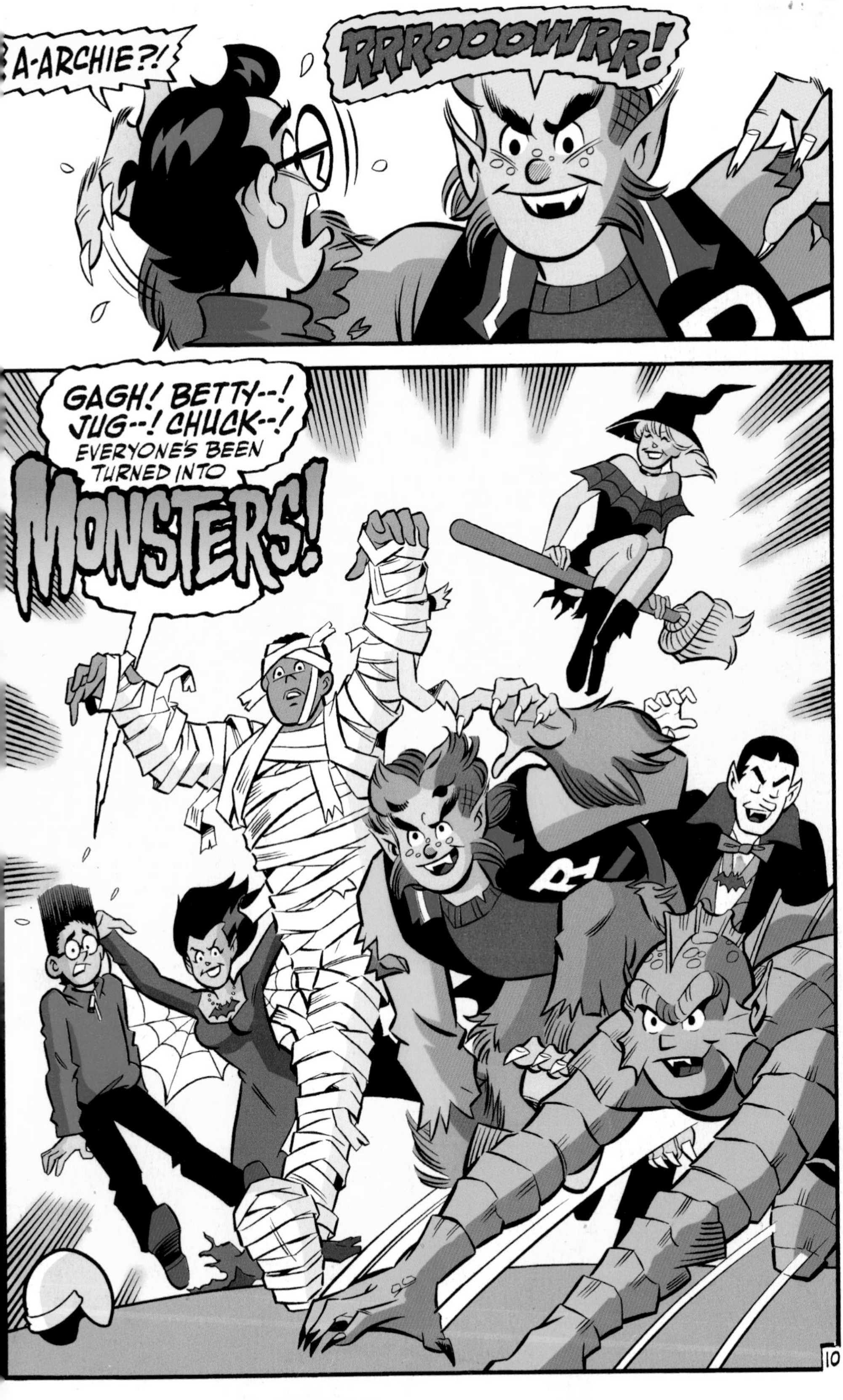
A-ARCHIE?!
RRROOOWRR!
GAGH! BETTY--! JUG--! CHUCK--! EVERYONE'S BEEN TURNED INTO MONSTERS!
10

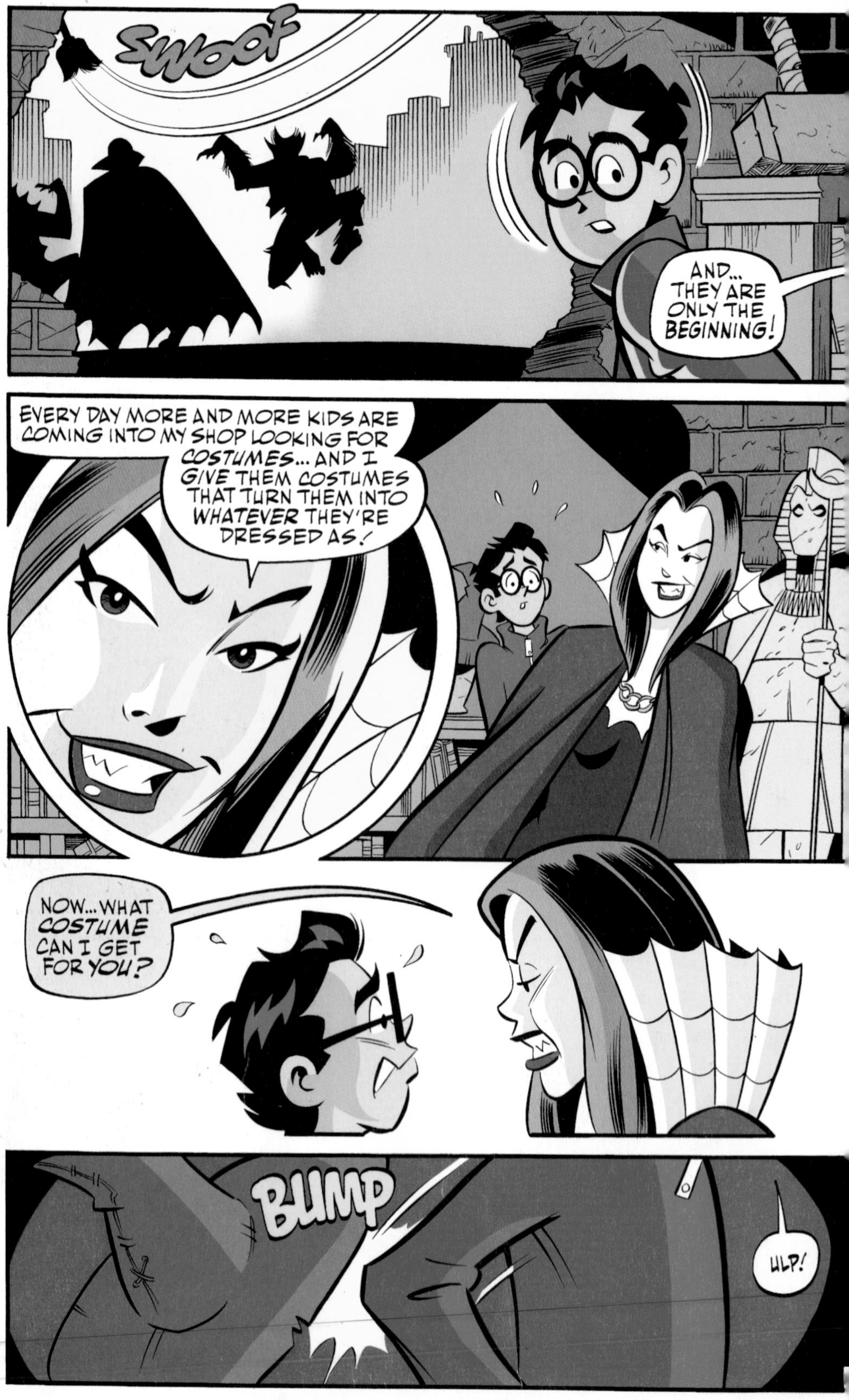
SWOOF
AND... THEY ARE ONLY THE BEGINNING!
EVERY DAY MORE AND MORE KIDS ARE COMING INTO MY SHOP LOOKING FOR COSTUMES... AND I GIVE THEM COSTUMES THAT TURN THEM INTO WHATEVER THEY'RE DRESSED AS!
NOW... WHAT COSTUME CAN I GET FOR YOU?
BUMP
ULP!

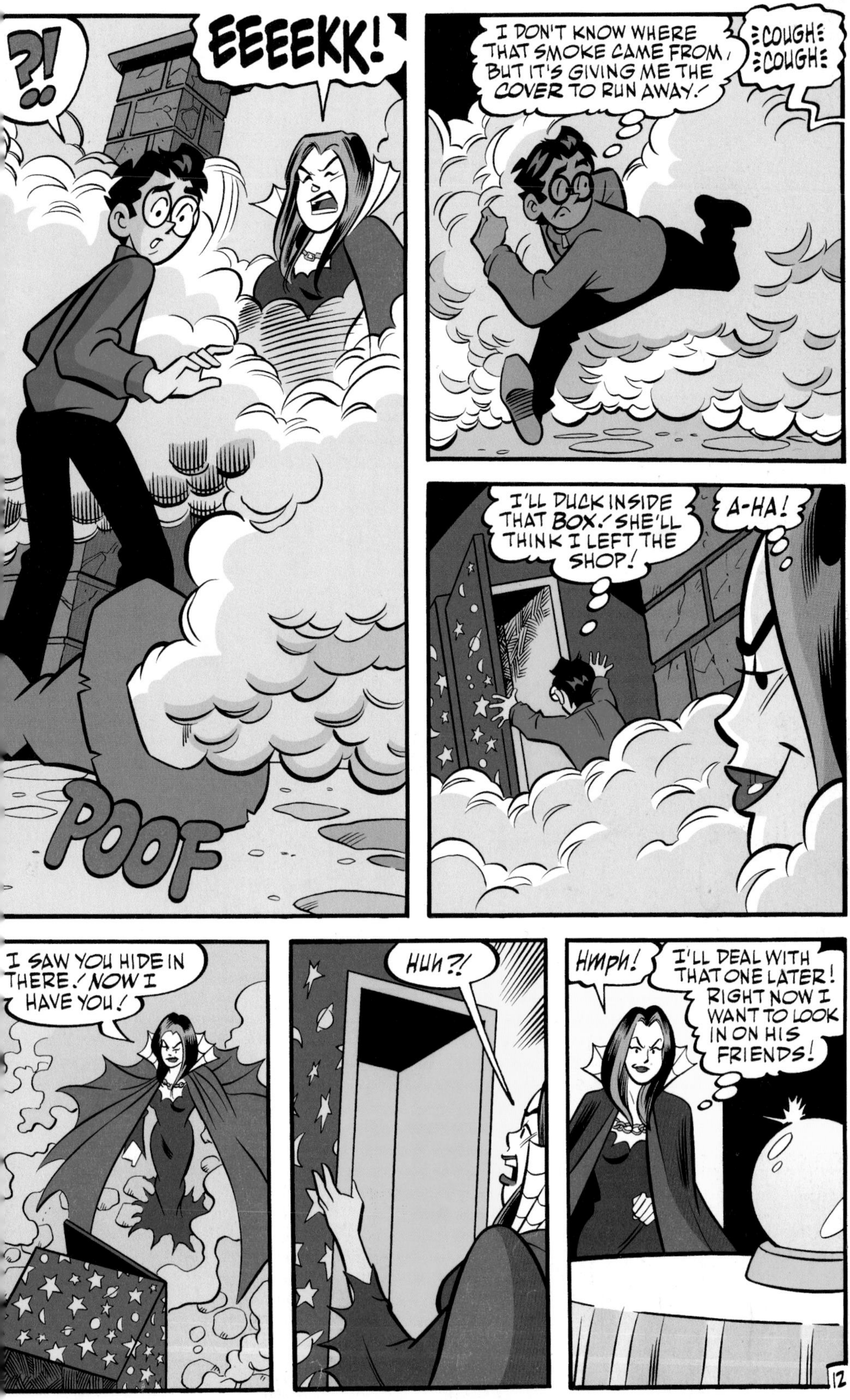
?!
EEEEKK!
POOF
I DON'T KNOW WHERE THAT SMOKE CAME FROM, BUT IT'S GIVING ME THE COVER TO RUN AWAY!
COUGH COUGH
I'LL DUCK INSIDE THAT BOX! SHE'LL THINK I LEFT THE SHOP!
A-HA!
I SAW YOU HIDE IN THERE! NOW I HAVE YOU!
HUH?!
HMPH!
I'LL DEAL WITH THAT ONE LATER! RIGHT NOW I WANT TO LOOK IN ON HIS FRIENDS!
12

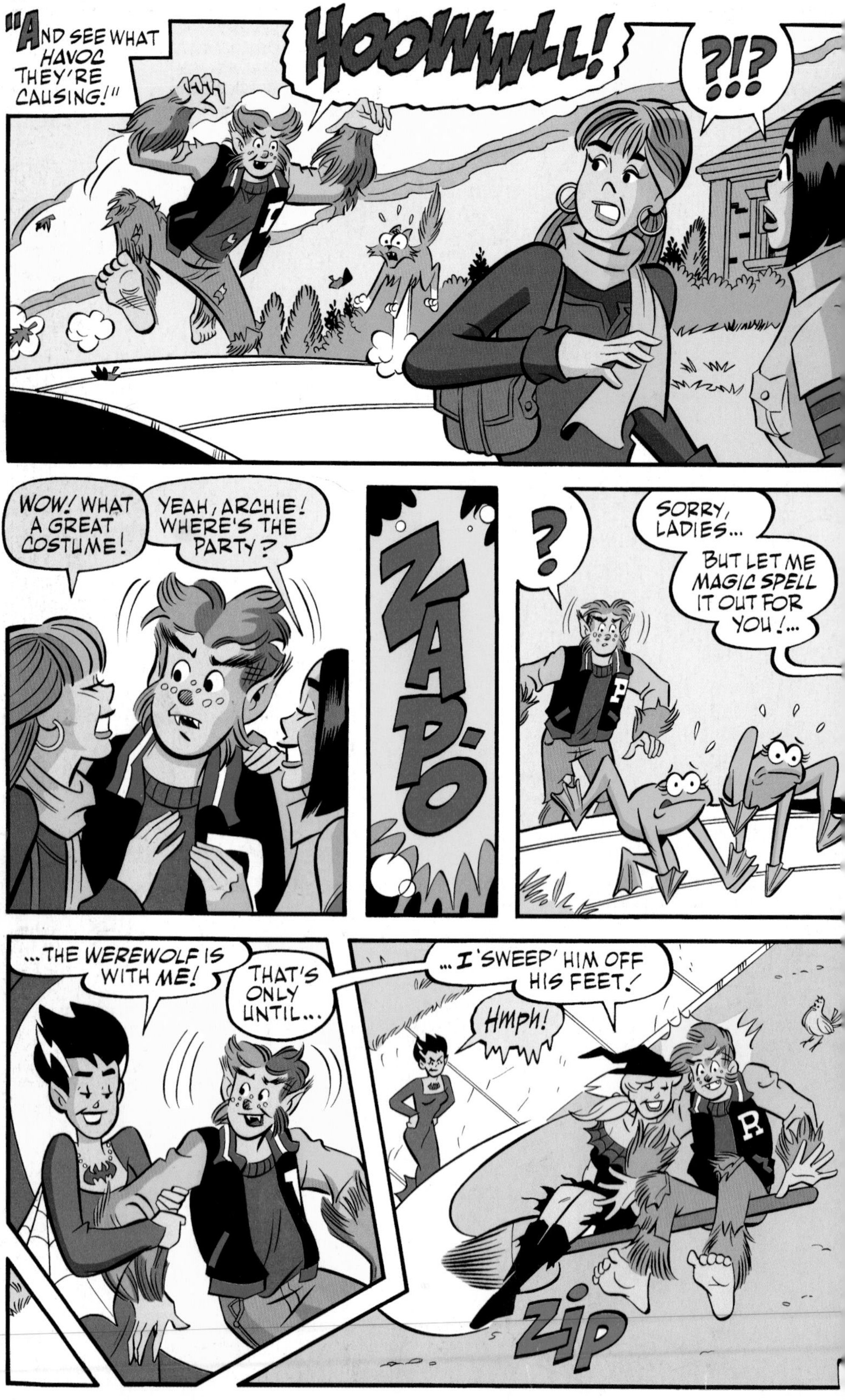
"AND SEE WHAT HAVOC THEY'RE CAUSING!"
HOOWWLL!
?!?
WOW! WHAT A GREAT COSTUME!
YEAH, ARCHIE! WHERE'S THE PARTY?
ZAPO
?
SORRY, LADIES...
BUT LET ME MAGIC SPELL IT OUT FOR YOU!...
...THE WEREWOLF IS WITH ME!
THAT'S ONLY UNTIL...
...I 'SWEEP' HIM OFF HIS FEET!
Hmph!
ZIP

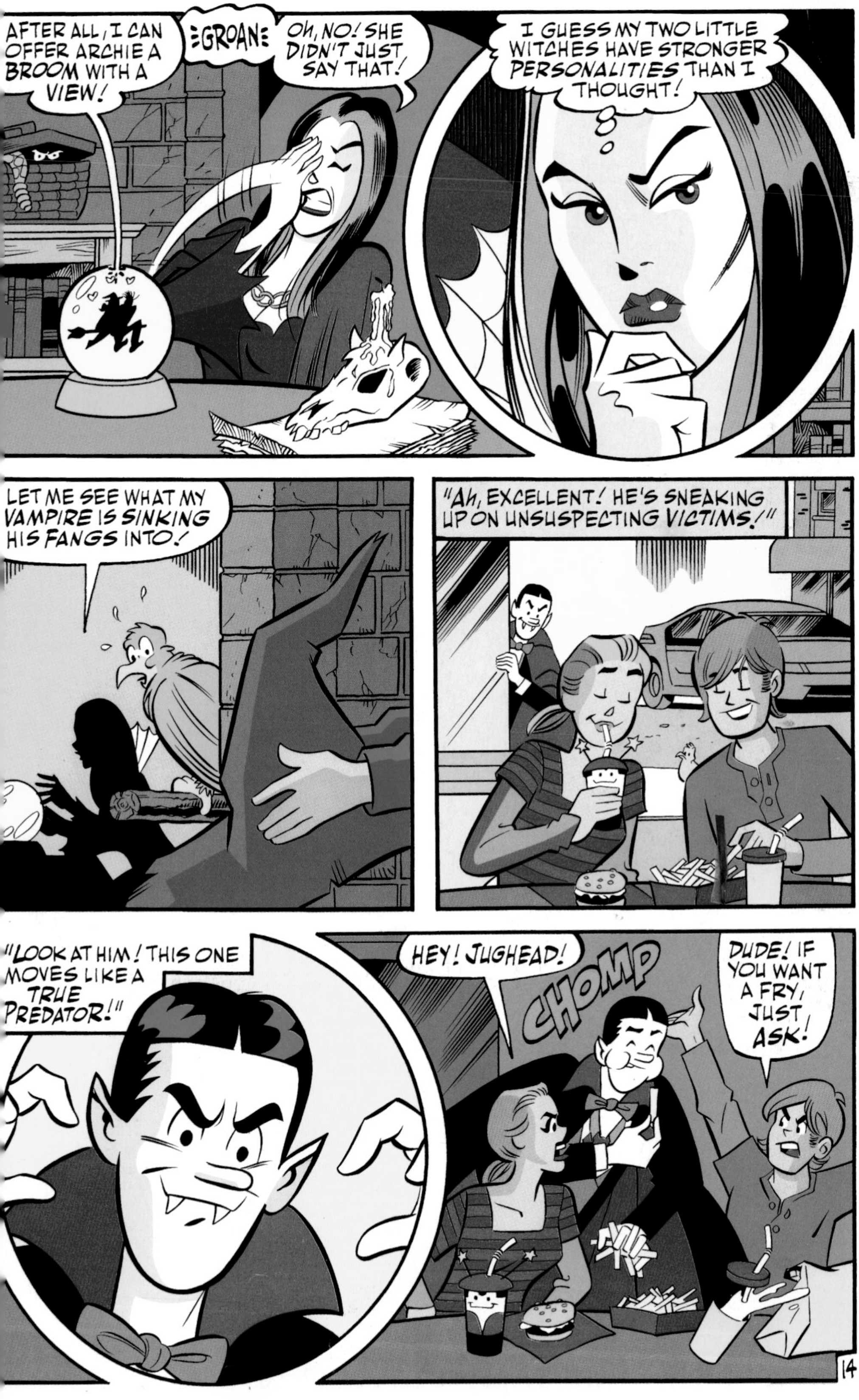
AFTER ALL, I CAN OFFER ARCHIE A BROOM WITH A VIEW!
GROAN
OH, NO! SHE DIDN'T JUST SAY THAT!
I GUESS MY TWO LITTLE WITCHES HAVE STRONGER PERSONALITIES THAN I THOUGHT!
LET ME SEE WHAT MY VAMPIRE IS SINKING HIS FANGS INTO!
"AH, EXCELLENT! HE'S SNEAKING UP ON UNSUSPECTING VICTIMS!"
"LOOK AT HIM! THIS ONE MOVES LIKE A TRUE PREDATOR!"
HEY! JUGHEAD!
CHOMP
DUDE! IF YOU WANT A FRY, JUST ASK!
14

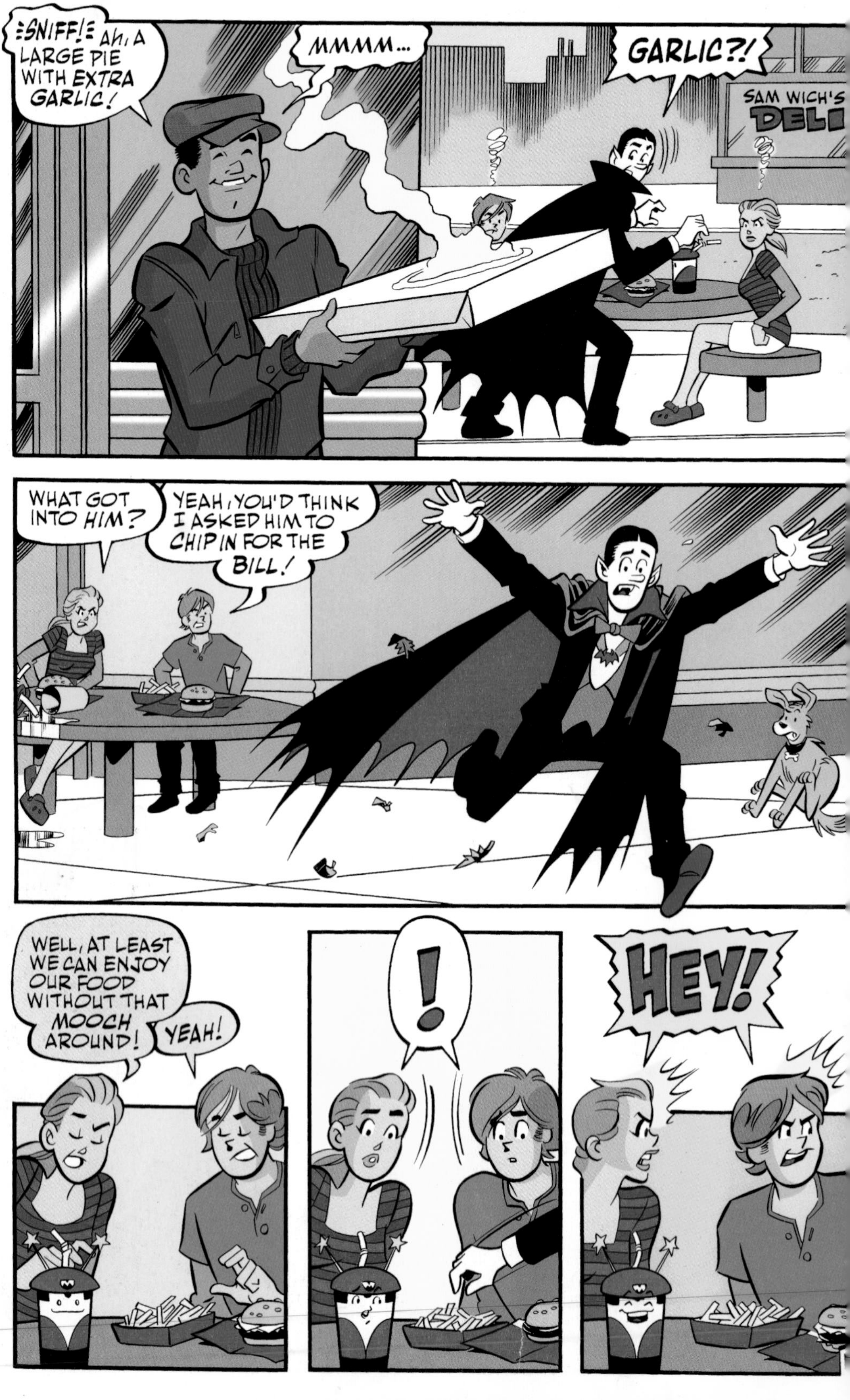
SNIFF! AH, A LARGE PIE WITH EXTRA GARLIC!
MMMM...
GARLIC?!
SAM WICH'S DELI
WHAT GOT INTO HIM?
YEAH, YOU'D THINK I ASKED HIM TO CHIP IN FOR THE BILL!
WELL, AT LEAST WE CAN ENJOY OUR FOOD WITHOUT THAT MOOCH AROUND!
YEAH!
!
HEY!

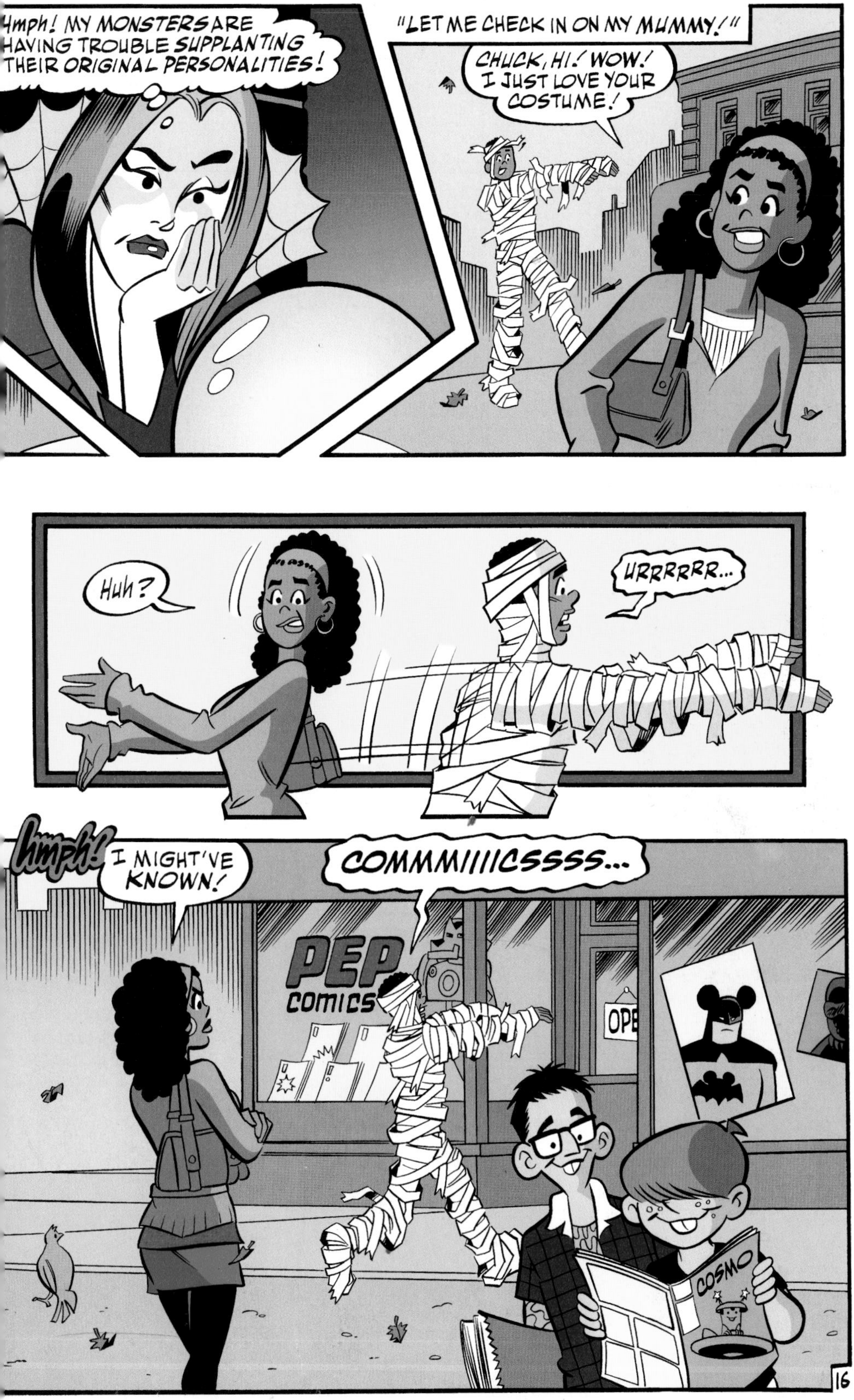
Hmph! MY MONSTERS ARE HAVING TROUBLE SUPPLANTING THEIR ORIGINAL PERSONALITIES!
"LET ME CHECK IN ON MY MUMMY!"
CHUCK, HI! WOW! I JUST LOVE YOUR COSTUME!
Huh?
URRRRRR...
Hmph!
I MIGHT'VE KNOWN!
COMMMIIIICSSSS...
PEP COMICS
OPE
COSMO

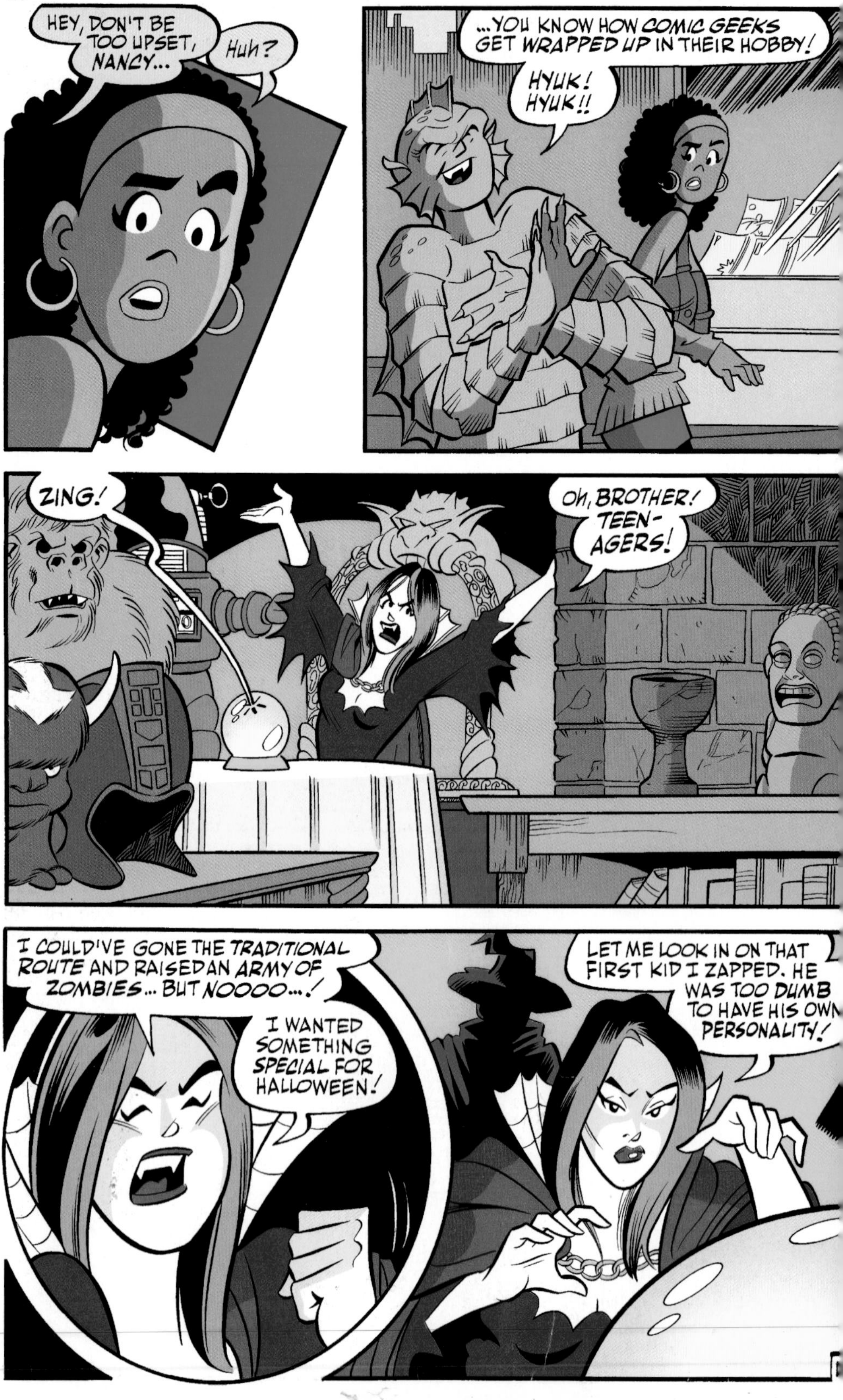
HEY, DON'T BE TOO UPSET, NANCY...
Huh?
...YOU KNOW HOW COMIC GEEKS GET WRAPPED UP IN THEIR HOBBY!
HYUK! HYUK!!
ZING!
Oh, BROTHER! TEEN-AGERS!
I COULD'VE GONE THE TRADITIONAL ROUTE AND RAISED AN ARMY OF ZOMBIES... BUT NOOOO...!
I WANTED SOMETHING SPECIAL FOR HALLOWEEN!
LET ME LOOK IN ON THAT FIRST KID I ZAPPED. HE WAS TOO DUMB TO HAVE HIS OWN PERSONALITY!

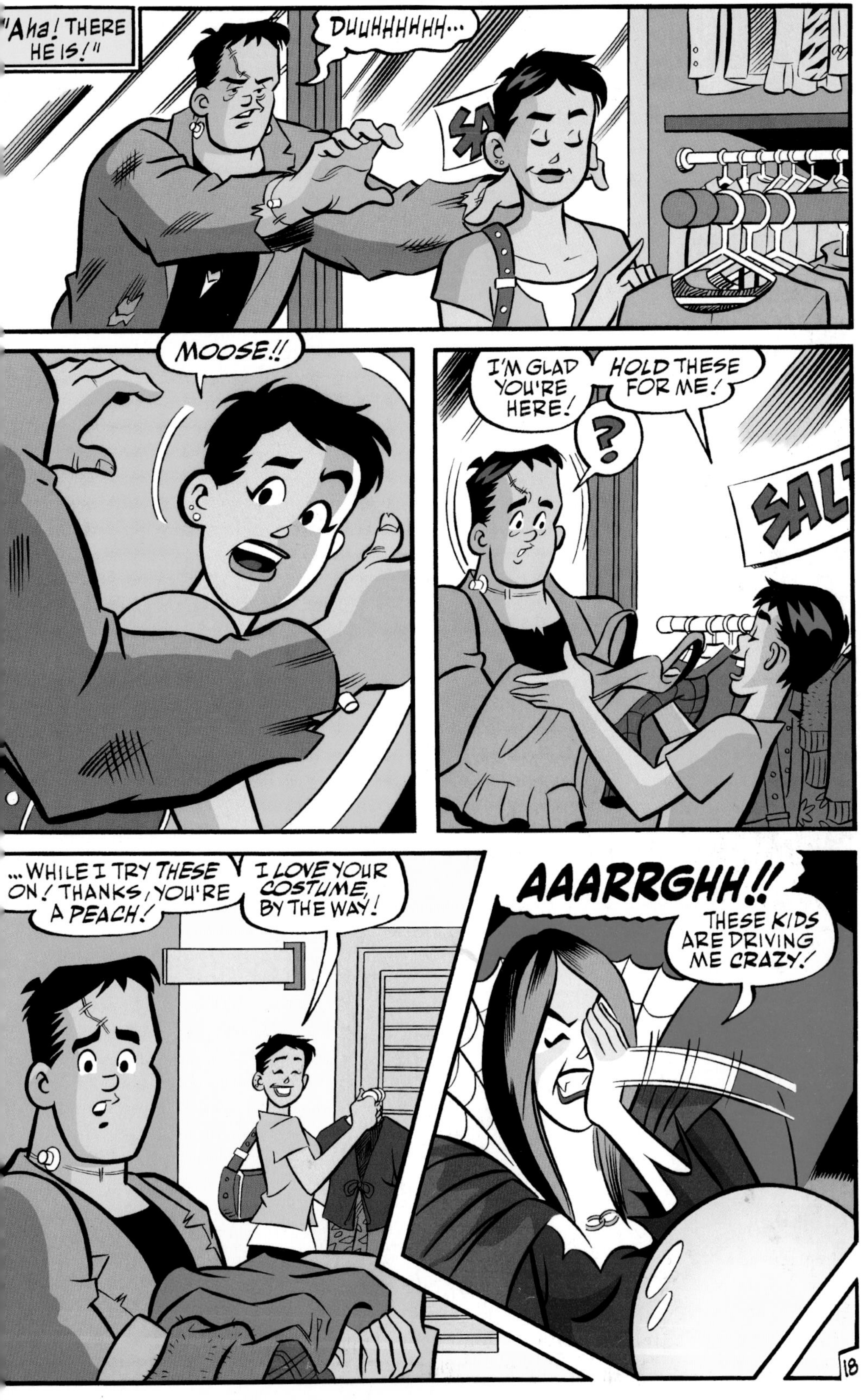
"AHA! THERE HE IS!"
DUUHHHHHH...
MOOSE!!
I'M GLAD YOU'RE HERE!
HOLD THESE FOR ME!
?
...WHILE I TRY THESE ON! THANKS, YOU'RE A PEACH!
I LOVE YOUR COSTUME, BY THE WAY!
AAARRGHH!!
THESE KIDS ARE DRIVING ME CRAZY!

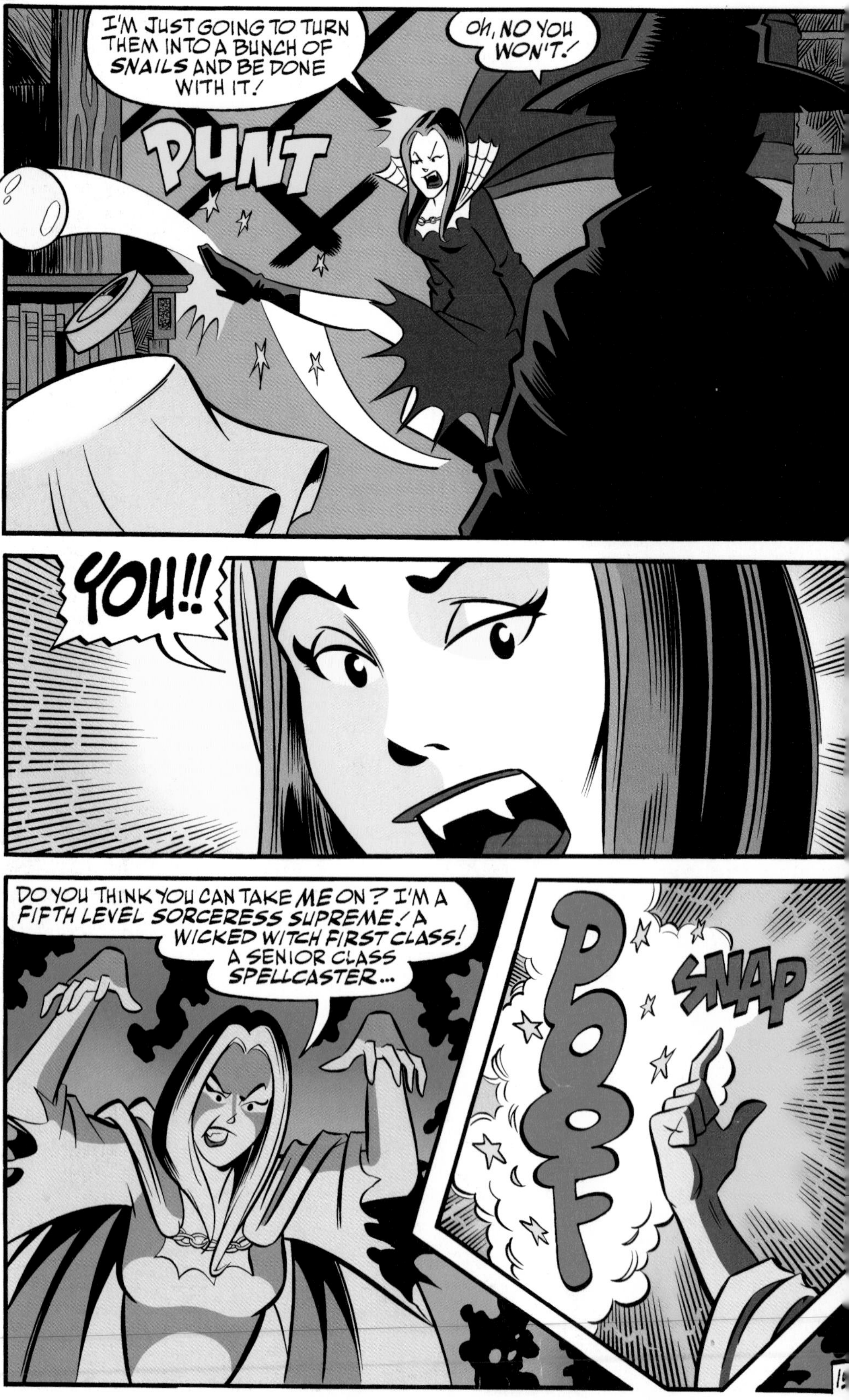
I'M JUST GOING TO TURN THEM INTO A BUNCH OF SNAILS AND BE DONE WITH IT!
OH, NO YOU WON'T!
PUNT
YOU!!
DO YOU THINK YOU CAN TAKE ME ON? I'M A FIFTH LEVEL SORCERESS SUPREME! A WICKED WITCH FIRST CLASS! A SENIOR CLASS SPELLCASTER...
POOF
SNAP

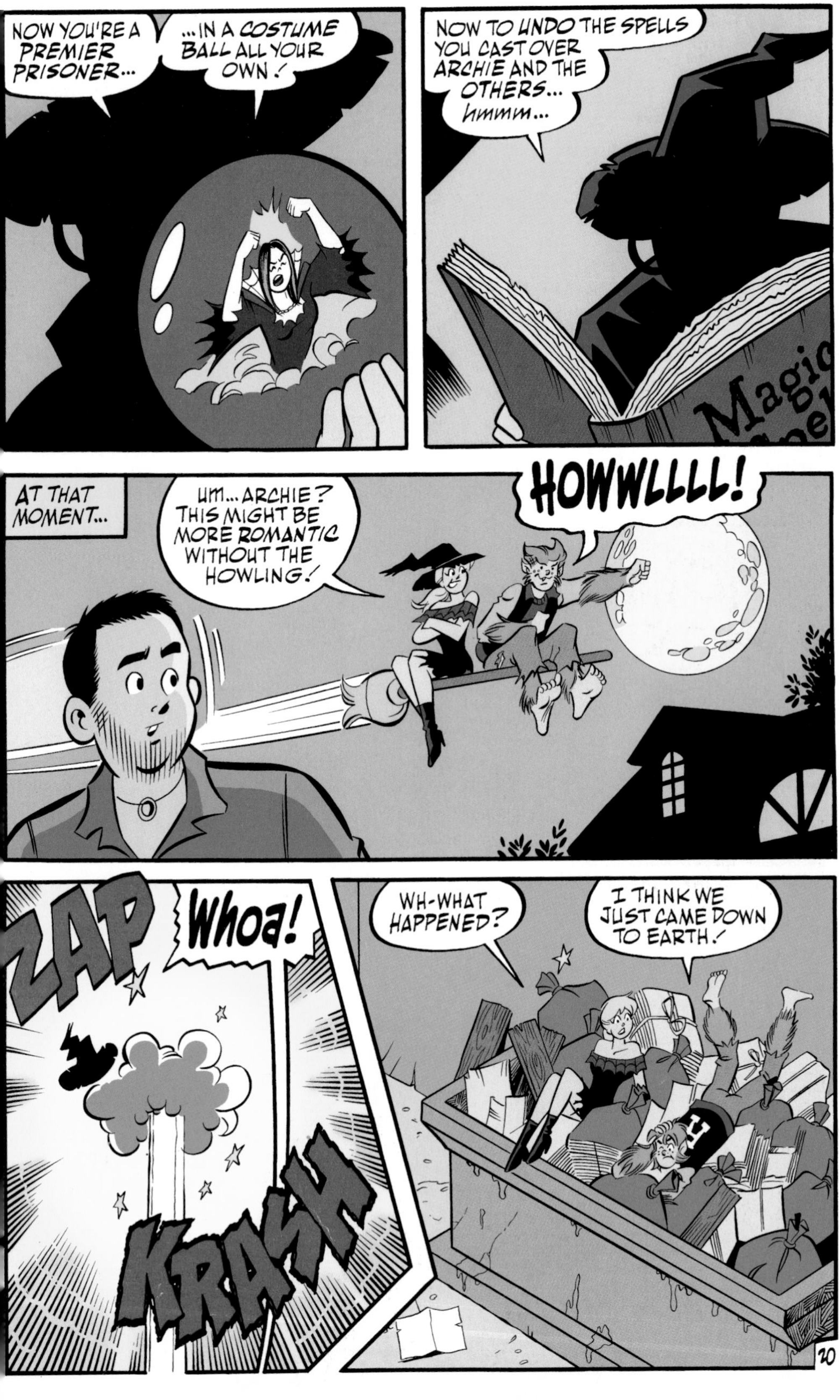
NOW YOU'RE A PREMIER PRISONER...
...IN A COSTUME BALL ALL YOUR OWN!
NOW TO UNDO THE SPELLS YOU CAST OVER ARCHIE AND THE OTHERS... hmmm...
Magic
AT THAT MOMENT...
UM... ARCHIE? THIS MIGHT BE MORE ROMANTIC WITHOUT THE HOWLING!
HOWWLLLL!
ZAP
Whoa!
KRASH
WH-WHAT HAPPENED?
I THINK WE JUST CAME DOWN TO EARTH!

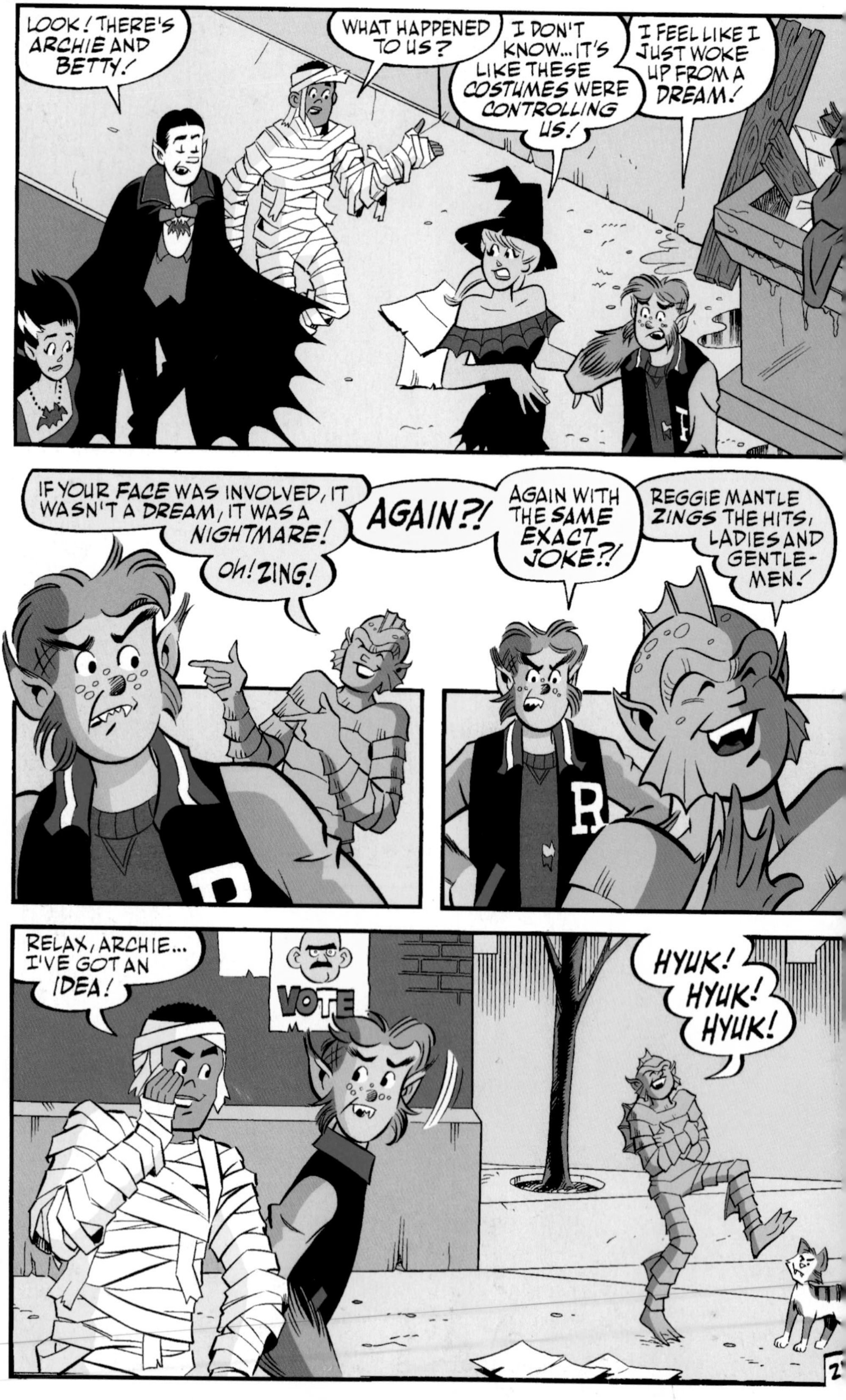

LOOK! THERE'S ARCHIE AND BETTY!
WHAT HAPPENED TO US?
I DON'T KNOW... IT'S LIKE THESE COSTUMES WERE CONTROLLING US!
I FEEL LIKE I JUST WOKE UP FROM A DREAM!
IF YOUR FACE WAS INVOLVED, IT WASN'T A DREAM, IT WAS A NIGHTMARE!
Oh! ZING!
AGAIN?!
AGAIN WITH THE SAME EXACT JOKE?!
REGGIE MANTLE ZINGS THE HITS, LADIES AND GENTLE-MEN!
RELAX, ARCHIE... I'VE GOT AN IDEA!
VOTE
HYUK! HYUK! HYUK!

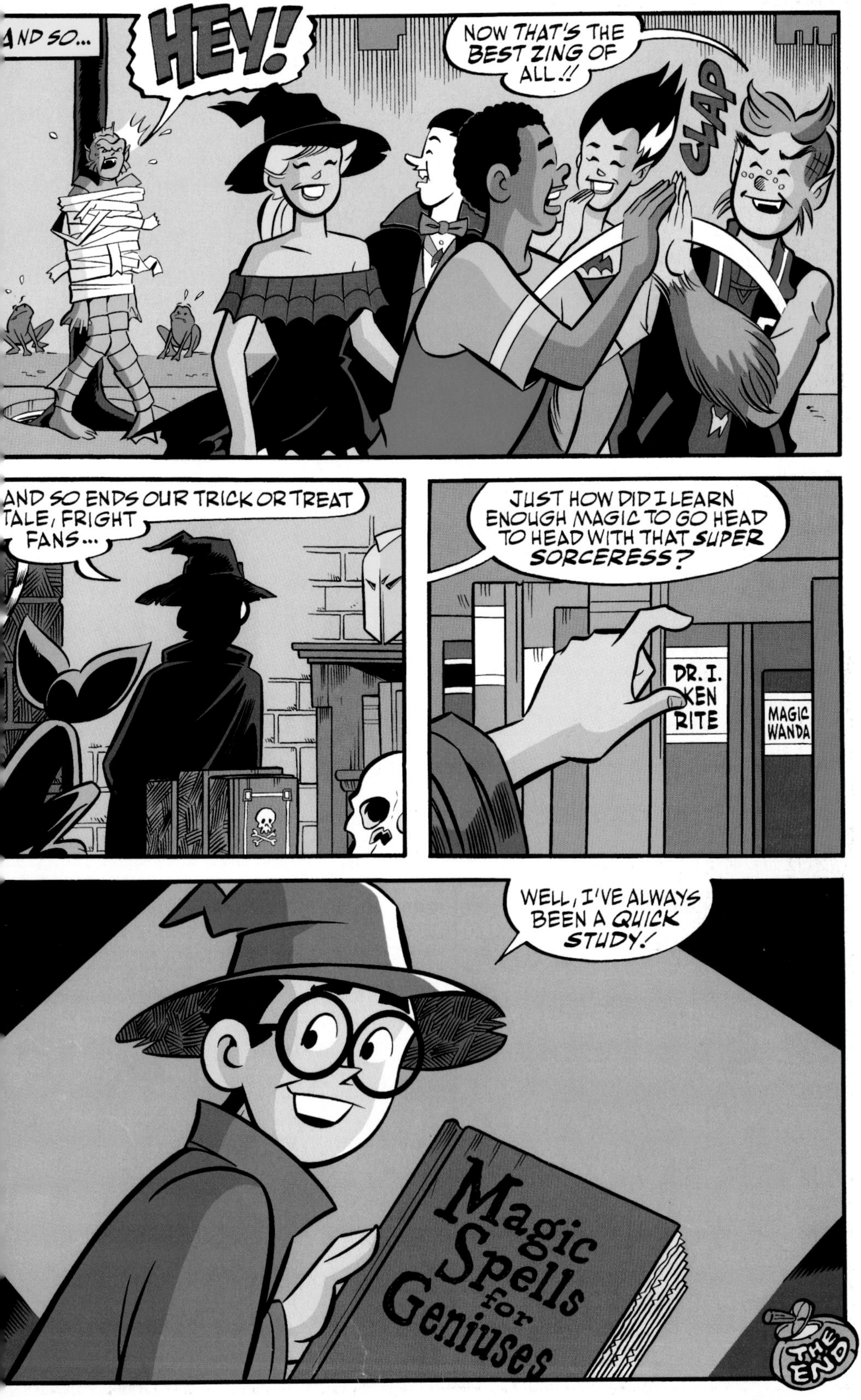
AND SO...
HEY!
NOW THAT'S THE BEST ZING OF ALL.!!
CLAP
AND SO ENDS OUR TRICK OR TREAT TALE, FRIGHT FANS...
JUST HOW DID I LEARN ENOUGH MAGIC TO GO HEAD TO HEAD WITH THAT SUPER SORCERESS?
DR. I. KEN RITE
MAGIC WANDA
WELL, I'VE ALWAYS BEEN A QUICK STUDY!
Magic Spells for Geniuses
THE END

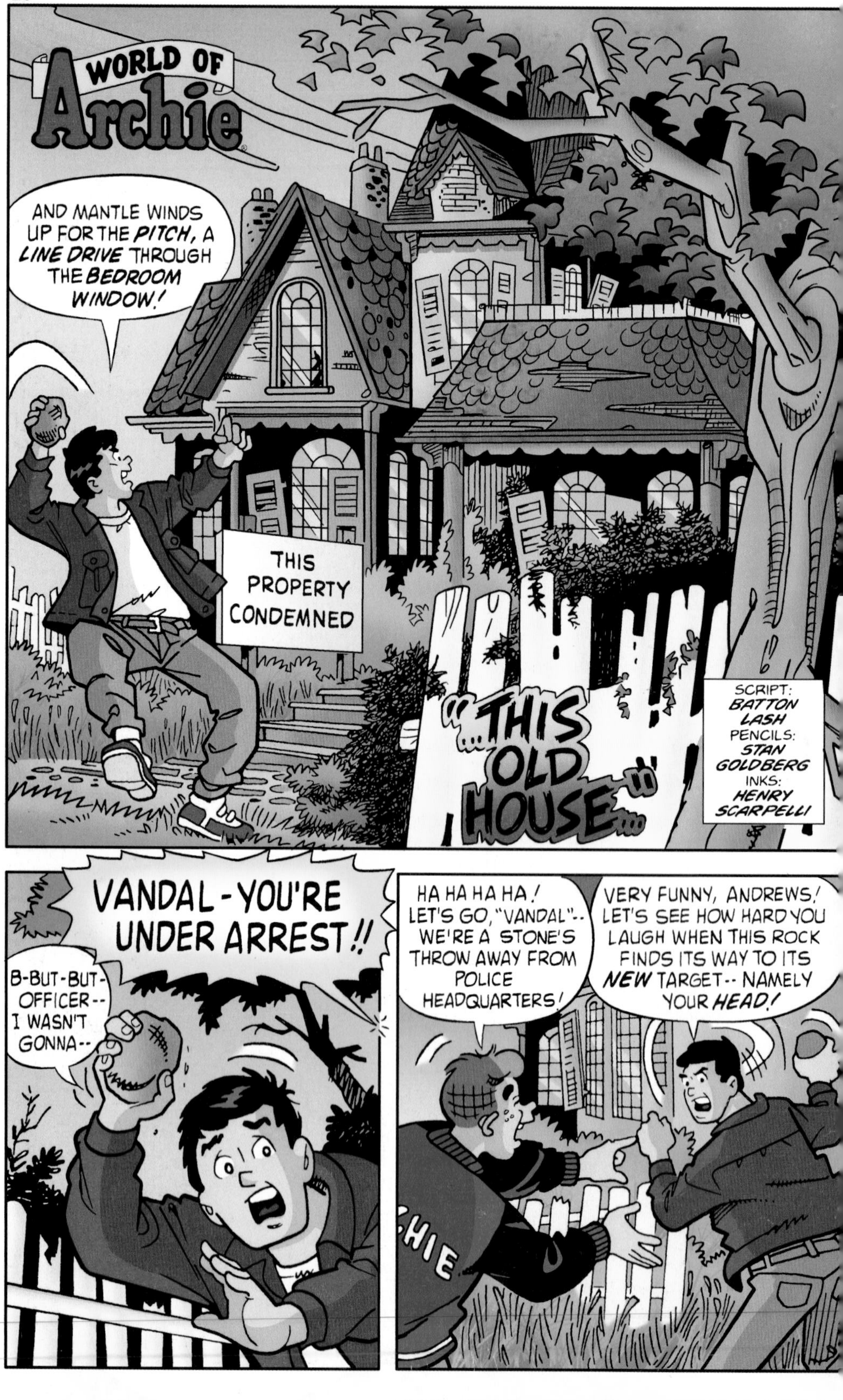
WORLD OF Archie
AND MANTLE WINDS UP FOR THE PITCH, A LINE DRIVE THROUGH THE BEDROOM WINDOW!
THIS PROPERTY CONDEMNED
"...THIS OLD HOUSE..."
SCRIPT: BATTON LASH PENCILS: STAN GOLDBERG INKS: HENRY SCARPELLI
VANDAL - YOU'RE UNDER ARREST!!
B-BUT-BUT-OFFICER-- I WASN'T GONNA--
HA HA HA HA! LET'S GO, "VANDAL"-- WE'RE A STONE'S THROW AWAY FROM POLICE HEADQUARTERS!
VERY FUNNY, ANDREWS! LET'S SEE HOW HARD YOU LAUGH WHEN THIS ROCK FINDS ITS WAY TO ITS NEW TARGET-- NAMELY YOUR HEAD!

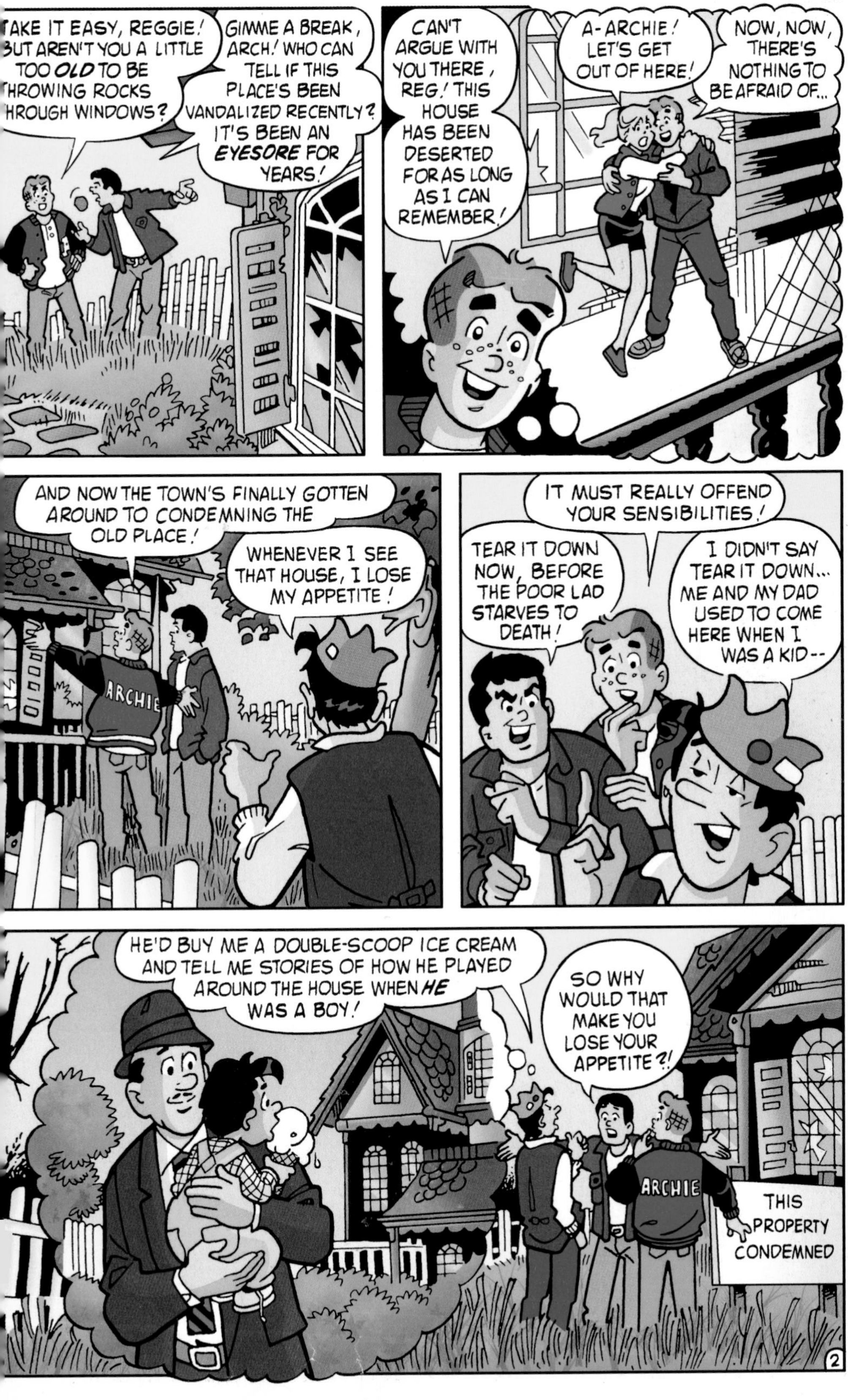
TAKE IT EASY, REGGIE! BUT AREN'T YOU A LITTLE TOO OLD TO BE THROWING ROCKS THROUGH WINDOWS?
GIMME A BREAK, ARCH! WHO CAN TELL IF THIS PLACE'S BEEN VANDALIZED RECENTLY? IT'S BEEN AN EYESORE FOR YEARS!
CAN'T ARGUE WITH YOU THERE, REG! THIS HOUSE HAS BEEN DESERTED FOR AS LONG AS I CAN REMEMBER!
A-ARCHIE! LET'S GET OUT OF HERE!
NOW, NOW, THERE'S NOTHING TO BE AFRAID OF...
AND NOW THE TOWN'S FINALLY GOTTEN AROUND TO CONDEMNING THE OLD PLACE!
WHENEVER I SEE THAT HOUSE, I LOSE MY APPETITE!
ARCHIE
IT MUST REALLY OFFEND YOUR SENSIBILITIES!
TEAR IT DOWN NOW, BEFORE THE POOR LAD STARVES TO DEATH!
I DIDN'T SAY TEAR IT DOWN... ME AND MY DAD USED TO COME HERE WHEN I WAS A KID--
HE'D BUY ME A DOUBLE-SCOOP ICE CREAM AND TELL ME STORIES OF HOW HE PLAYED AROUND THE HOUSE WHEN HE WAS A BOY!
SO WHY WOULD THAT MAKE YOU LOSE YOUR APPETITE?!
ARCHIE
THIS PROPERTY CONDEMNED
2

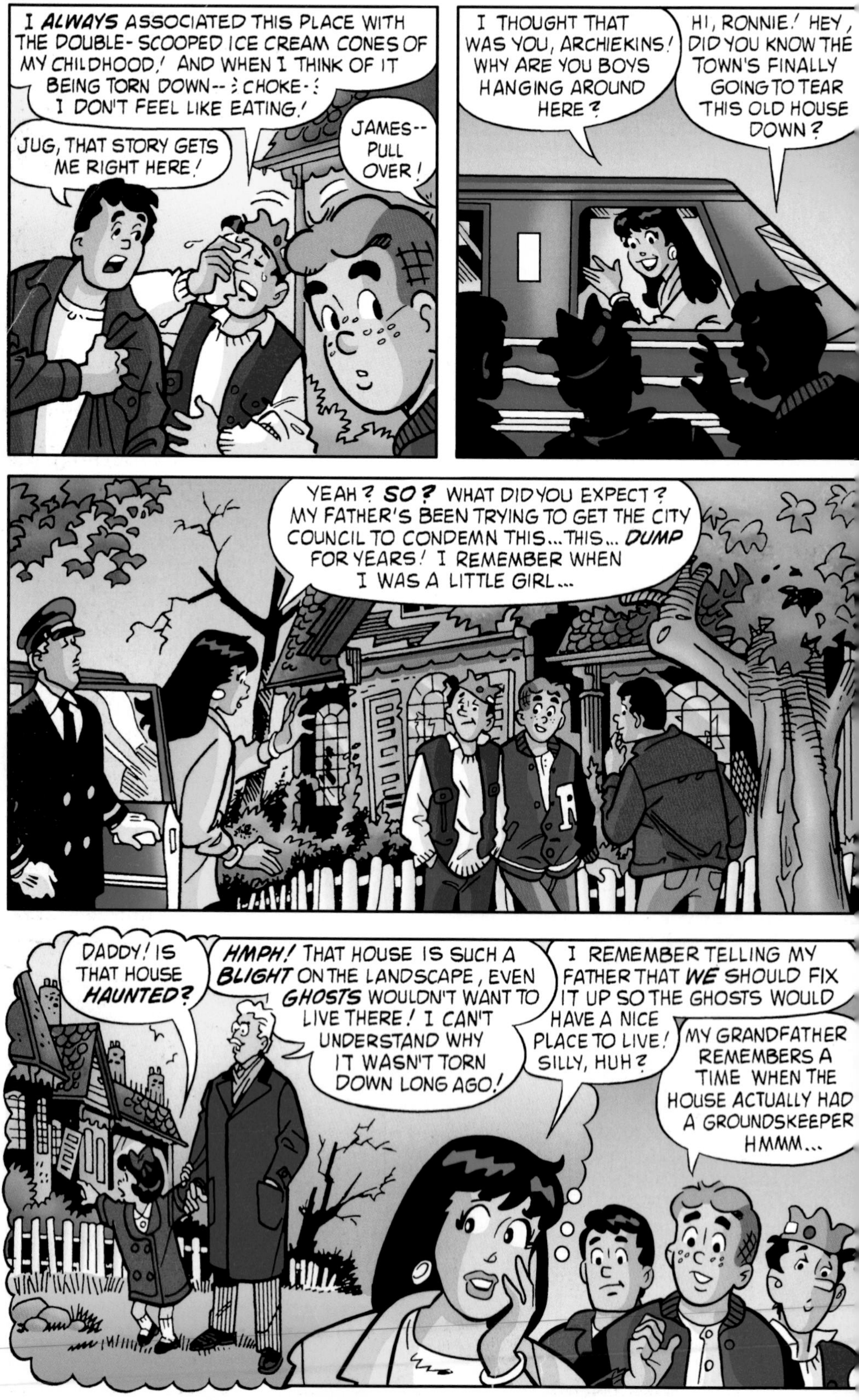
I ALWAYS ASSOCIATED THIS PLACE WITH THE DOUBLE-SCOOPED ICE CREAM CONES OF MY CHILDHOOD! AND WHEN I THINK OF IT BEING TORN DOWN-- CHOKE- I DON'T FEEL LIKE EATING!
JUG, THAT STORY GETS ME RIGHT HERE!
JAMES-- PULL OVER!
I THOUGHT THAT WAS YOU, ARCHIEKINS! WHY ARE YOU BOYS HANGING AROUND HERE?
HI, RONNIE! HEY, DID YOU KNOW THE TOWN'S FINALLY GOING TO TEAR THIS OLD HOUSE DOWN?
YEAH? SO? WHAT DID YOU EXPECT? MY FATHER'S BEEN TRYING TO GET THE CITY COUNCIL TO CONDEMN THIS...THIS... DUMP FOR YEARS! I REMEMBER WHEN I WAS A LITTLE GIRL...
DADDY! IS THAT HOUSE HAUNTED?
HMPH! THAT HOUSE IS SUCH A BLIGHT ON THE LANDSCAPE, EVEN GHOSTS WOULDN'T WANT TO LIVE THERE! I CAN'T UNDERSTAND WHY IT WASN'T TORN DOWN LONG AGO!
I REMEMBER TELLING MY FATHER THAT WE SHOULD FIX IT UP SO THE GHOSTS WOULD HAVE A NICE PLACE TO LIVE! SILLY, HUH?
MY GRANDFATHER REMEMBERS A TIME WHEN THE HOUSE ACTUALLY HAD A GROUNDSKEEPER HMMM...

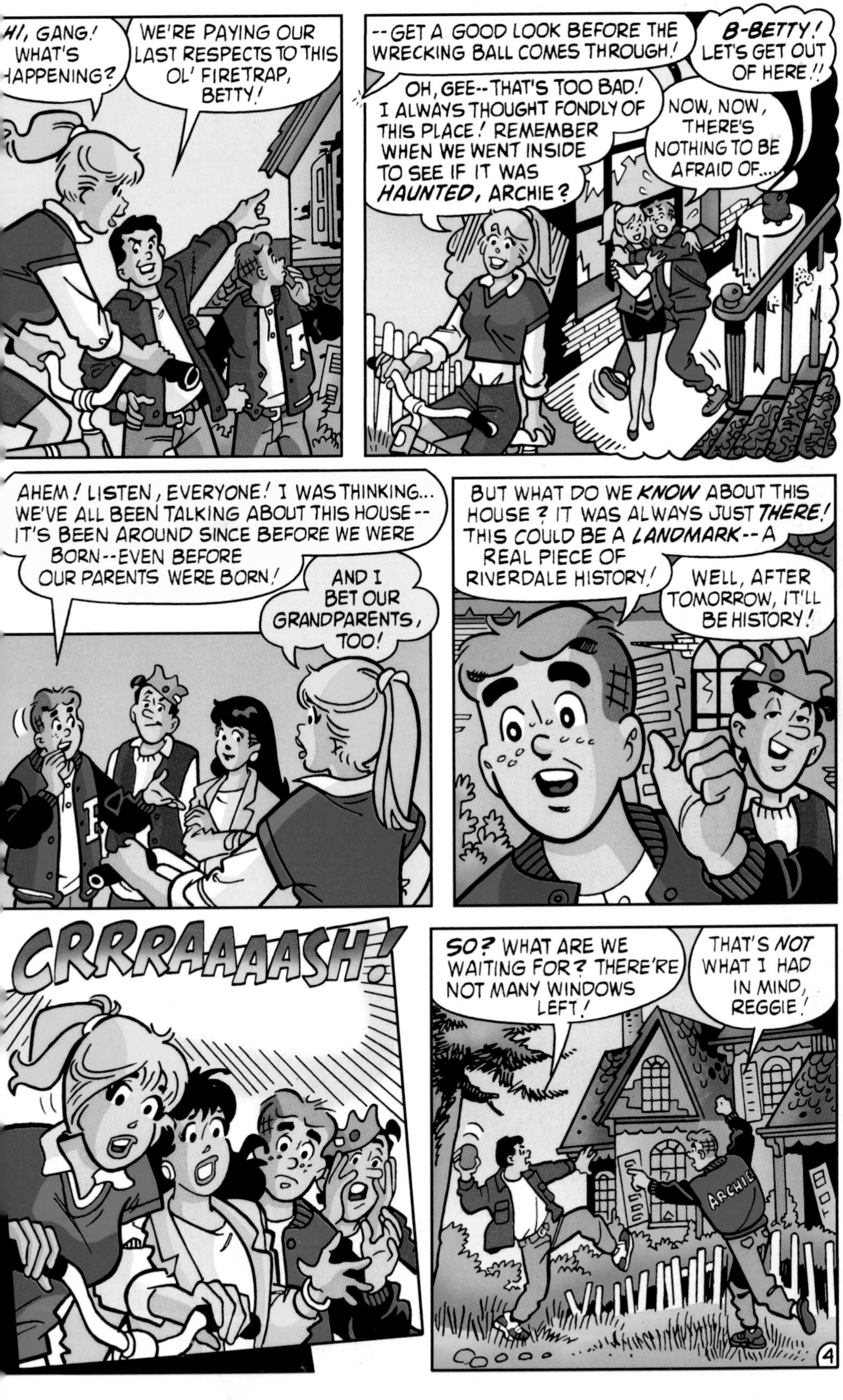
HI, GANG! WHAT'S HAPPENING?
WE'RE PAYING OUR LAST RESPECTS TO THIS OL' FIRETRAP, BETTY!
--GET A GOOD LOOK BEFORE THE WRECKING BALL COMES THROUGH!
OH, GEE--THAT'S TOO BAD! I ALWAYS THOUGHT FONDLY OF THIS PLACE! REMEMBER WHEN WE WENT INSIDE TO SEE IF IT WAS HAUNTED, ARCHIE?
B-BETTY! LET'S GET OUT OF HERE!!
NOW, NOW, THERE'S NOTHING TO BE AFRAID OF...
AHEM! LISTEN, EVERYONE! I WAS THINKING... WE'VE ALL BEEN TALKING ABOUT THIS HOUSE--IT'S BEEN AROUND SINCE BEFORE WE WERE BORN--EVEN BEFORE OUR PARENTS WERE BORN!
AND I BET OUR GRANDPARENTS, TOO!
BUT WHAT DO WE KNOW ABOUT THIS HOUSE? IT WAS ALWAYS JUST THERE! THIS COULD BE A LANDMARK--A REAL PIECE OF RIVERDALE HISTORY!
WELL, AFTER TOMORROW, IT'LL BE HISTORY!
CRRRAAAAASH!
SO? WHAT ARE WE WAITING FOR? THERE'RE NOT MANY WINDOWS LEFT!
THAT'S NOT WHAT I HAD IN MIND, REGGIE!
ARCHIE
4

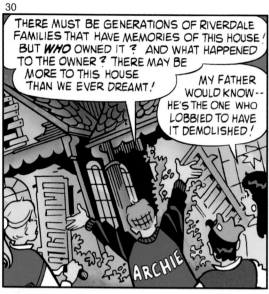

THERE MUST BE GENERATIONS OF RIVERDALE FAMILIES THAT HAVE MEMORIES OF THIS HOUSE! BUT *WHO* OWNED IT? AND WHAT HAPPENED TO THE OWNER? THERE MAY BE MORE TO THIS HOUSE THAN WE EVER DREAMT!

MY FATHER WOULD KNOW-- HE'S THE ONE WHO LOBBIED TO HAVE IT DEMOLISHED!

RONNIE, CAN YOU DROP ME OFF AT THE *HALL* OF *RECORDS*? I WANT TO DO SOME RESEARCH!

I'LL MEET YOU THERE, ARCH!

RONNIE, DROP ME OFF AT *POP'S*-- I HAVE THIS SUDDEN CRAVING FOR A DOUBLE-SCOOPED ICE CREAM CONE!

YOU GUYS ARE *NUTS*!

WHO CARES WHO LIVED HERE? DO YOU THINK HIS *GHOST* IS HANGING AROUND? HAW HAW HAW! WELL, HE HASN'T BEEN ANSWERING *MY* MESSAGES!

BOING!

HEY, YOU GUYS!! WAIT FOR ME!!

The END...?

NOT ON YOUR LIFE! THIS IS JUST THE *BEGINNING*! YOU'LL BE AMAZED HOW THIS CONDEMNED HOUSE WILL AFFECT EVERY SINGLE PERSON IN RIVERDALE!

KEEP READING... IF YOU DARE!

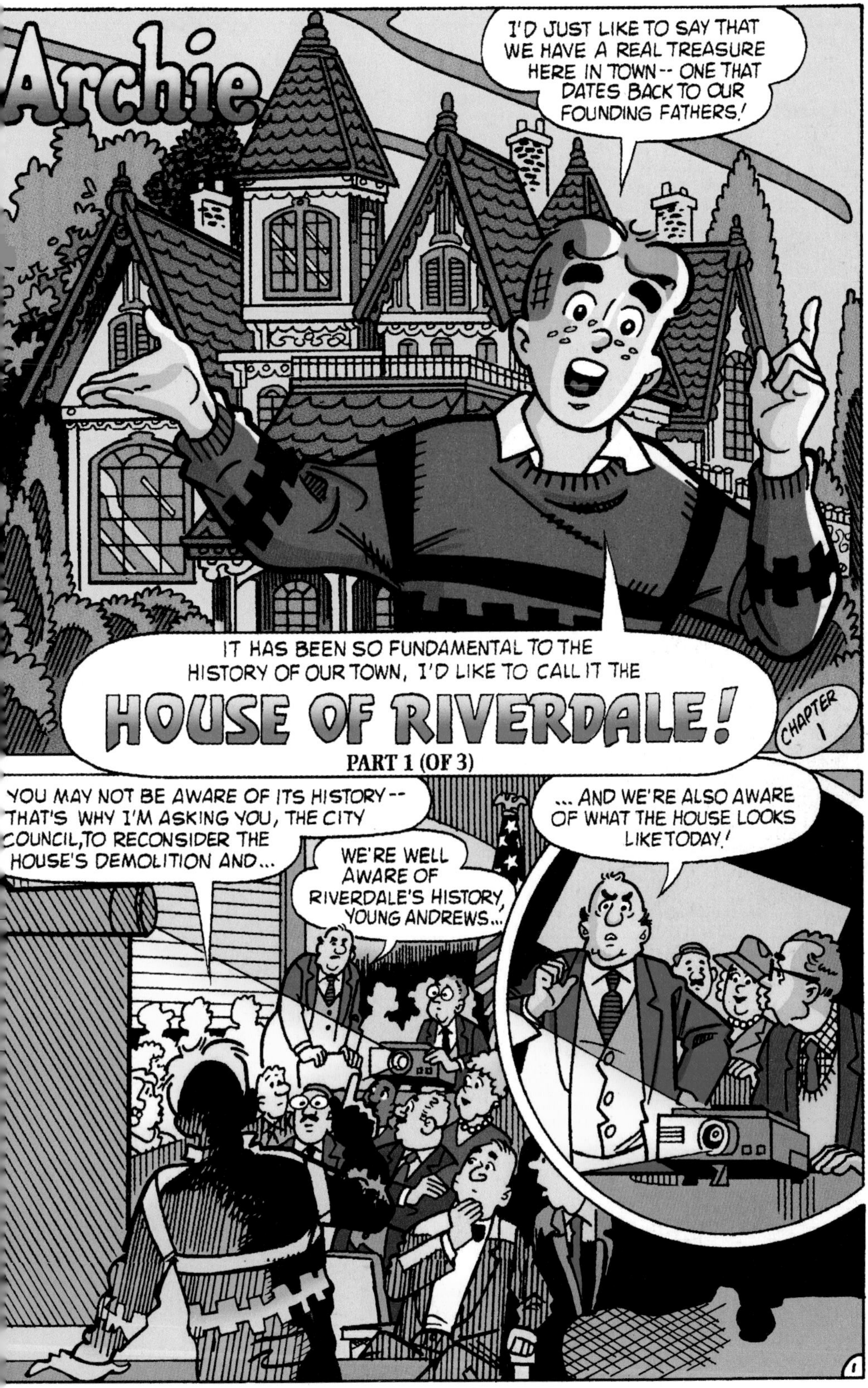
Archie
I'D JUST LIKE TO SAY THAT WE HAVE A REAL TREASURE HERE IN TOWN -- ONE THAT DATES BACK TO OUR FOUNDING FATHERS!
IT HAS BEEN SO FUNDAMENTAL TO THE HISTORY OF OUR TOWN, I'D LIKE TO CALL IT THE
HOUSE OF RIVERDALE!
CHAPTER 1
PART 1 (OF 3)
YOU MAY NOT BE AWARE OF ITS HISTORY -- THAT'S WHY I'M ASKING YOU, THE CITY COUNCIL, TO RECONSIDER THE HOUSE'S DEMOLITION AND...
WE'RE WELL AWARE OF RIVERDALE'S HISTORY, YOUNG ANDREWS...
... AND WE'RE ALSO AWARE OF WHAT THE HOUSE LOOKS LIKE TODAY!
1

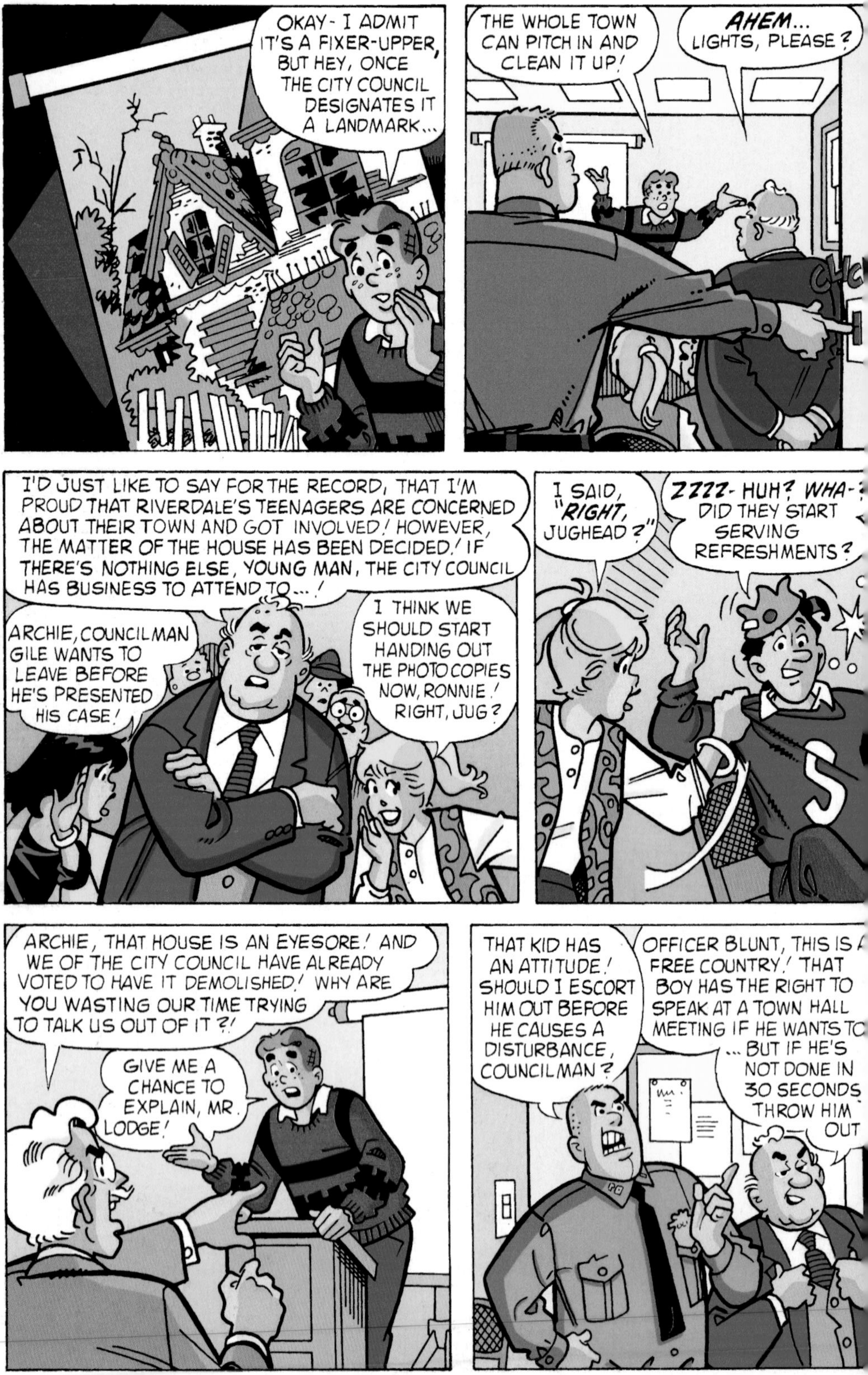
OKAY- I ADMIT IT'S A FIXER-UPPER, BUT HEY, ONCE THE CITY COUNCIL DESIGNATES IT A LANDMARK...
THE WHOLE TOWN CAN PITCH IN AND CLEAN IT UP!
AHEM... LIGHTS, PLEASE?
I'D JUST LIKE TO SAY FOR THE RECORD, THAT I'M PROUD THAT RIVERDALE'S TEENAGERS ARE CONCERNED ABOUT THEIR TOWN AND GOT INVOLVED! HOWEVER, THE MATTER OF THE HOUSE HAS BEEN DECIDED! IF THERE'S NOTHING ELSE, YOUNG MAN, THE CITY COUNCIL HAS BUSINESS TO ATTEND TO...!
ARCHIE, COUNCILMAN GILE WANTS TO LEAVE BEFORE HE'S PRESENTED HIS CASE!
I THINK WE SHOULD START HANDING OUT THE PHOTOCOPIES NOW, RONNIE! RIGHT, JUG?
I SAID, "RIGHT, JUGHEAD?"
ZZZZ- HUH? WHA-? DID THEY START SERVING REFRESHMENTS?
ARCHIE, THAT HOUSE IS AN EYESORE! AND WE OF THE CITY COUNCIL HAVE ALREADY VOTED TO HAVE IT DEMOLISHED! WHY ARE YOU WASTING OUR TIME TRYING TO TALK US OUT OF IT?!
GIVE ME A CHANCE TO EXPLAIN, MR. LODGE!
THAT KID HAS AN ATTITUDE! SHOULD I ESCORT HIM OUT BEFORE HE CAUSES A DISTURBANCE, COUNCILMAN?
OFFICER BLUNT, THIS IS FREE COUNTRY! THAT BOY HAS THE RIGHT TO SPEAK AT A TOWN HALL MEETING IF HE WANTS T
...BUT IF HE'S NOT DONE IN 30 SECONDS THROW HIM OUT

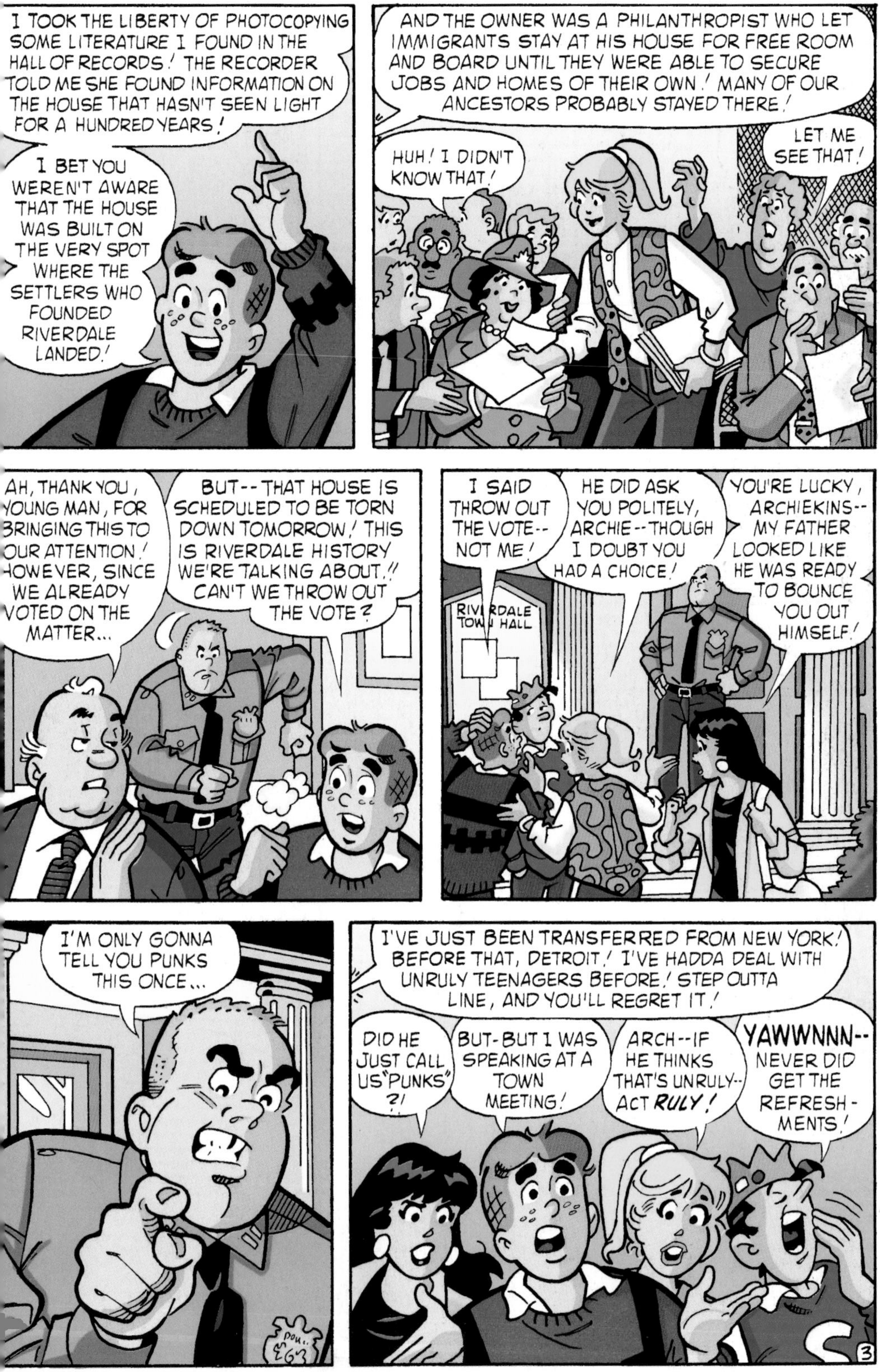
I TOOK THE LIBERTY OF PHOTOCOPYING SOME LITERATURE I FOUND IN THE HALL OF RECORDS! THE RECORDER TOLD ME SHE FOUND INFORMATION ON THE HOUSE THAT HASN'T SEEN LIGHT FOR A HUNDRED YEARS!
I BET YOU WEREN'T AWARE THAT THE HOUSE WAS BUILT ON THE VERY SPOT WHERE THE SETTLERS WHO FOUNDED RIVERDALE LANDED!
AND THE OWNER WAS A PHILANTHROPIST WHO LET IMMIGRANTS STAY AT HIS HOUSE FOR FREE ROOM AND BOARD UNTIL THEY WERE ABLE TO SECURE JOBS AND HOMES OF THEIR OWN! MANY OF OUR ANCESTORS PROBABLY STAYED THERE!
HUH! I DIDN'T KNOW THAT!
LET ME SEE THAT!
AH, THANK YOU, YOUNG MAN, FOR BRINGING THIS TO OUR ATTENTION! HOWEVER, SINCE WE ALREADY VOTED ON THE MATTER...
BUT-- THAT HOUSE IS SCHEDULED TO BE TORN DOWN TOMORROW! THIS IS RIVERDALE HISTORY WE'RE TALKING ABOUT!! CAN'T WE THROW OUT THE VOTE?
I SAID THROW OUT THE VOTE-- NOT ME!
HE DID ASK YOU POLITELY, ARCHIE-- THOUGH I DOUBT YOU HAD A CHOICE!
YOU'RE LUCKY, ARCHIEKINS-- MY FATHER LOOKED LIKE HE WAS READY TO BOUNCE YOU OUT HIMSELF!
I'M ONLY GONNA TELL YOU PUNKS THIS ONCE...
I'VE JUST BEEN TRANSFERRED FROM NEW YORK! BEFORE THAT, DETROIT! I'VE HADDA DEAL WITH UNRULY TEENAGERS BEFORE! STEP OUTTA LINE, AND YOU'LL REGRET IT!
DID HE JUST CALL US "PUNKS" ?!
BUT-BUT I WAS SPEAKING AT A TOWN MEETING!
ARCH-- IF HE THINKS THAT'S UNRULY-- ACT RULY!
YAWWNNN-- NEVER DID GET THE REFRESH-MENTS!

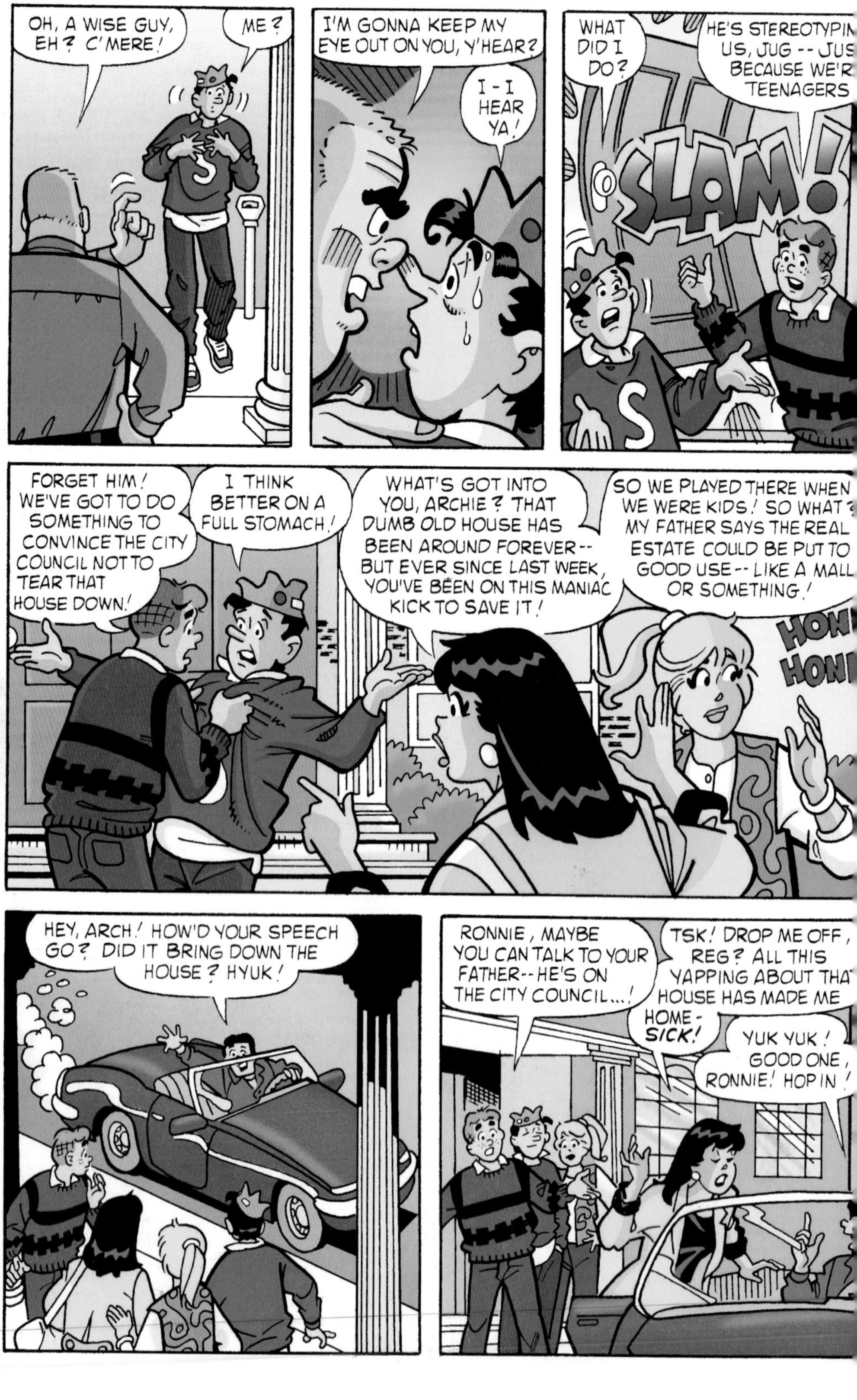
OH, A WISE GUY, EH? C'MERE!
ME?
I'M GONNA KEEP MY EYE OUT ON YOU, Y'HEAR?
I-I HEAR YA!
WHAT DID I DO?
HE'S STEREOTYPIN US, JUG -- JUS BECAUSE WE'R TEENAGERS
SLAM!
FORGET HIM! WE'VE GOT TO DO SOMETHING TO CONVINCE THE CITY COUNCIL NOT TO TEAR THAT HOUSE DOWN!
I THINK BETTER ON A FULL STOMACH!
WHAT'S GOT INTO YOU, ARCHIE? THAT DUMB OLD HOUSE HAS BEEN AROUND FOREVER -- BUT EVER SINCE LAST WEEK, YOU'VE BEEN ON THIS MANIAC KICK TO SAVE IT!
SO WE PLAYED THERE WHEN WE WERE KIDS! SO WHAT? MY FATHER SAYS THE REAL ESTATE COULD BE PUT TO GOOD USE -- LIKE A MALL OR SOMETHING!
HON
HON
HEY, ARCH! HOW'D YOUR SPEECH GO? DID IT BRING DOWN THE HOUSE? HYUK!
RONNIE, MAYBE YOU CAN TALK TO YOUR FATHER -- HE'S ON THE CITY COUNCIL...!
TSK! DROP ME OFF, REG? ALL THIS YAPPING ABOUT THA HOUSE HAS MADE ME HOME-SICK!
YUK YUK! GOOD ONE, RONNIE! HOP IN!

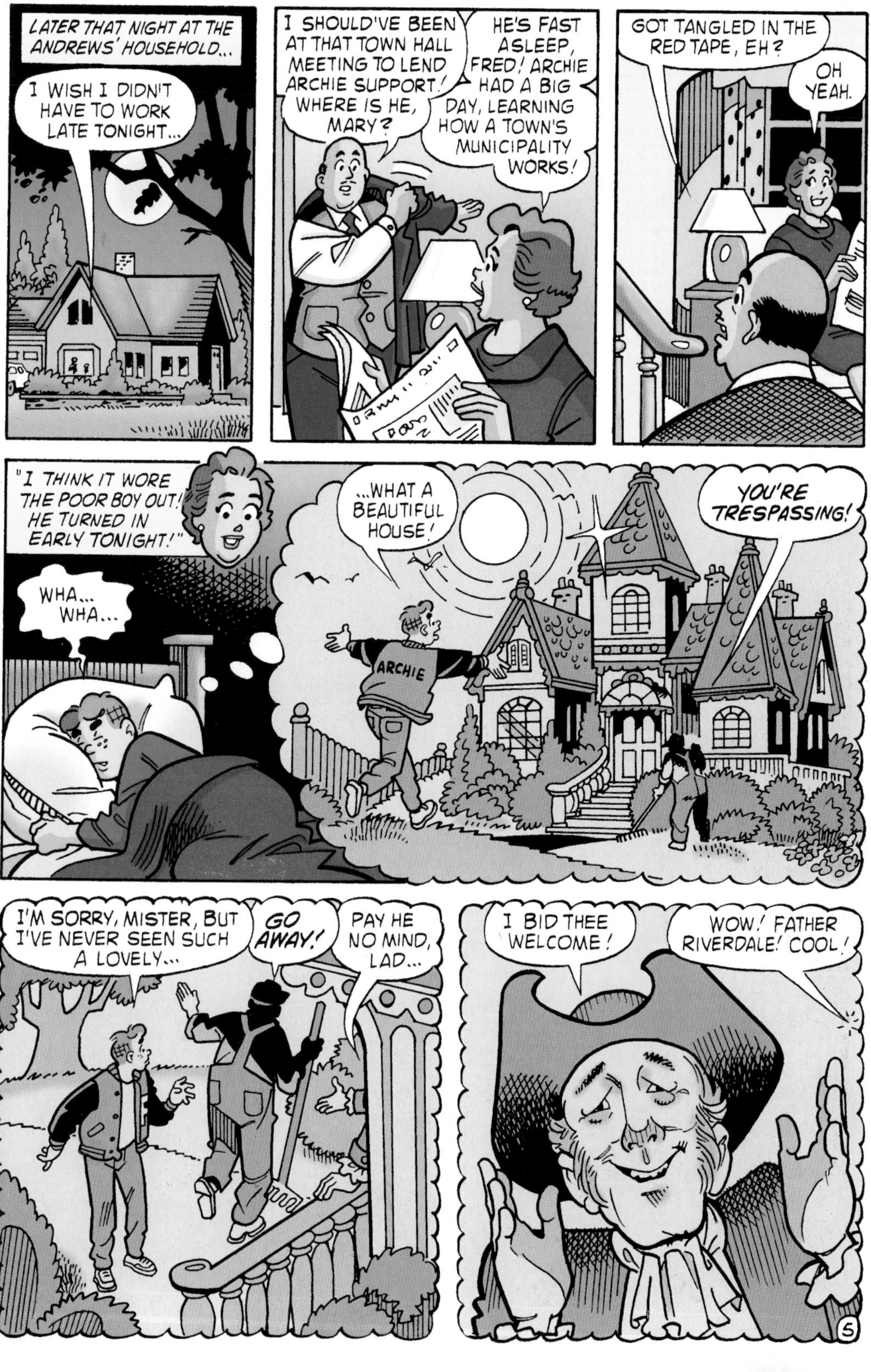
LATER THAT NIGHT AT THE ANDREWS' HOUSEHOLD...
I WISH I DIDN'T HAVE TO WORK LATE TONIGHT...
I SHOULD'VE BEEN AT THAT TOWN HALL MEETING TO LEND ARCHIE SUPPORT! WHERE IS HE, MARY?
HE'S FAST ASLEEP, FRED! ARCHIE HAD A BIG DAY, LEARNING HOW A TOWN'S MUNICIPALITY WORKS!
GOT TANGLED IN THE RED TAPE, EH?
OH YEAH.
"I THINK IT WORE THE POOR BOY OUT! HE TURNED IN EARLY TONIGHT!"
WHA... WHA...
...WHAT A BEAUTIFUL HOUSE!
ARCHIE
YOU'RE TRESPASSING!
I'M SORRY, MISTER, BUT I'VE NEVER SEEN SUCH A LOVELY...
GO AWAY!
PAY HE NO MIND, LAD...
I BID THEE WELCOME!
WOW! FATHER RIVERDALE! COOL!
5

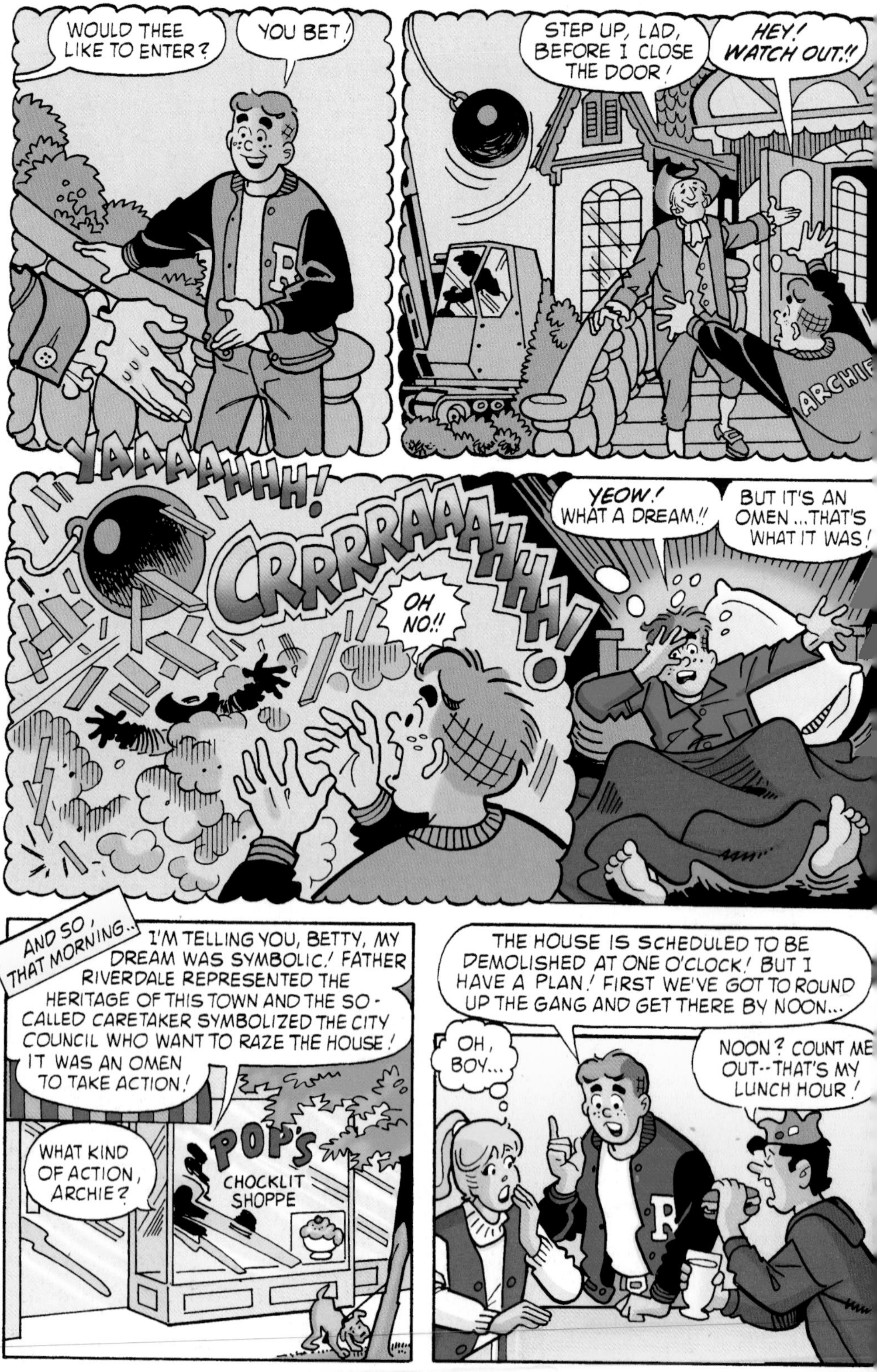
WOULD THEE LIKE TO ENTER?
YOU BET!
STEP UP, LAD, BEFORE I CLOSE THE DOOR!
HEY! WATCH OUT!!
ARCHIE
YAAAAAHHHH!
CRRRRAAAAHHHH!
OH NO!!
YEOW! WHAT A DREAM!!
BUT IT'S AN OMEN ...THAT'S WHAT IT WAS!
AND SO, THAT MORNING...
I'M TELLING YOU, BETTY, MY DREAM WAS SYMBOLIC! FATHER RIVERDALE REPRESENTED THE HERITAGE OF THIS TOWN AND THE SO-CALLED CARETAKER SYMBOLIZED THE CITY COUNCIL WHO WANT TO RAZE THE HOUSE! IT WAS AN OMEN TO TAKE ACTION!
WHAT KIND OF ACTION, ARCHIE?
POP'S CHOCKLIT SHOPPE
THE HOUSE IS SCHEDULED TO BE DEMOLISHED AT ONE O'CLOCK! BUT I HAVE A PLAN! FIRST WE'VE GOT TO ROUND UP THE GANG AND GET THERE BY NOON...
OH, BOY...
NOON? COUNT ME OUT--THAT'S MY LUNCH HOUR!

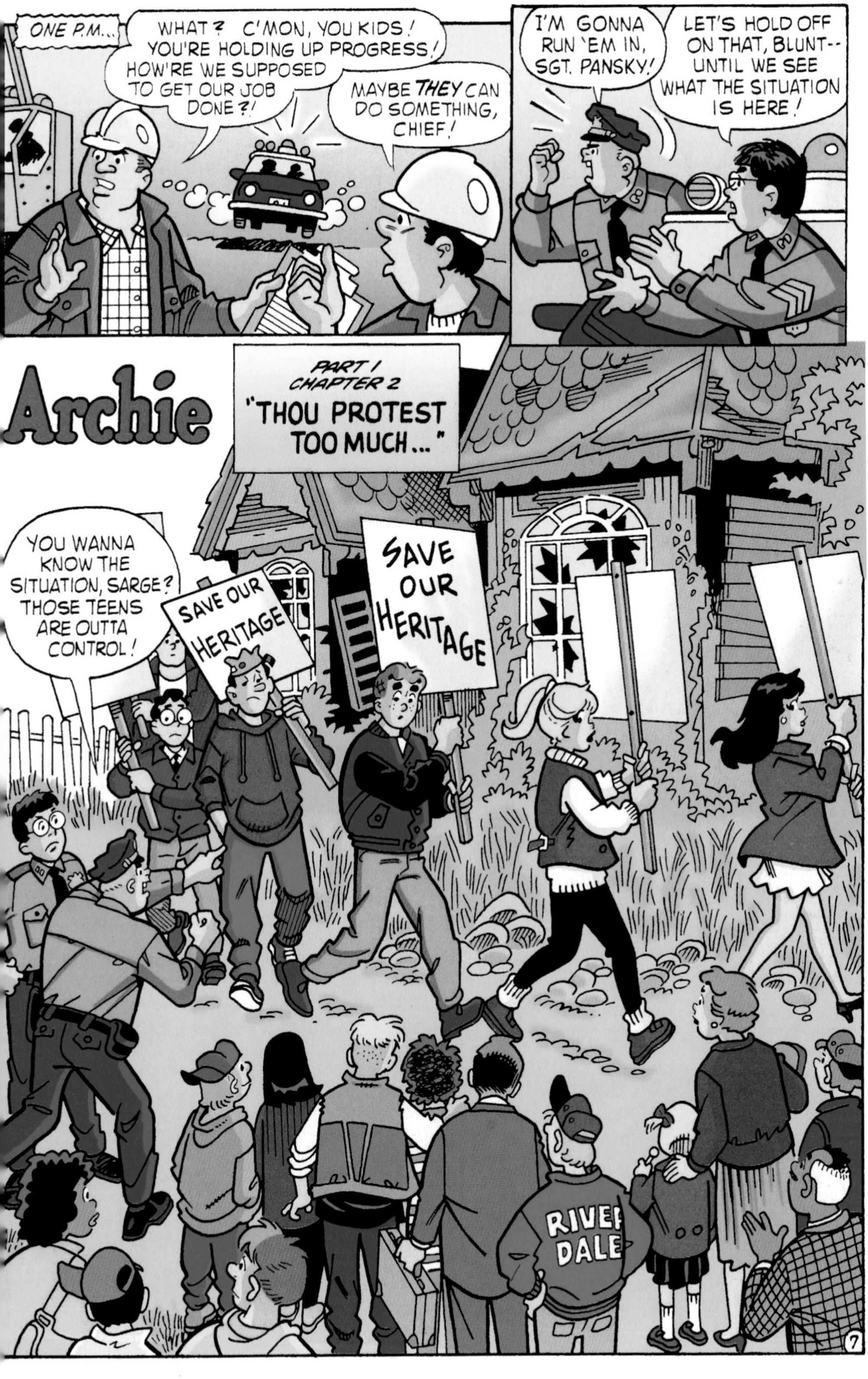
ONE P.M...
WHAT? C'MON, YOU KIDS! YOU'RE HOLDING UP PROGRESS! HOW'RE WE SUPPOSED TO GET OUR JOB DONE?!
MAYBE THEY CAN DO SOMETHING, CHIEF!
I'M GONNA RUN 'EM IN, SGT. PANSKY!
LET'S HOLD OFF ON THAT, BLUNT-- UNTIL WE SEE WHAT THE SITUATION IS HERE!
Archie
PART 1 CHAPTER 2 "THOU PROTEST TOO MUCH..."
YOU WANNA KNOW THE SITUATION, SARGE? THOSE TEENS ARE OUTTA CONTROL!
SAVE OUR HERITAGE
SAVE OUR HERITAGE
RIVER DALE
7

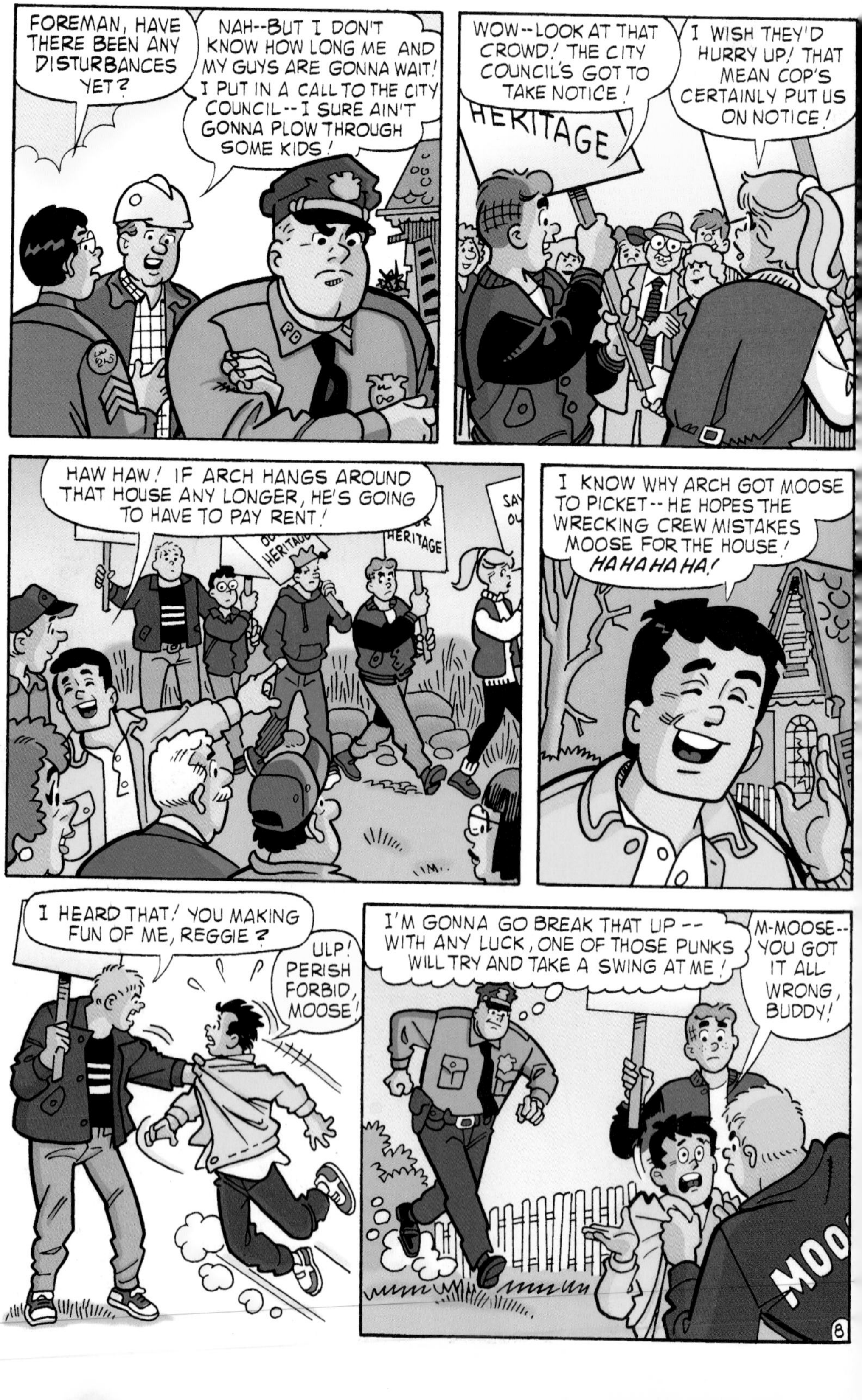
FOREMAN, HAVE THERE BEEN ANY DISTURBANCES YET?
NAH--BUT I DON'T KNOW HOW LONG ME AND MY GUYS ARE GONNA WAIT! I PUT IN A CALL TO THE CITY COUNCIL--I SURE AIN'T GONNA PLOW THROUGH SOME KIDS!
WOW--LOOK AT THAT CROWD! THE CITY COUNCIL'S GOT TO TAKE NOTICE!
HERITAGE
I WISH THEY'D HURRY UP! THAT MEAN COP'S CERTAINLY PUT US ON NOTICE!
HAW HAW! IF ARCH HANGS AROUND THAT HOUSE ANY LONGER, HE'S GOING TO HAVE TO PAY RENT!
HERITAGE
I KNOW WHY ARCH GOT MOOSE TO PICKET--HE HOPES THE WRECKING CREW MISTAKES MOOSE FOR THE HOUSE! HA HA HA HA HA!
I HEARD THAT! YOU MAKING FUN OF ME, REGGIE?
ULP! PERISH FORBID, MOOSE!
I'M GONNA GO BREAK THAT UP--WITH ANY LUCK, ONE OF THOSE PUNKS WILL TRY AND TAKE A SWING AT ME!
M-MOOSE--YOU GOT IT ALL WRONG, BUDDY!
MOO
8

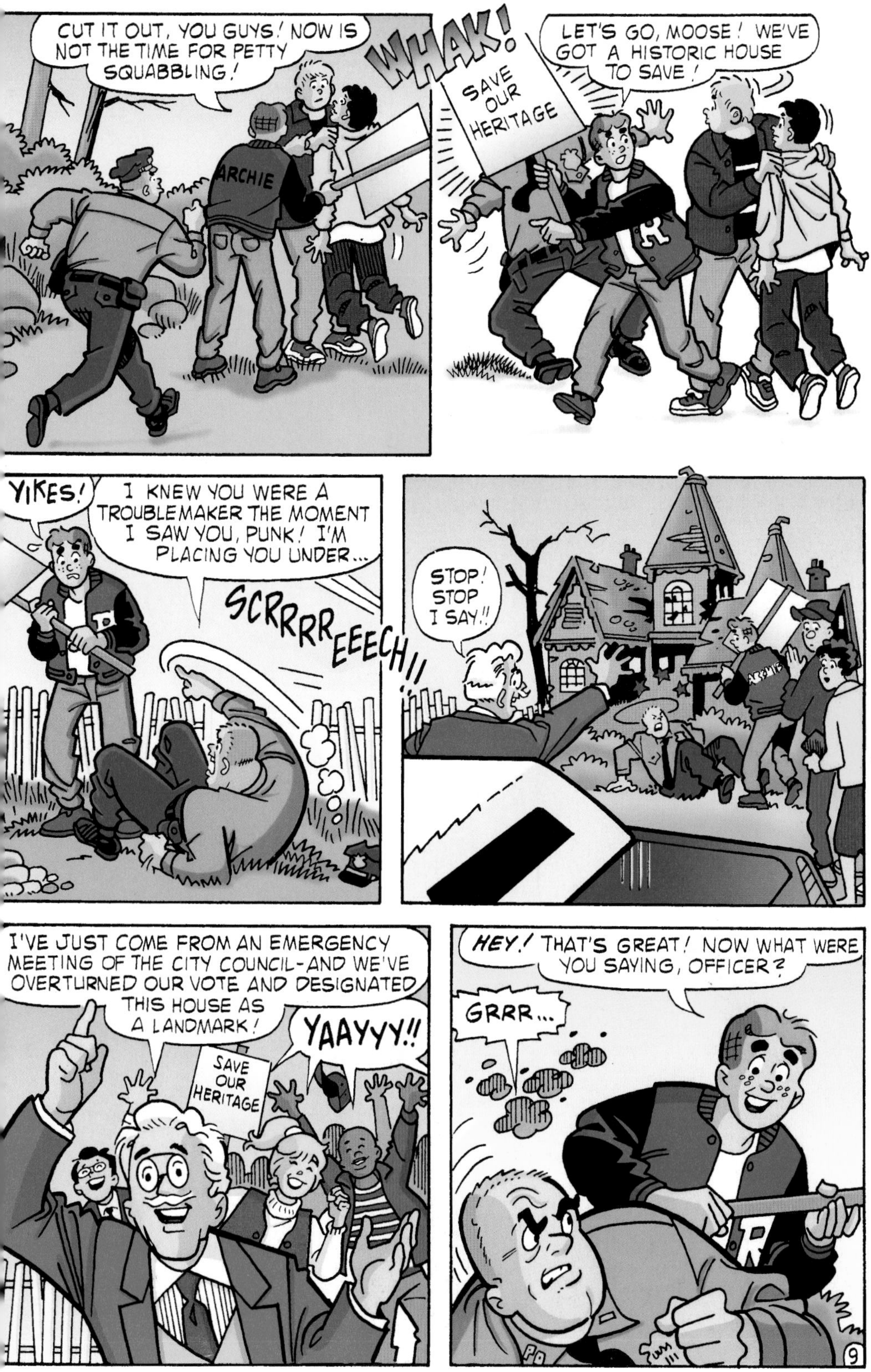
CUT IT OUT, YOU GUYS! NOW IS NOT THE TIME FOR PETTY SQUABBLING!
ARCHIE
WHAK!
SAVE OUR HERITAGE
LET'S GO, MOOSE! WE'VE GOT A HISTORIC HOUSE TO SAVE!
YIKES!
I KNEW YOU WERE A TROUBLEMAKER THE MOMENT I SAW YOU, PUNK! I'M PLACING YOU UNDER...
SCRRRREEECH!!
STOP! STOP I SAY!!
I'VE JUST COME FROM AN EMERGENCY MEETING OF THE CITY COUNCIL-AND WE'VE OVERTURNED OUR VOTE AND DESIGNATED THIS HOUSE AS A LANDMARK!
SAVE OUR HERITAGE
YAAYYY!!
HEY! THAT'S GREAT! NOW WHAT WERE YOU SAYING, OFFICER?
GRRR...
9

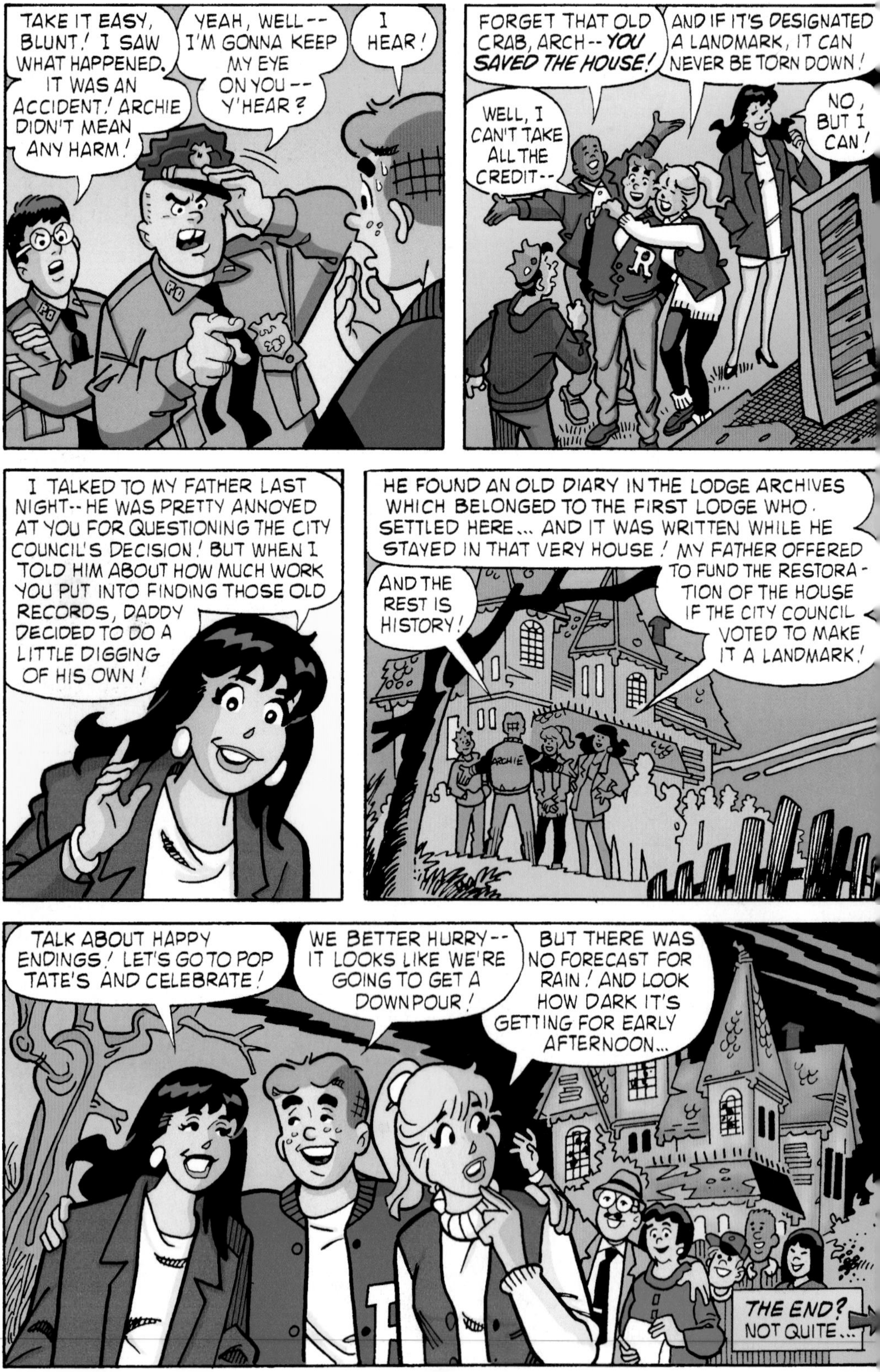
TAKE IT EASY, BLUNT! I SAW WHAT HAPPENED. IT WAS AN ACCIDENT! ARCHIE DIDN'T MEAN ANY HARM!
YEAH, WELL -- I'M GONNA KEEP MY EYE ON YOU -- Y'HEAR?
I HEAR!
FORGET THAT OLD CRAB, ARCH -- YOU SAVED THE HOUSE!
AND IF IT'S DESIGNATED A LANDMARK, IT CAN NEVER BE TORN DOWN!
WELL, I CAN'T TAKE ALL THE CREDIT --
NO, BUT I CAN!
I TALKED TO MY FATHER LAST NIGHT -- HE WAS PRETTY ANNOYED AT YOU FOR QUESTIONING THE CITY COUNCIL'S DECISION! BUT WHEN I TOLD HIM ABOUT HOW MUCH WORK YOU PUT INTO FINDING THOSE OLD RECORDS, DADDY DECIDED TO DO A LITTLE DIGGING OF HIS OWN!
HE FOUND AN OLD DIARY IN THE LODGE ARCHIVES WHICH BELONGED TO THE FIRST LODGE WHO SETTLED HERE... AND IT WAS WRITTEN WHILE HE STAYED IN THAT VERY HOUSE!
MY FATHER OFFERED TO FUND THE RESTORATION OF THE HOUSE IF THE CITY COUNCIL VOTED TO MAKE IT A LANDMARK!
AND THE REST IS HISTORY!
ARCHIE
TALK ABOUT HAPPY ENDINGS! LET'S GO TO POP TATE'S AND CELEBRATE!
WE BETTER HURRY -- IT LOOKS LIKE WE'RE GOING TO GET A DOWNPOUR!
BUT THERE WAS NO FORECAST FOR RAIN! AND LOOK HOW DARK IT'S GETTING FOR EARLY AFTERNOON...
THE END? NOT QUITE...

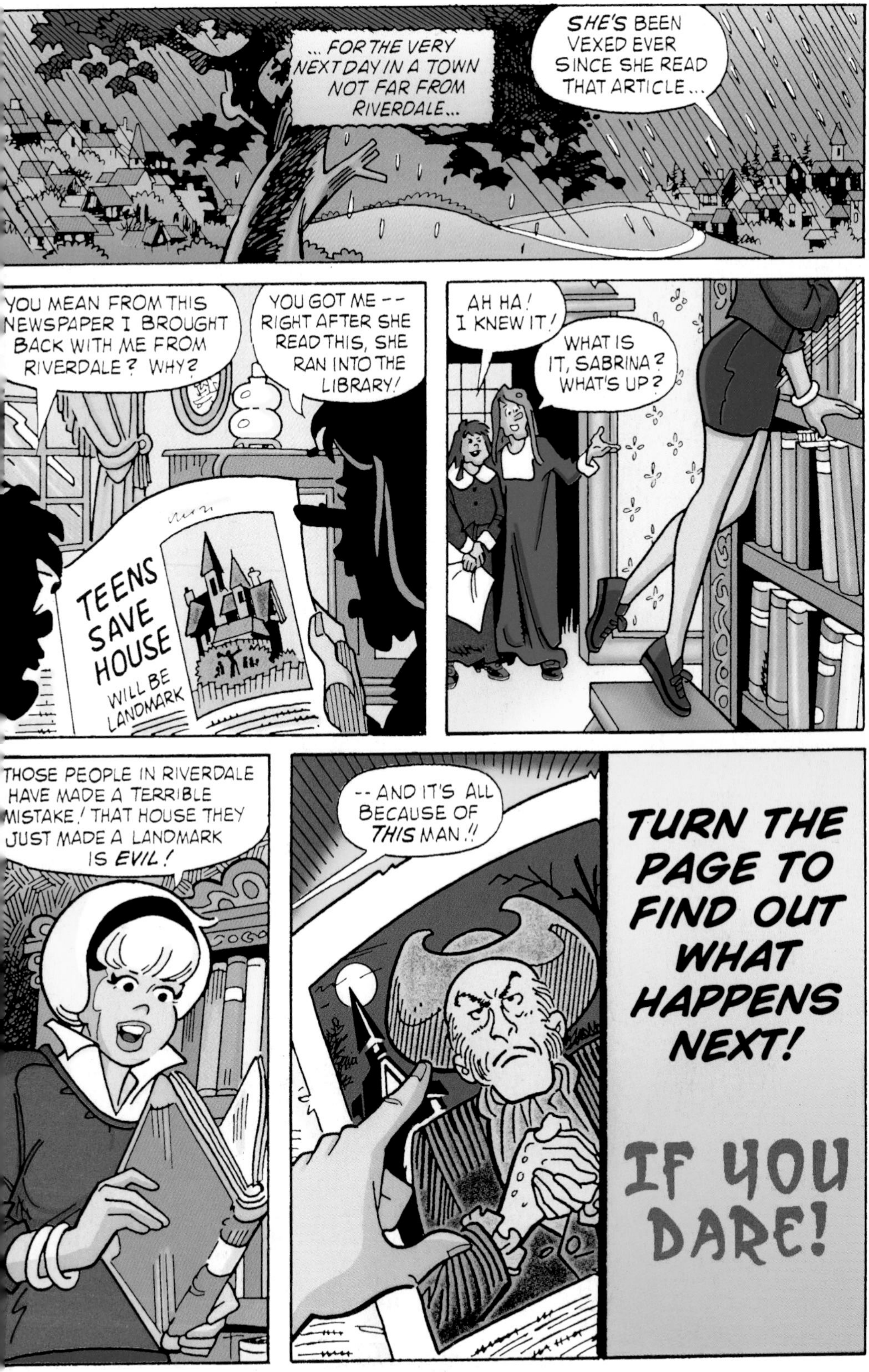
...FOR THE VERY NEXT DAY IN A TOWN NOT FAR FROM RIVERDALE...
SHE'S BEEN VEXED EVER SINCE SHE READ THAT ARTICLE...
YOU MEAN FROM THIS NEWSPAPER I BROUGHT BACK WITH ME FROM RIVERDALE? WHY?
YOU GOT ME -- RIGHT AFTER SHE READ THIS, SHE RAN INTO THE LIBRARY!
TEENS SAVE HOUSE
WILL BE LANDMARK
AH HA! I KNEW IT!
WHAT IS IT, SABRINA? WHAT'S UP?
THOSE PEOPLE IN RIVERDALE HAVE MADE A TERRIBLE MISTAKE! THAT HOUSE THEY JUST MADE A LANDMARK IS EVIL!
-- AND IT'S ALL BECAUSE OF THIS MAN!!
TURN THE PAGE TO FIND OUT WHAT HAPPENS NEXT!
IF YOU DARE!

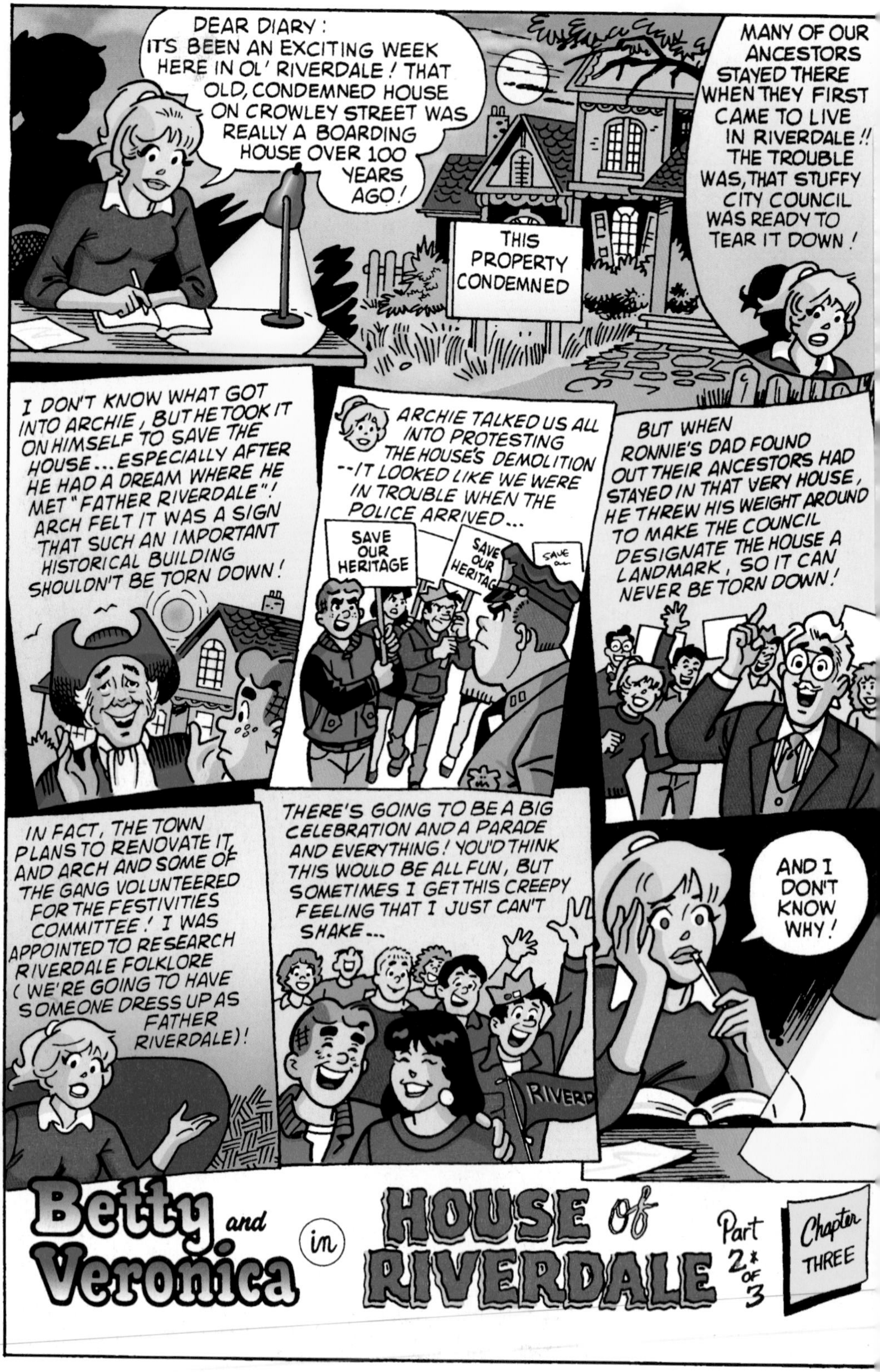
DEAR DIARY: IT'S BEEN AN EXCITING WEEK HERE IN OL' RIVERDALE! THAT OLD, CONDEMNED HOUSE ON CROWLEY STREET WAS REALLY A BOARDING HOUSE OVER 100 YEARS AGO!
THIS PROPERTY CONDEMNED
MANY OF OUR ANCESTORS STAYED THERE WHEN THEY FIRST CAME TO LIVE IN RIVERDALE!! THE TROUBLE WAS, THAT STUFFY CITY COUNCIL WAS READY TO TEAR IT DOWN!
I DON'T KNOW WHAT GOT INTO ARCHIE, BUT HE TOOK IT ON HIMSELF TO SAVE THE HOUSE... ESPECIALLY AFTER HE HAD A DREAM WHERE HE MET "FATHER RIVERDALE"! ARCH FELT IT WAS A SIGN THAT SUCH AN IMPORTANT HISTORICAL BUILDING SHOULDN'T BE TORN DOWN!
ARCHIE TALKED US ALL INTO PROTESTING THE HOUSE'S DEMOLITION --IT LOOKED LIKE WE WERE IN TROUBLE WHEN THE POLICE ARRIVED...
SAVE OUR HERITAGE
BUT WHEN RONNIE'S DAD FOUND OUT THEIR ANCESTORS HAD STAYED IN THAT VERY HOUSE, HE THREW HIS WEIGHT AROUND TO MAKE THE COUNCIL DESIGNATE THE HOUSE A LANDMARK, SO IT CAN NEVER BE TORN DOWN!
IN FACT, THE TOWN PLANS TO RENOVATE IT, AND ARCH AND SOME OF THE GANG VOLUNTEERED FOR THE FESTIVITIES COMMITTEE! I WAS APPOINTED TO RESEARCH RIVERDALE FOLKLORE (WE'RE GOING TO HAVE SOMEONE DRESS UP AS FATHER RIVERDALE)!
THERE'S GOING TO BE A BIG CELEBRATION AND A PARADE AND EVERYTHING! YOU'D THINK THIS WOULD BE ALL FUN, BUT SOMETIMES I GET THIS CREEPY FEELING THAT I JUST CAN'T SHAKE...
AND I DON'T KNOW WHY!
Betty and Veronica in HOUSE of RIVERDALE
Part 2* of 3
Chapter THREE

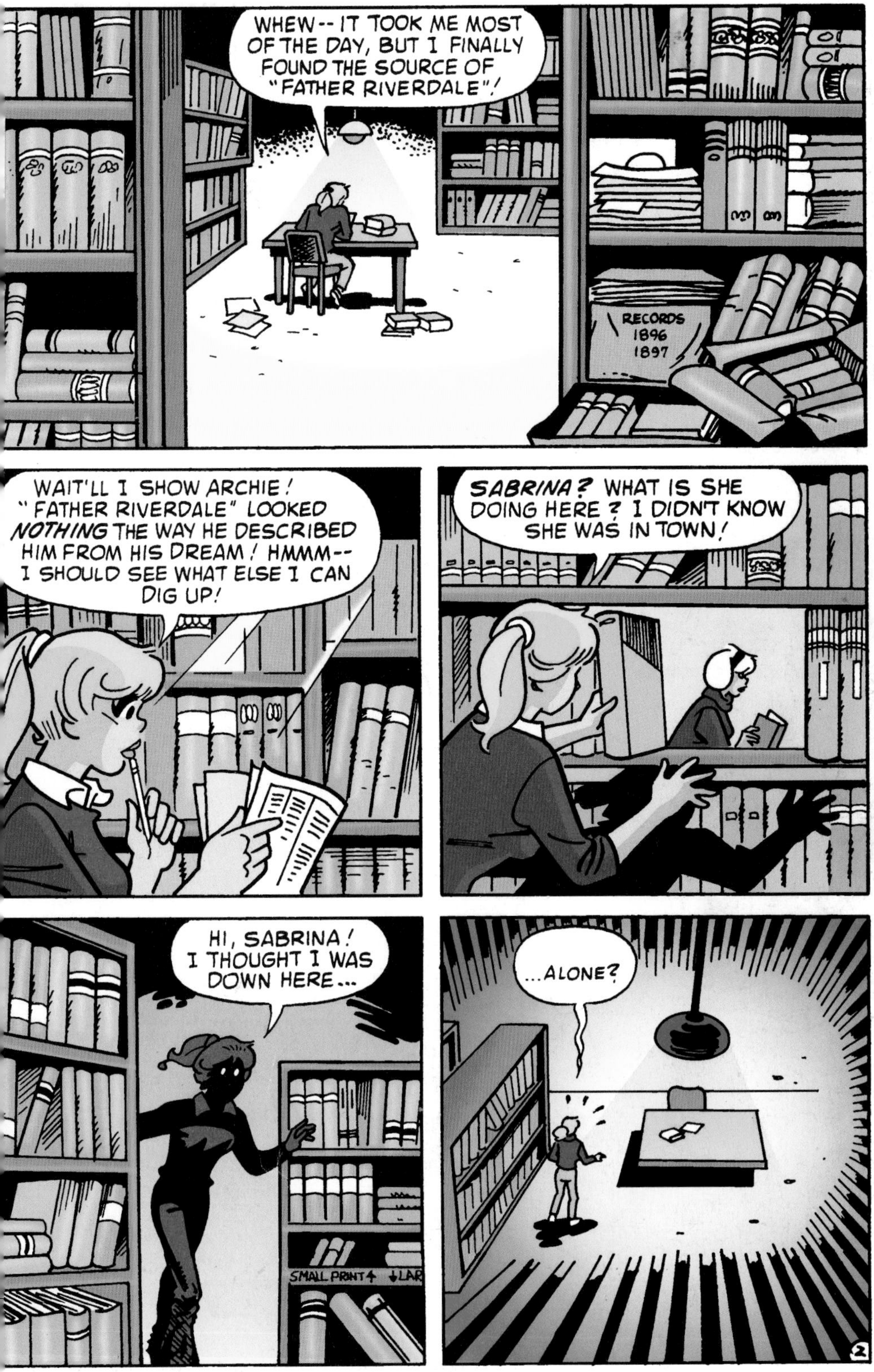
WHEW-- IT TOOK ME MOST OF THE DAY, BUT I FINALLY FOUND THE SOURCE OF "FATHER RIVERDALE"!
RECORDS 1896 1897
WAIT'LL I SHOW ARCHIE! "FATHER RIVERDALE" LOOKED NOTHING THE WAY HE DESCRIBED HIM FROM HIS DREAM! HMMM-- I SHOULD SEE WHAT ELSE I CAN DIG UP!
SABRINA? WHAT IS SHE DOING HERE? I DIDN'T KNOW SHE WAS IN TOWN!
HI, SABRINA! I THOUGHT I WAS DOWN HERE...
SMALL PRINT ↑ ↓LAR
...ALONE?
2

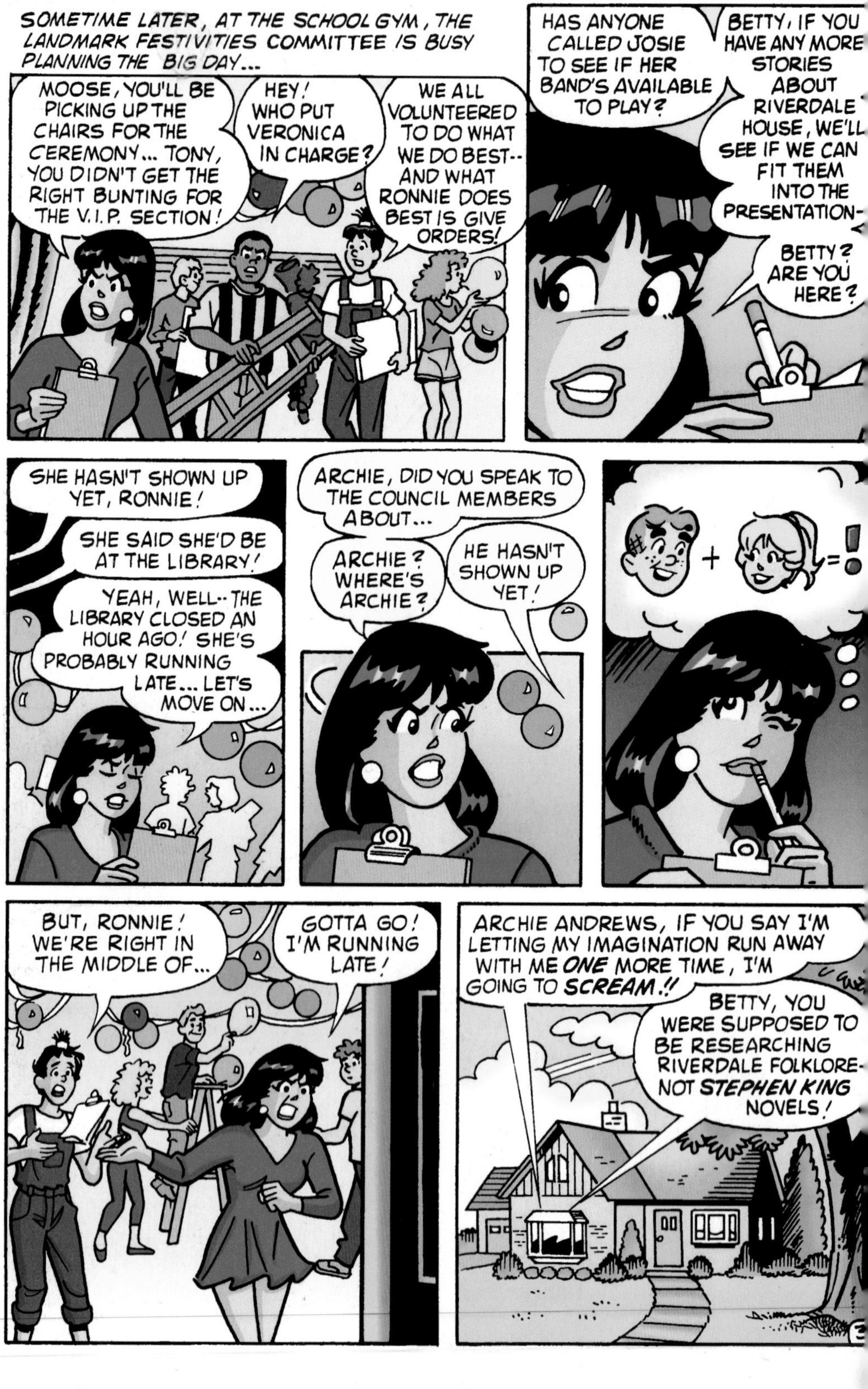
SOMETIME LATER, AT THE SCHOOL GYM, THE LANDMARK FESTIVITIES COMMITTEE IS BUSY PLANNING THE BIG DAY...
MOOSE, YOU'LL BE PICKING UP THE CHAIRS FOR THE CEREMONY... TONY, YOU DIDN'T GET THE RIGHT BUNTING FOR THE V.I.P. SECTION!
HEY! WHO PUT VERONICA IN CHARGE?
WE ALL VOLUNTEERED TO DO WHAT WE DO BEST-- AND WHAT RONNIE DOES BEST IS GIVE ORDERS!
HAS ANYONE CALLED JOSIE TO SEE IF HER BAND'S AVAILABLE TO PLAY?
BETTY, IF YOU HAVE ANY MORE STORIES ABOUT RIVERDALE HOUSE, WE'LL SEE IF WE CAN FIT THEM INTO THE PRESENTATION--
BETTY? ARE YOU HERE?
SHE HASN'T SHOWN UP YET, RONNIE!
SHE SAID SHE'D BE AT THE LIBRARY!
YEAH, WELL-- THE LIBRARY CLOSED AN HOUR AGO! SHE'S PROBABLY RUNNING LATE... LET'S MOVE ON...
ARCHIE, DID YOU SPEAK TO THE COUNCIL MEMBERS ABOUT...
ARCHIE? WHERE'S ARCHIE?
HE HASN'T SHOWN UP YET!
+ = !
BUT, RONNIE! WE'RE RIGHT IN THE MIDDLE OF...
GOTTA GO! I'M RUNNING LATE!
ARCHIE ANDREWS, IF YOU SAY I'M LETTING MY IMAGINATION RUN AWAY WITH ME ONE MORE TIME, I'M GOING TO SCREAM!!
BETTY, YOU WERE SUPPOSED TO BE RESEARCHING RIVERDALE FOLKLORE- NOT STEPHEN KING NOVELS!

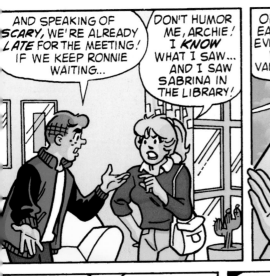

AND SPEAKING OF *SCARY*, WE'RE ALREADY *LATE* FOR THE MEETING! IF WE KEEP RONNIE WAITING...

DON'T HUMOR ME, ARCHIE! I *KNOW* WHAT I SAW... AND I SAW SABRINA IN THE LIBRARY!

OKAY--OKAY! TAKE IT EASY! BUT SHE DOESN'T EVEN LIVE IN RIVERDALE! WHAT DID SHE DO... VANISH INTO THIN AIR?

ARCHIE, WE MAY NOT KNOW SABRINA WELL, BUT DON'T THE *ODDEST* THINGS HAPPEN WHENEVER SHE'S AROUND?

THE ODDEST THING BEING THAT SHE NEVER WANTED TO GO OUT WITH ME!

YEAH, WELL... ANYWAY, WHY WERE THESE PAPERS AND DIARY LEFT ON THE TABLE WHERE SHE WAS SITTING?

THIS STUFF LOOKS PRETTY OLD! I'M SURPRISED THE LIBRARY LENT IT TO YOU!

LENDING'S *NOT* THE RIGHT WORD!

I...AH, BORROWED IT!

BETTY! DID THE ODOR OF MUSTY OLD PAPERS AFFECT YOUR BRAIN?

TAKE A LOOK, WISE GUY--*LEANDER VAN DERMEULEN!* HE WAS A DRIFTER WHO SETTLED IN RIVERDALE ... PAGE AFTER PAGE HE WROTE HOW MUCH HE RESENTED *PROGRESS!*

PROGRESS?

4

OCT. 19, 1895 THE TOWNSPEOPLE DO THEIR LAND AN INJUSTICE; THEY HAVE SUCCUMBED TO INDUSTRY... I HAVE FOUND THE PSYCHIC NEXUS WHICH THEY HAVE CHOSEN TO IGNORE... THEY ARE BUT CHILDREN AND I, THEIR PROTECTIVE PATRIARCH... WHY WILL THEY NOT ACKNOWLEDGE THAT FACT?!

WEIRD-- BUT SO WHAT? IT'S A GOOD THING NO ONE LISTENED TO HIM! WE'D BE WATCHING CABLE TV BY CANDLE LIGHT!

THE DIARY IS FILLED WITH RANTING LIKE THIS-- BUT THERE WAS ALSO A NEWSPAPER CLIPPING...

VAN DERMEULEN WAS TRAINING THE YOUTH OF RIVERDALE IN THE PSYCHIC SCIENCES-- *SORCERY* TO FIGHT INDUSTRY IN THE 20TH CENTURY!

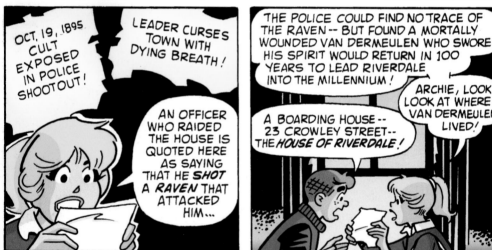

OCT. 19, 1895. CULT EXPOSED IN POLICE SHOOTOUT!

LEADER CURSES TOWN WITH DYING BREATH!

AN OFFICER WHO RAIDED THE HOUSE IS QUOTED HERE AS SAYING THAT HE *SHOT* A *RAVEN* THAT ATTACKED HIM...

THE POLICE COULD FIND NO TRACE OF THE RAVEN -- BUT FOUND A MORTALLY WOUNDED VAN DERMEULEN WHO SWORE HIS SPIRIT WOULD RETURN IN 100 YEARS TO LEAD RIVERDALE INTO THE MILLENNIUM!

A BOARDING HOUSE -- 23 CROWLEY STREET-- THE *HOUSE OF RIVERDALE!*

ARCHIE, LOOK, LOOK AT WHERE VAN DERMEULEN LIVED!

C'MON, BETTY! WHAT ARE YOU TRYING TO SAY? IT'S JUST A COINCIDENCE! JUST BECAUSE THIS VAN DERMEULEN CHARACTER WAS ABLE TO GET SOME KIDS TO JOIN HIS CULT DOESN'T MEAN HE WAS A SORCERER!

I DON'T KNOW, ARCHIE... THERE WAS AN OLD PHOTO OF VAN DERMEULEN TUCKED AWAY IN THE DIARY--- HE LOOKS LIKE HE'S READY TO CONJURE UP SOMETHING BAD!

F- FATHER RIVERDALE!

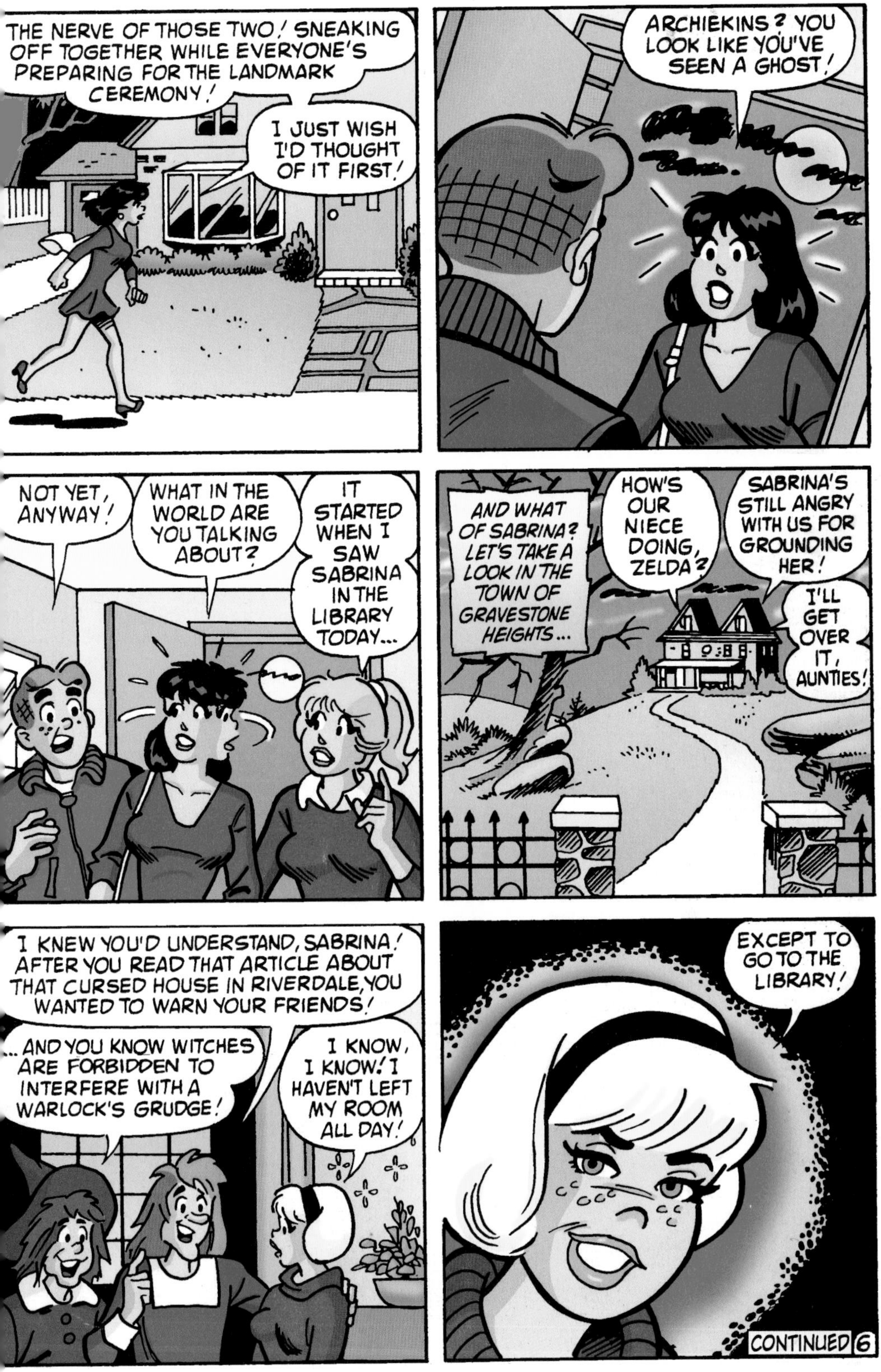
THE NERVE OF THOSE TWO! SNEAKING OFF TOGETHER WHILE EVERYONE'S PREPARING FOR THE LANDMARK CEREMONY!
I JUST WISH I'D THOUGHT OF IT FIRST!
ARCHIEKINS? YOU LOOK LIKE YOU'VE SEEN A GHOST!
NOT YET, ANYWAY!
WHAT IN THE WORLD ARE YOU TALKING ABOUT?
IT STARTED WHEN I SAW SABRINA IN THE LIBRARY TODAY...
AND WHAT OF SABRINA? LET'S TAKE A LOOK IN THE TOWN OF GRAVESTONE HEIGHTS...
HOW'S OUR NIECE DOING, ZELDA?
SABRINA'S STILL ANGRY WITH US FOR GROUNDING HER!
I'LL GET OVER IT, AUNTIES!
I KNEW YOU'D UNDERSTAND, SABRINA! AFTER YOU READ THAT ARTICLE ABOUT THAT CURSED HOUSE IN RIVERDALE, YOU WANTED TO WARN YOUR FRIENDS!
...AND YOU KNOW WITCHES ARE FORBIDDEN TO INTERFERE WITH A WARLOCK'S GRUDGE!
I KNOW, I KNOW! I HAVEN'T LEFT MY ROOM ALL DAY!
EXCEPT TO GO TO THE LIBRARY!
CONTINUED 6

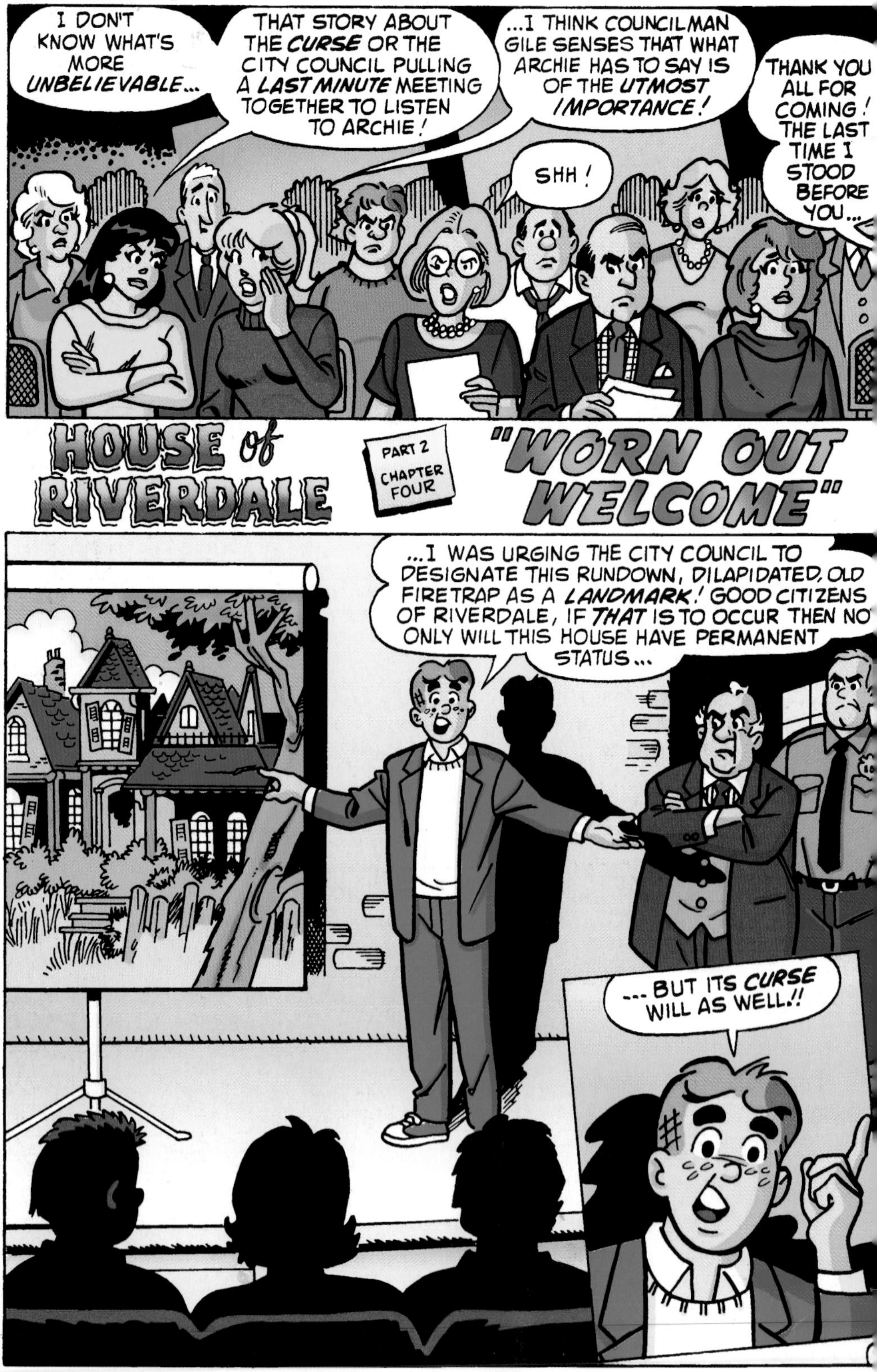
I DON'T KNOW WHAT'S MORE UNBELIEVABLE...
THAT STORY ABOUT THE CURSE OR THE CITY COUNCIL PULLING A LAST MINUTE MEETING TOGETHER TO LISTEN TO ARCHIE!
...I THINK COUNCILMAN GILE SENSES THAT WHAT ARCHIE HAS TO SAY IS OF THE UTMOST IMPORTANCE!
SHH!
THANK YOU ALL FOR COMING! THE LAST TIME I STOOD BEFORE YOU...
HOUSE of RIVERDALE
PART 2 CHAPTER FOUR
"WORN OUT WELCOME"
...I WAS URGING THE CITY COUNCIL TO DESIGNATE THIS RUNDOWN, DILAPIDATED, OLD FIRETRAP AS A LANDMARK! GOOD CITIZENS OF RIVERDALE, IF THAT IS TO OCCUR THEN NO ONLY WILL THIS HOUSE HAVE PERMANENT STATUS...
... BUT ITS CURSE WILL AS WELL!!

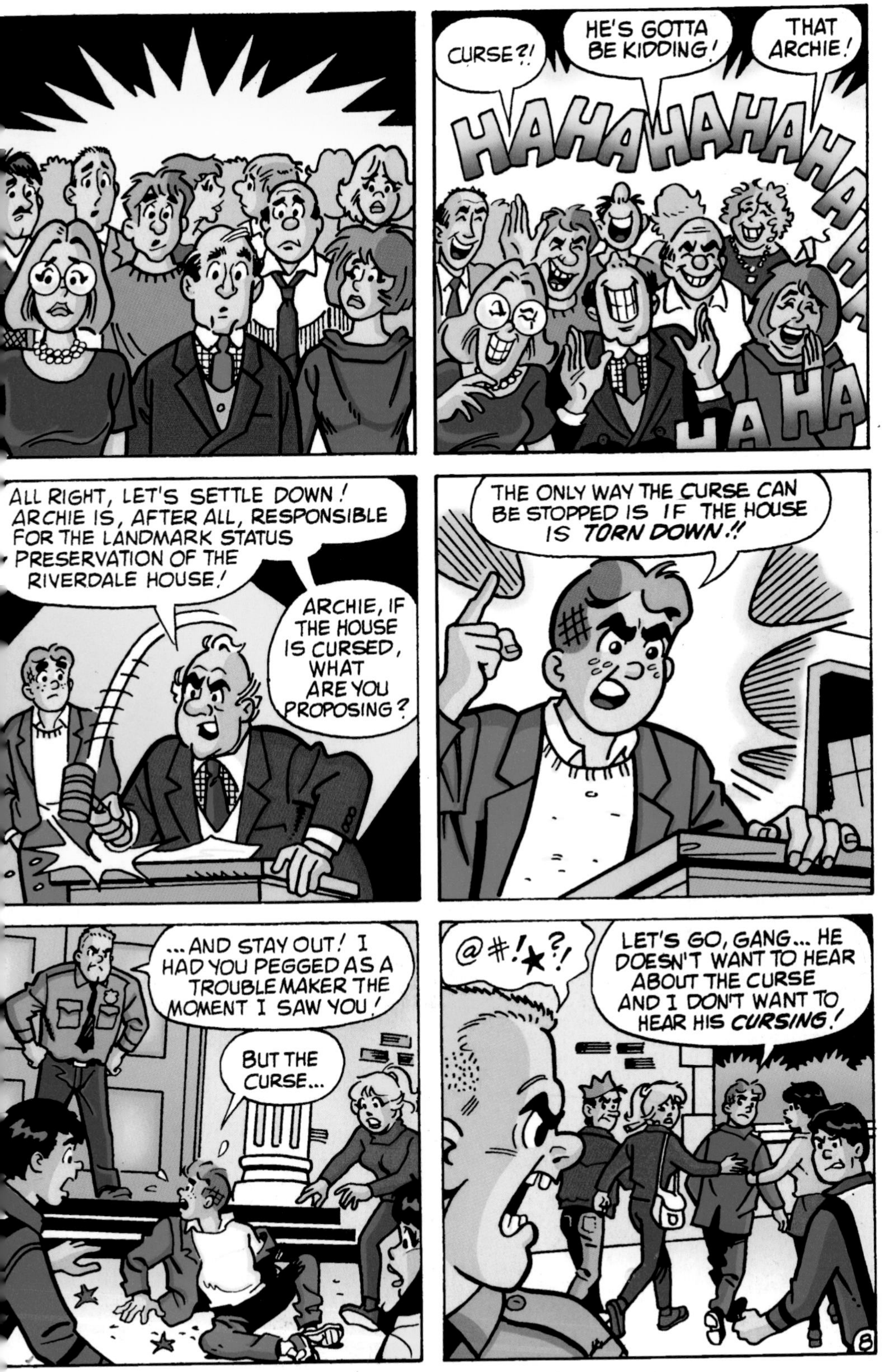
CURSE?!
HE'S GOTTA BE KIDDING!
THAT ARCHIE!
HAHAHAHAHAHAHAHA
HAHA
ALL RIGHT, LET'S SETTLE DOWN! ARCHIE IS, AFTER ALL, RESPONSIBLE FOR THE LANDMARK STATUS PRESERVATION OF THE RIVERDALE HOUSE!
ARCHIE, IF THE HOUSE IS CURSED, WHAT ARE YOU PROPOSING?
THE ONLY WAY THE CURSE CAN BE STOPPED IS IF THE HOUSE IS TORN DOWN!!
...AND STAY OUT! I HAD YOU PEGGED AS A TROUBLEMAKER THE MOMENT I SAW YOU!
BUT THE CURSE...
@#!★?!
LET'S GO, GANG... HE DOESN'T WANT TO HEAR ABOUT THE CURSE AND I DON'T WANT TO HEAR HIS CURSING!
8

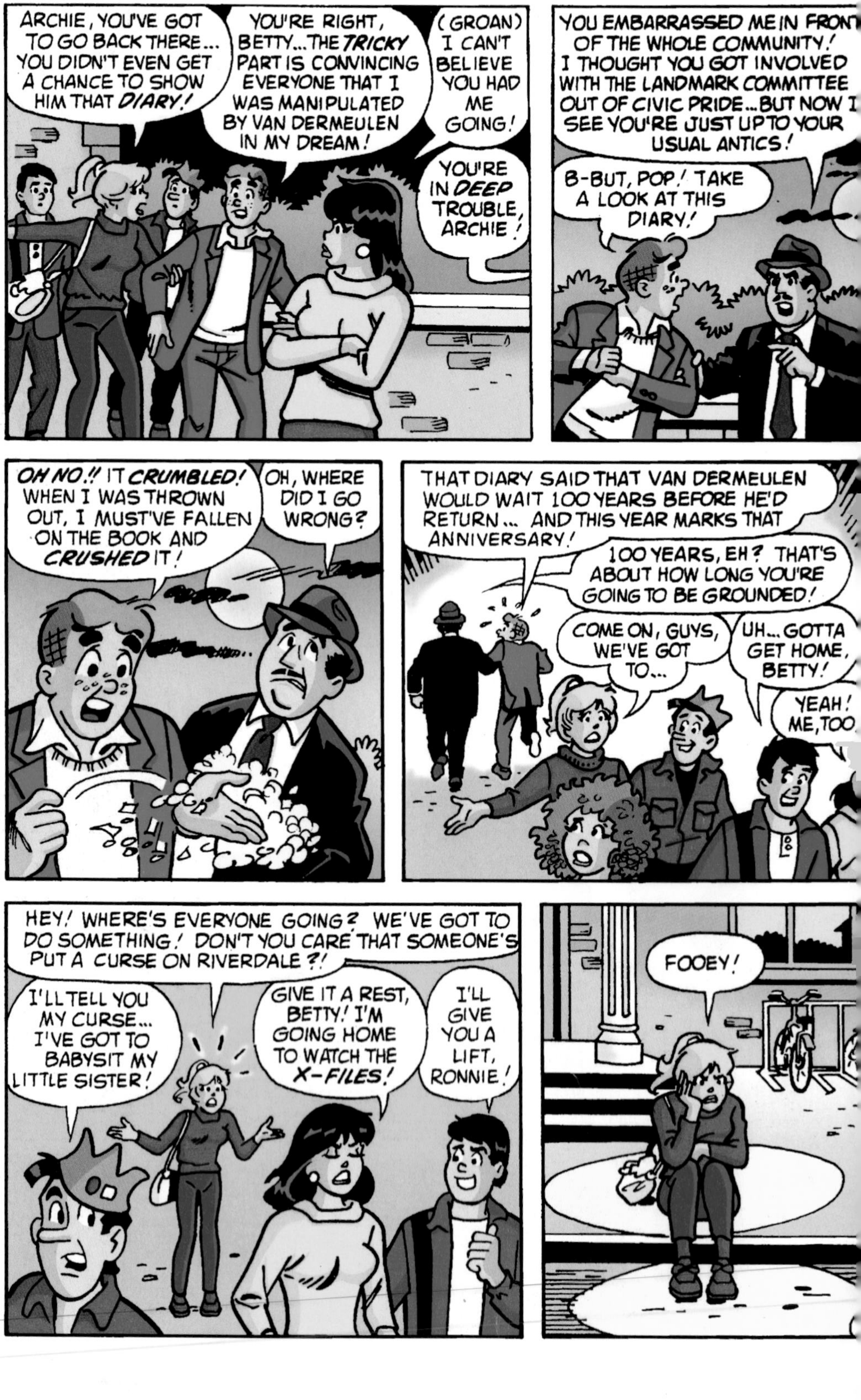
ARCHIE, YOU'VE GOT TO GO BACK THERE... YOU DIDN'T EVEN GET A CHANCE TO SHOW HIM THAT DIARY!
YOU'RE RIGHT, BETTY...THE TRICKY PART IS CONVINCING EVERYONE THAT I WAS MANIPULATED BY VAN DERMEULEN IN MY DREAM!
(GROAN) I CAN'T BELIEVE YOU HAD ME GOING!
YOU'RE IN DEEP TROUBLE, ARCHIE!
YOU EMBARRASSED ME IN FRONT OF THE WHOLE COMMUNITY! I THOUGHT YOU GOT INVOLVED WITH THE LANDMARK COMMITTEE OUT OF CIVIC PRIDE...BUT NOW I SEE YOU'RE JUST UP TO YOUR USUAL ANTICS!
B-BUT, POP! TAKE A LOOK AT THIS DIARY!
OH NO!! IT CRUMBLED! WHEN I WAS THROWN OUT, I MUST'VE FALLEN ON THE BOOK AND CRUSHED IT!
OH, WHERE DID I GO WRONG?
THAT DIARY SAID THAT VAN DERMEULEN WOULD WAIT 100 YEARS BEFORE HE'D RETURN... AND THIS YEAR MARKS THAT ANNIVERSARY!
100 YEARS, EH? THAT'S ABOUT HOW LONG YOU'RE GOING TO BE GROUNDED!
COME ON, GUYS, WE'VE GOT TO...
UH...GOTTA GET HOME, BETTY!
YEAH! ME, TOO
HEY! WHERE'S EVERYONE GOING? WE'VE GOT TO DO SOMETHING! DON'T YOU CARE THAT SOMEONE'S PUT A CURSE ON RIVERDALE?!
I'LL TELL YOU MY CURSE... I'VE GOT TO BABYSIT MY LITTLE SISTER!
GIVE IT A REST, BETTY! I'M GOING HOME TO WATCH THE X-FILES!
I'LL GIVE YOU A LIFT, RONNIE!
FOOEY!

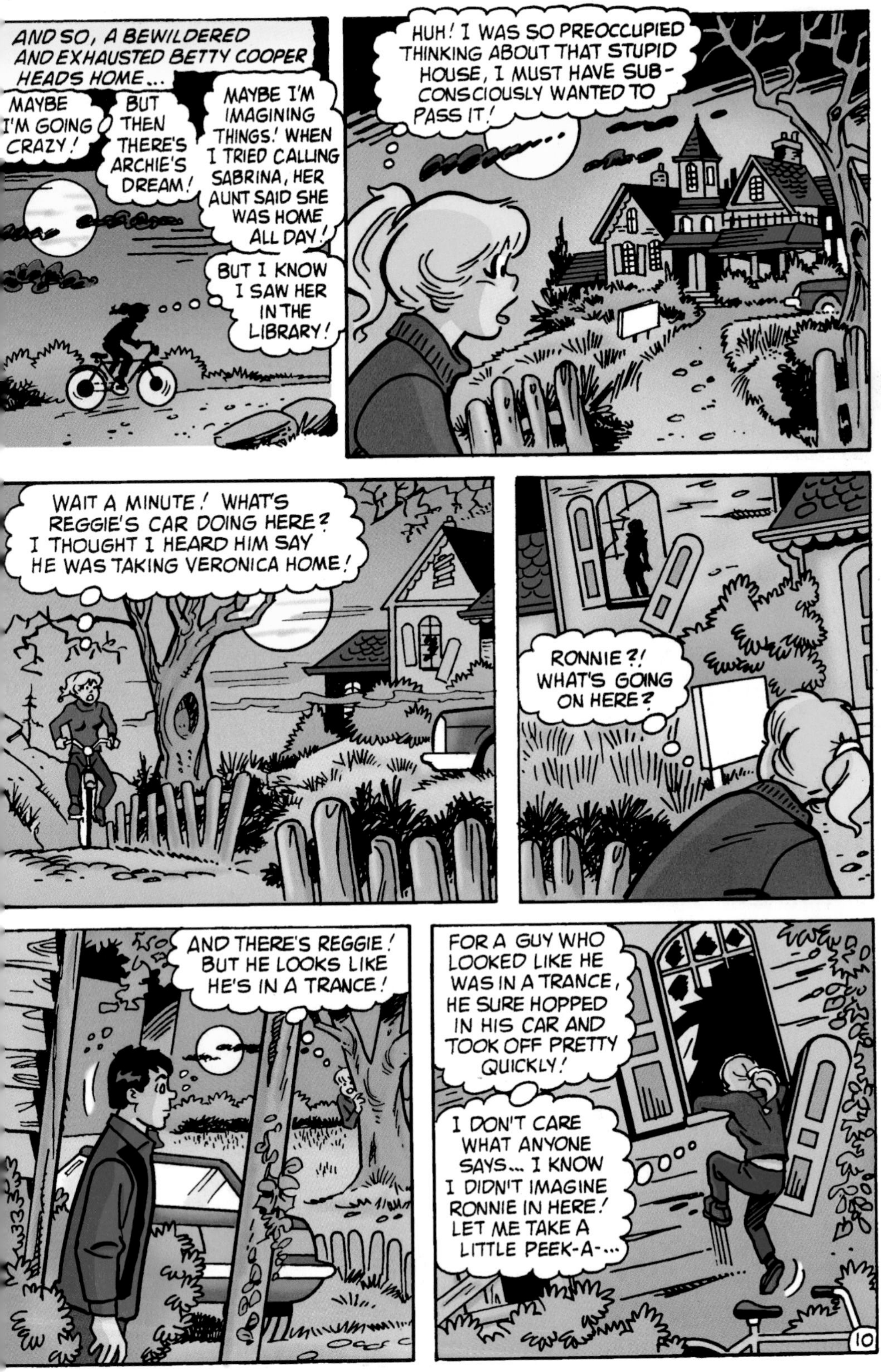
AND SO, A BEWILDERED AND EXHAUSTED BETTY COOPER HEADS HOME...
MAYBE I'M GOING CRAZY!
BUT THEN THERE'S ARCHIE'S DREAM!
MAYBE I'M IMAGINING THINGS! WHEN I TRIED CALLING SABRINA, HER AUNT SAID SHE WAS HOME ALL DAY!
BUT I KNOW I SAW HER IN THE LIBRARY!
HUH! I WAS SO PREOCCUPIED THINKING ABOUT THAT STUPID HOUSE, I MUST HAVE SUB-CONSCIOUSLY WANTED TO PASS IT!
WAIT A MINUTE! WHAT'S REGGIE'S CAR DOING HERE? I THOUGHT I HEARD HIM SAY HE WAS TAKING VERONICA HOME!
RONNIE?! WHAT'S GOING ON HERE?
AND THERE'S REGGIE! BUT HE LOOKS LIKE HE'S IN A TRANCE!
FOR A GUY WHO LOOKED LIKE HE WAS IN A TRANCE, HE SURE HOPPED IN HIS CAR AND TOOK OFF PRETTY QUICKLY!
I DON'T CARE WHAT ANYONE SAYS... I KNOW I DIDN'T IMAGINE RONNIE IN HERE! LET ME TAKE A LITTLE PEEK-A-...
10

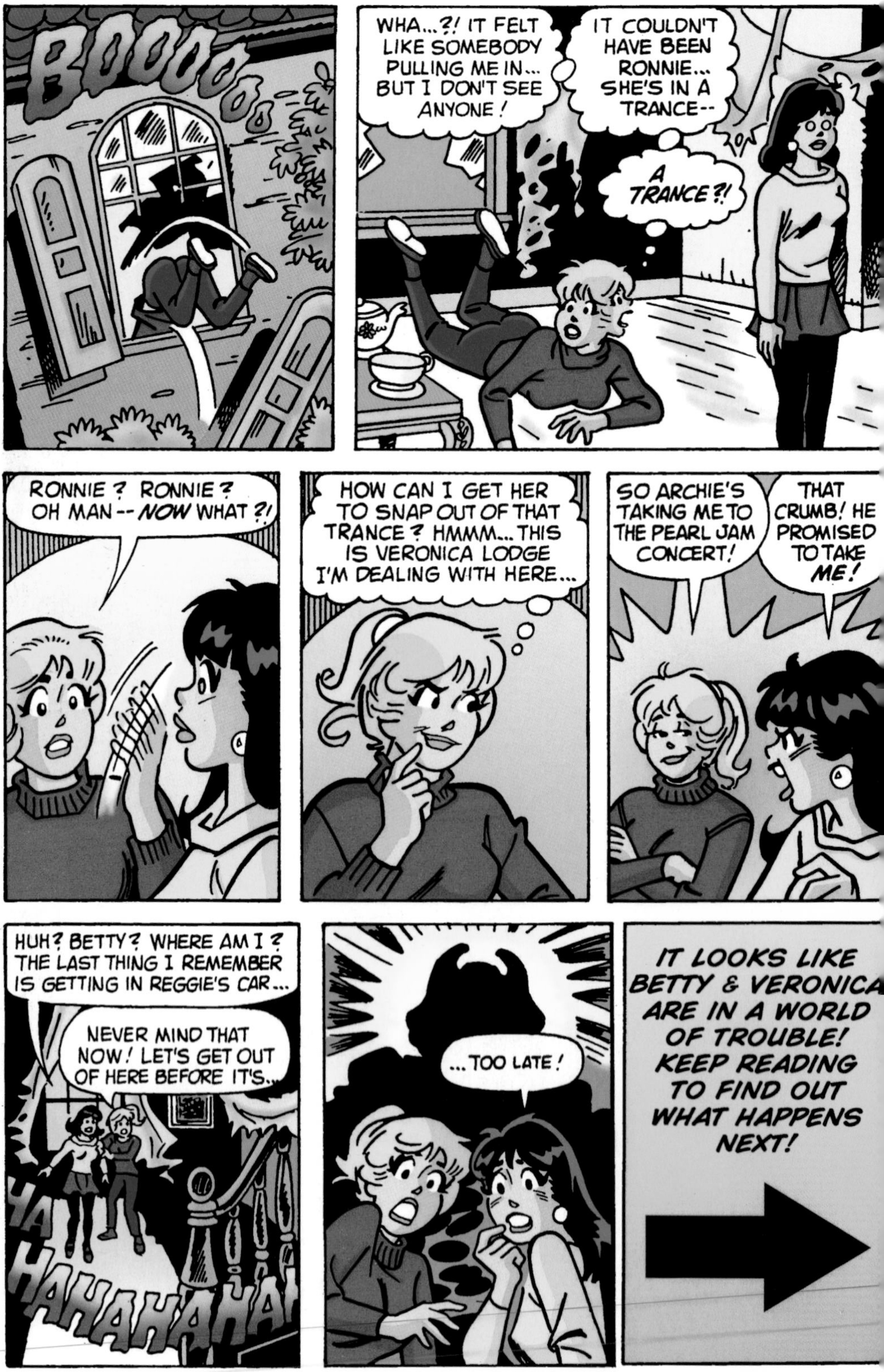
BOOOOoo
WHA...?! IT FELT LIKE SOMEBODY PULLING ME IN... BUT I DON'T SEE ANYONE!
IT COULDN'T HAVE BEEN RONNIE... SHE'S IN A TRANCE--
A TRANCE?!
RONNIE? RONNIE? OH MAN--NOW WHAT?!
HOW CAN I GET HER TO SNAP OUT OF THAT TRANCE? HMMM... THIS IS VERONICA LODGE I'M DEALING WITH HERE...
SO ARCHIE'S TAKING ME TO THE PEARL JAM CONCERT!
THAT CRUMB! HE PROMISED TO TAKE ME!
HUH? BETTY? WHERE AM I? THE LAST THING I REMEMBER IS GETTING IN REGGIE'S CAR...
NEVER MIND THAT NOW! LET'S GET OUT OF HERE BEFORE IT'S...
HAHAHAHAHA
...TOO LATE!
IT LOOKS LIKE BETTY & VERONICA ARE IN A WORLD OF TROUBLE! KEEP READING TO FIND OUT WHAT HAPPENS NEXT!

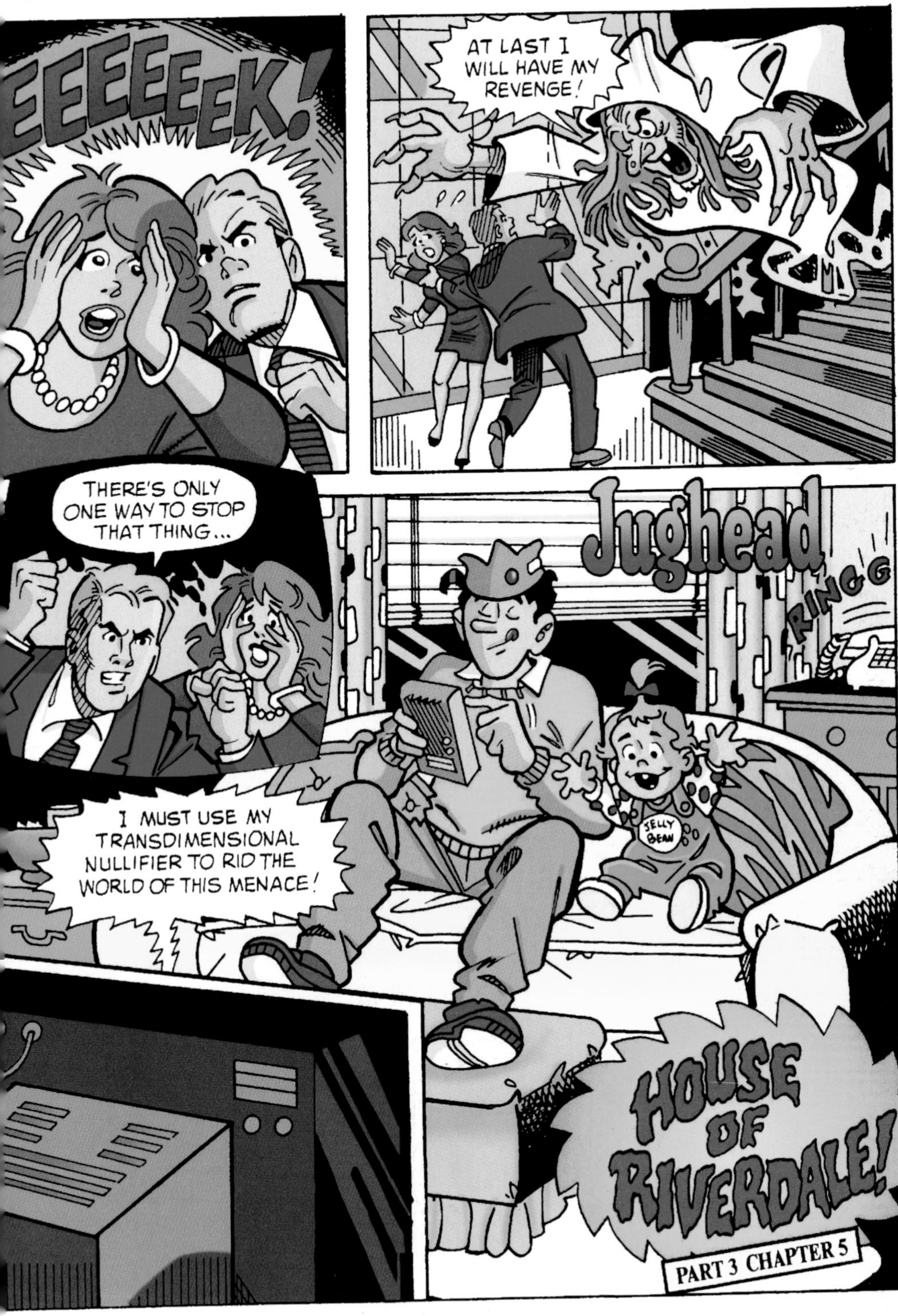
EEEEEEEK!
AT LAST I WILL HAVE MY REVENGE!
THERE'S ONLY ONE WAY TO STOP THAT THING...
I MUST USE MY TRANSDIMENSIONAL NULLIFIER TO RID THE WORLD OF THIS MENACE!
Jughead
RINGG
JELLY BEAN
HOUSE OF RIVERDALE!
PART 3 CHAPTER 5

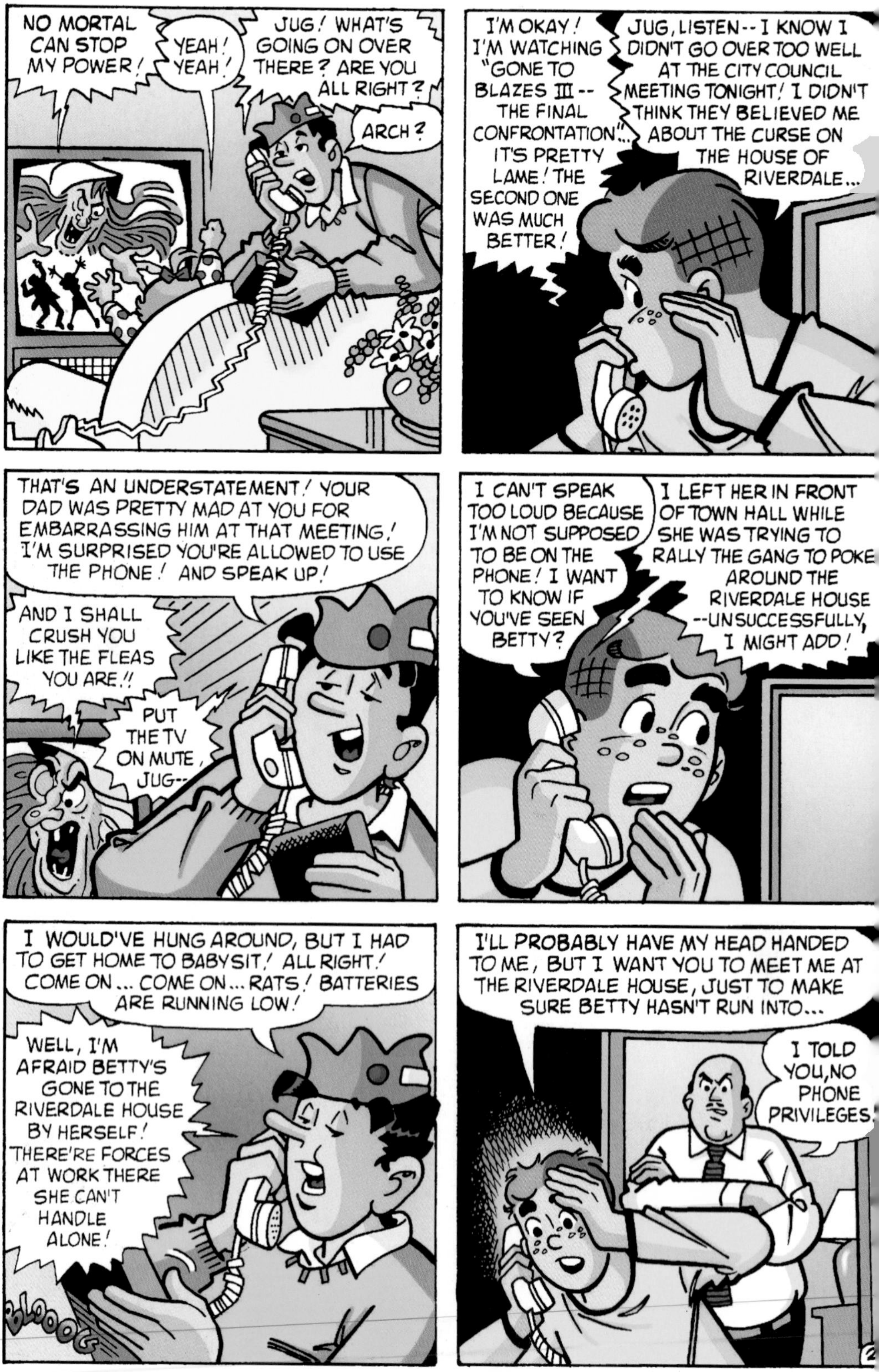
NO MORTAL CAN STOP MY POWER!
YEAH! YEAH!
JUG! WHAT'S GOING ON OVER THERE? ARE YOU ALL RIGHT?
ARCH?
I'M OKAY! I'M WATCHING "GONE TO BLAZES III -- THE FINAL CONFRONTATION"... IT'S PRETTY LAME! THE SECOND ONE WAS MUCH BETTER!
JUG, LISTEN-- I KNOW I DIDN'T GO OVER TOO WELL AT THE CITY COUNCIL MEETING TONIGHT! I DIDN'T THINK THEY BELIEVED ME ABOUT THE CURSE ON THE HOUSE OF RIVERDALE...
THAT'S AN UNDERSTATEMENT! YOUR DAD WAS PRETTY MAD AT YOU FOR EMBARRASSING HIM AT THAT MEETING! I'M SURPRISED YOU'RE ALLOWED TO USE THE PHONE! AND SPEAK UP!
AND I SHALL CRUSH YOU LIKE THE FLEAS YOU ARE!!
PUT THE TV ON MUTE, JUG--
I CAN'T SPEAK TOO LOUD BECAUSE I'M NOT SUPPOSED TO BE ON THE PHONE! I WANT TO KNOW IF YOU'VE SEEN BETTY?
I LEFT HER IN FRONT OF TOWN HALL WHILE SHE WAS TRYING TO RALLY THE GANG TO POKE AROUND THE RIVERDALE HOUSE --UNSUCCESSFULLY, I MIGHT ADD!
I WOULD'VE HUNG AROUND, BUT I HAD TO GET HOME TO BABYSIT! ALL RIGHT! COME ON... COME ON... RATS! BATTERIES ARE RUNNING LOW!
WELL, I'M AFRAID BETTY'S GONE TO THE RIVERDALE HOUSE BY HERSELF! THERE'RE FORCES AT WORK THERE SHE CAN'T HANDLE ALONE!
I'LL PROBABLY HAVE MY HEAD HANDED TO ME, BUT I WANT YOU TO MEET ME AT THE RIVERDALE HOUSE, JUST TO MAKE SURE BETTY HASN'T RUN INTO...
I TOLD YOU, NO PHONE PRIVILEGES!

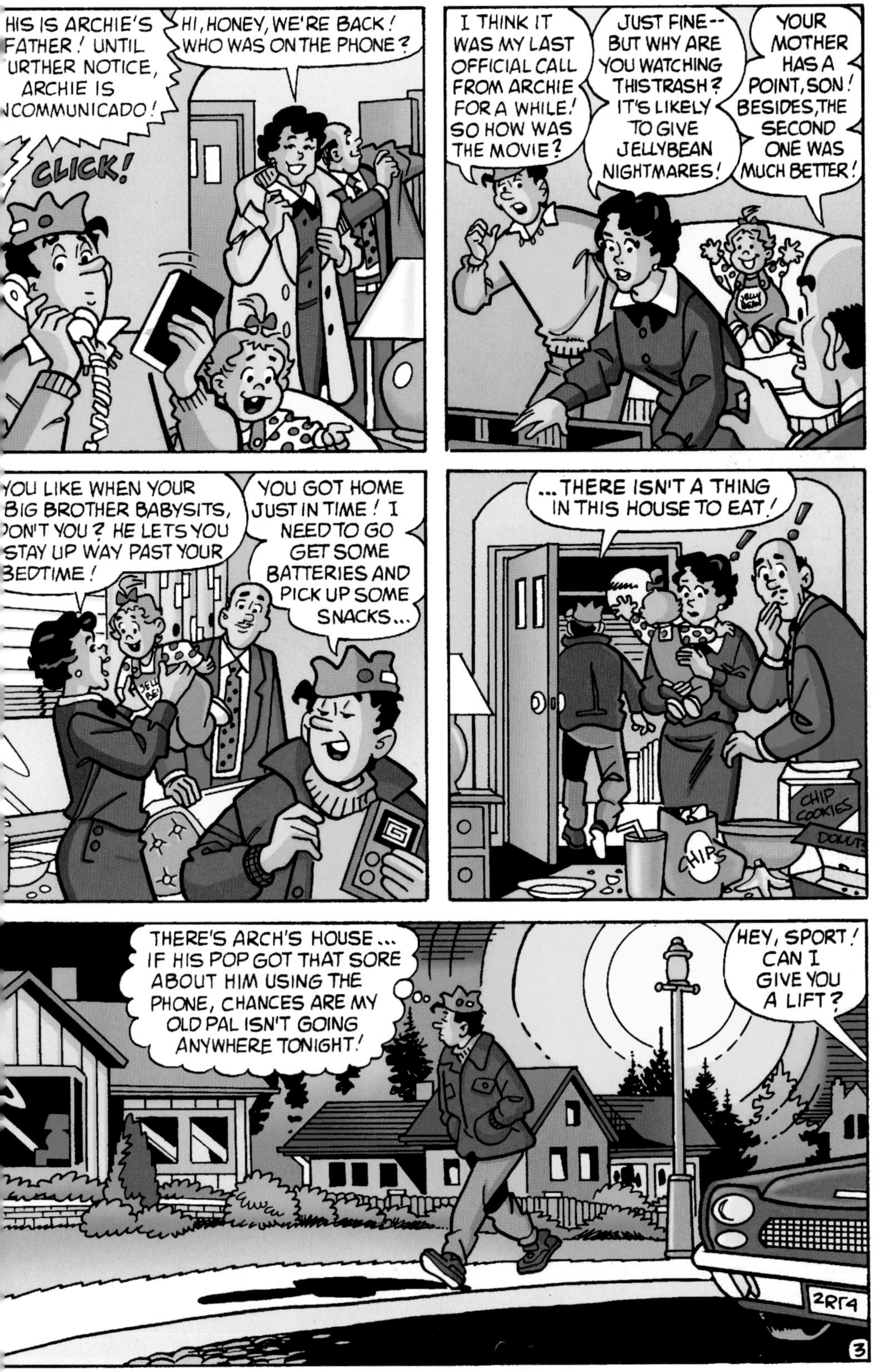
HIS IS ARCHIE'S FATHER! UNTIL URTHER NOTICE, ARCHIE IS ICOMMUNICADO!
CLICK!
HI, HONEY, WE'RE BACK! WHO WAS ON THE PHONE?
I THINK IT WAS MY LAST OFFICIAL CALL FROM ARCHIE FOR A WHILE! SO HOW WAS THE MOVIE?
JUST FINE-- BUT WHY ARE YOU WATCHING THIS TRASH? IT'S LIKELY TO GIVE JELLYBEAN NIGHTMARES!
YOUR MOTHER HAS A POINT, SON! BESIDES, THE SECOND ONE WAS MUCH BETTER!
YOU LIKE WHEN YOUR BIG BROTHER BABYSITS, DON'T YOU? HE LETS YOU STAY UP WAY PAST YOUR BEDTIME!
YOU GOT HOME JUST IN TIME! I NEED TO GO GET SOME BATTERIES AND PICK UP SOME SNACKS...
...THERE ISN'T A THING IN THIS HOUSE TO EAT!
CHIP COOKIES
DONUTS
CHIPS
THERE'S ARCH'S HOUSE... IF HIS POP GOT THAT SORE ABOUT HIM USING THE PHONE, CHANCES ARE MY OLD PAL ISN'T GOING ANYWHERE TONIGHT!
HEY, SPORT! CAN I GIVE YOU A LIFT?
2RT4
3

REGGIE? *YOU'RE* OFFERING ME A RIDE? WHAT'S THE CATCH?

NO CATCH, BUDDY! I TRIED CALLING ON ANDREWS, BUT HE'S GROUNDED! I SAW YOU GOING MY WAY, SO HOP IN!

SURE, WHY NOT? I'M HEADING FOR THE CONVENIENCE STORE!

BUCKLE UP-- I KNOW A SHORTCUT...

EVEN THOUGH MY DAD MADE ME TURN REGGIE AWAY, I COULD TELL SOMETHING WASN'T RIGHT WITH HIM! THERE WAS A VACANT LOOK IN HIS EYES, AS IF HE WAS IN A TRANCE!

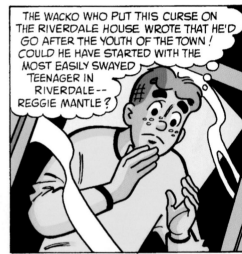

THE WACKO WHO PUT THIS CURSE ON THE RIVERDALE HOUSE WROTE THAT HE'D GO AFTER THE YOUTH OF THE TOWN! COULD HE HAVE STARTED WITH THE MOST EASILY SWAYED TEENAGER IN RIVERDALE-- REGGIE MANTLE?

SOMETHING TELLS ME I BETTER GET TO THE RIVERDALE HOUSE, AND PRONTO!

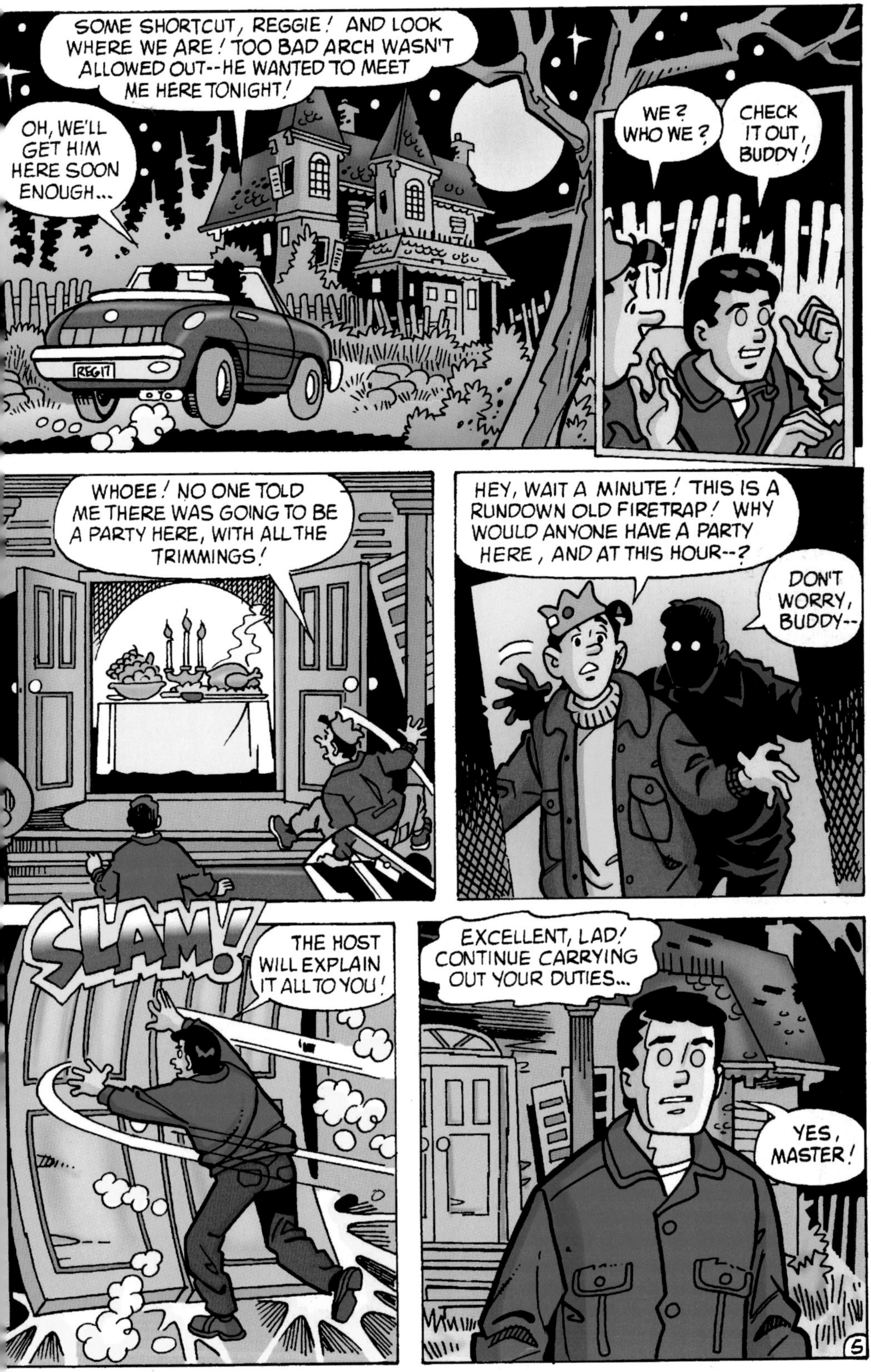
SOME SHORTCUT, REGGIE! AND LOOK WHERE WE ARE! TOO BAD ARCH WASN'T ALLOWED OUT--HE WANTED TO MEET ME HERE TONIGHT!
OH, WE'LL GET HIM HERE SOON ENOUGH...
REG17
WE? WHO WE?
CHECK IT OUT, BUDDY!
WHOEE! NO ONE TOLD ME THERE WAS GOING TO BE A PARTY HERE, WITH ALL THE TRIMMINGS!
HEY, WAIT A MINUTE! THIS IS A RUNDOWN OLD FIRETRAP! WHY WOULD ANYONE HAVE A PARTY HERE, AND AT THIS HOUR--?
DON'T WORRY, BUDDY--
SLAM!
THE HOST WILL EXPLAIN IT ALL TO YOU!
EXCELLENT, LAD! CONTINUE CARRYING OUT YOUR DUTIES...
YES, MASTER!
5

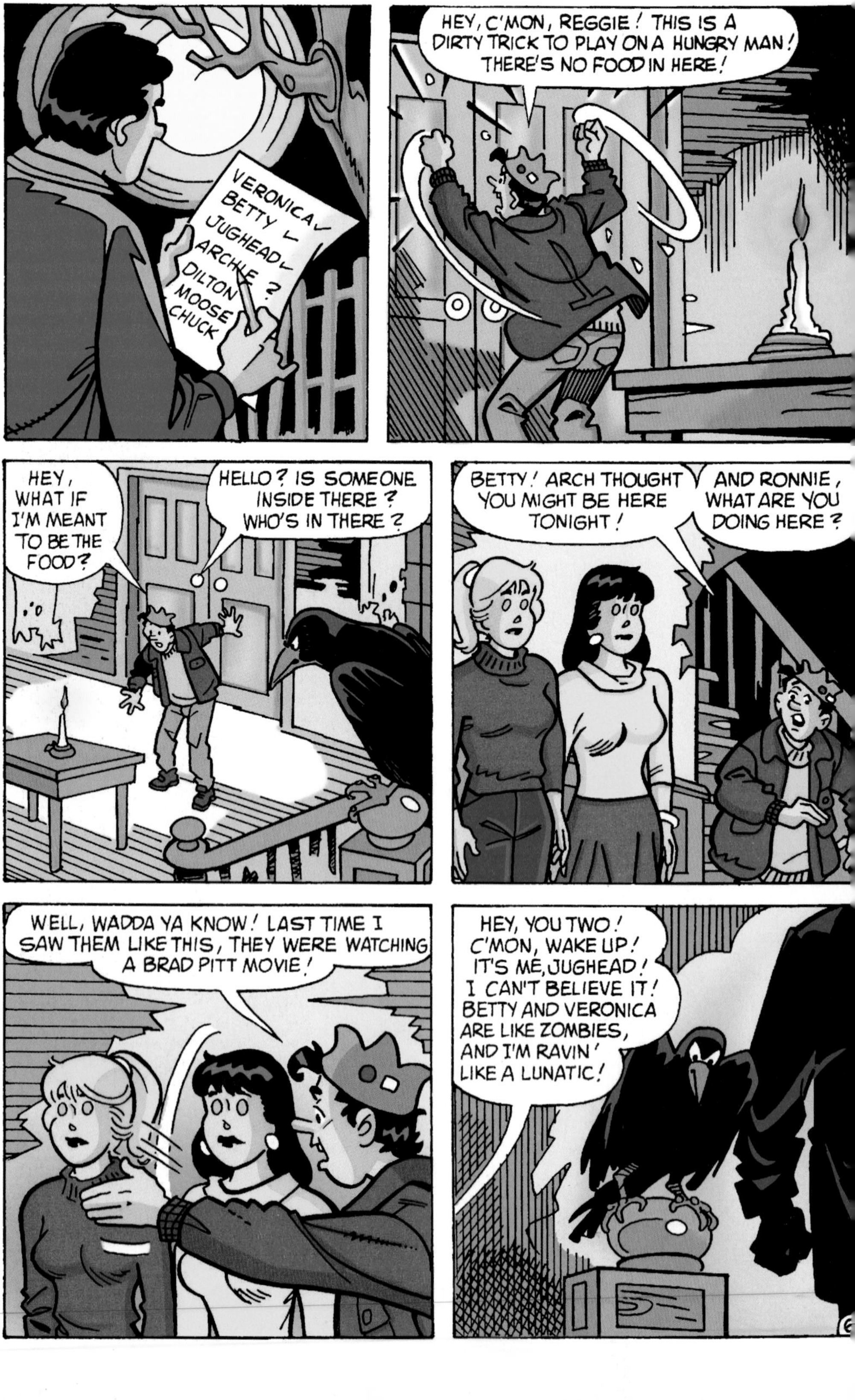
VERONICA
BETTY
JUGHEAD
ARCHIE ?
DILTON
MOOSE
CHUCK
HEY, C'MON, REGGIE! THIS IS A DIRTY TRICK TO PLAY ON A HUNGRY MAN! THERE'S NO FOOD IN HERE!
HEY, WHAT IF I'M MEANT TO BE THE FOOD?
HELLO? IS SOMEONE INSIDE THERE? WHO'S IN THERE?
BETTY! ARCH THOUGHT YOU MIGHT BE HERE TONIGHT!
AND RONNIE, WHAT ARE YOU DOING HERE?
WELL, WADDA YA KNOW! LAST TIME I SAW THEM LIKE THIS, THEY WERE WATCHING A BRAD PITT MOVIE!
HEY, YOU TWO! C'MON, WAKE UP! IT'S ME, JUGHEAD! I CAN'T BELIEVE IT! BETTY AND VERONICA ARE LIKE ZOMBIES, AND I'M RAVIN' LIKE A LUNATIC!

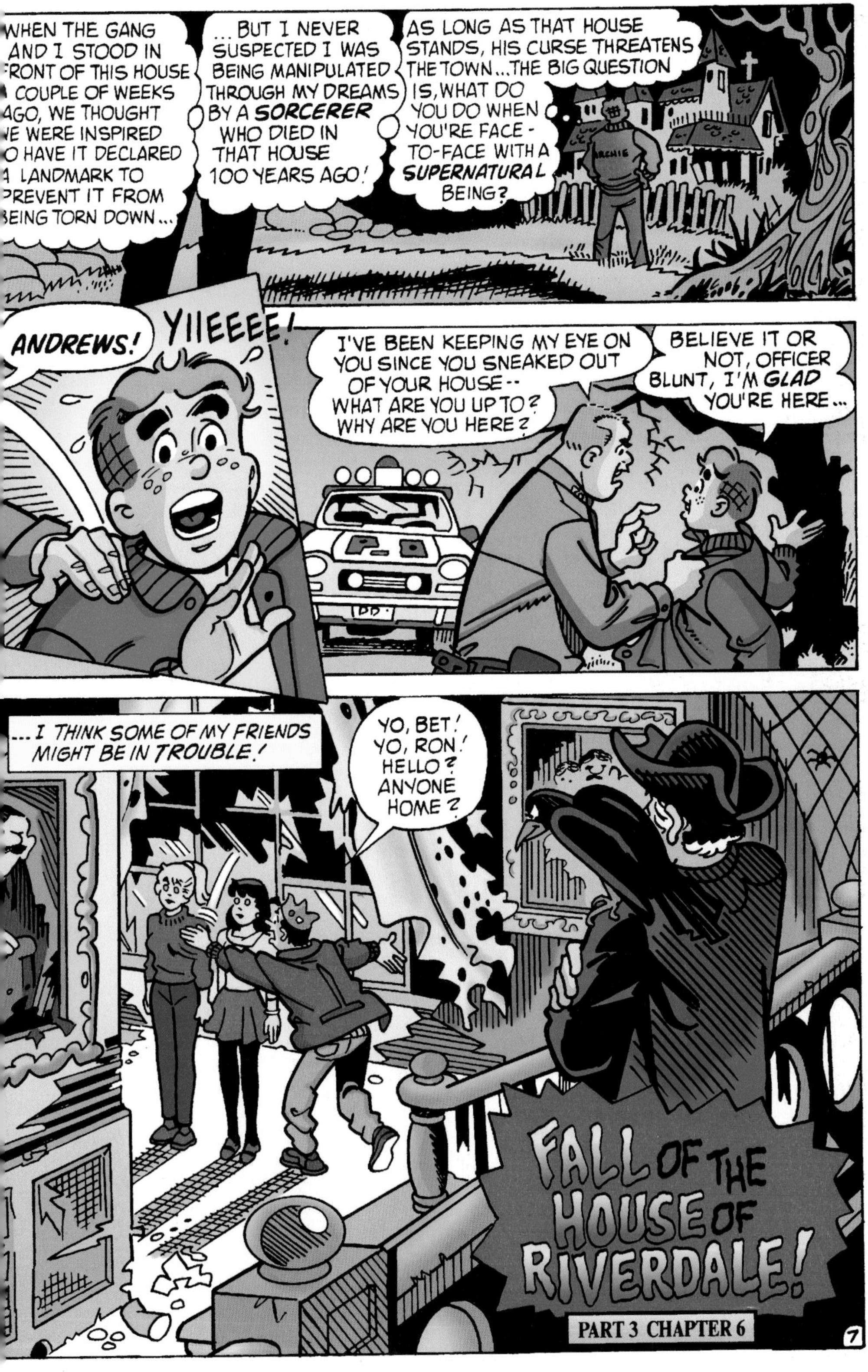
WHEN THE GANG AND I STOOD IN FRONT OF THIS HOUSE A COUPLE OF WEEKS AGO, WE THOUGHT WE WERE INSPIRED TO HAVE IT DECLARED A LANDMARK TO PREVENT IT FROM BEING TORN DOWN...
... BUT I NEVER SUSPECTED I WAS BEING MANIPULATED THROUGH MY DREAMS BY A SORCERER WHO DIED IN THAT HOUSE 100 YEARS AGO!
AS LONG AS THAT HOUSE STANDS, HIS CURSE THREATENS THE TOWN... THE BIG QUESTION IS, WHAT DO YOU DO WHEN YOU'RE FACE-TO-FACE WITH A SUPERNATURAL BEING?
ANDREWS!
YIIEEEE!
I'VE BEEN KEEPING MY EYE ON YOU SINCE YOU SNEAKED OUT OF YOUR HOUSE -- WHAT ARE YOU UP TO? WHY ARE YOU HERE?
BELIEVE IT OR NOT, OFFICER BLUNT, I'M GLAD YOU'RE HERE...
... I THINK SOME OF MY FRIENDS MIGHT BE IN TROUBLE!
YO, BET! YO, RON! HELLO? ANYONE HOME?
FALL OF THE HOUSE OF RIVERDALE!
PART 3 CHAPTER 6
7

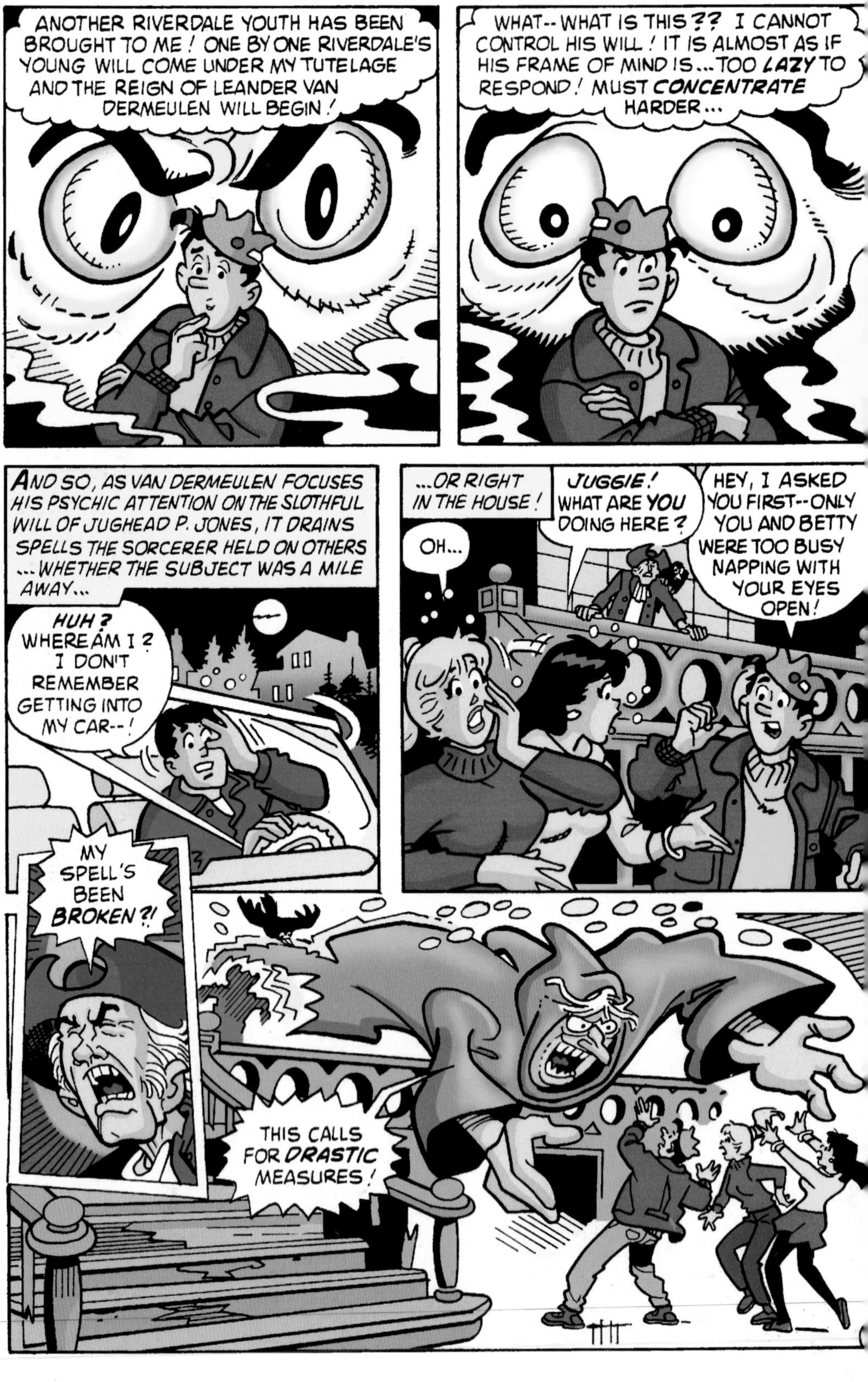
ANOTHER RIVERDALE YOUTH HAS BEEN BROUGHT TO ME! ONE BY ONE RIVERDALE'S YOUNG WILL COME UNDER MY TUTELAGE AND THE REIGN OF LEANDER VAN DERMEULEN WILL BEGIN!
WHAT--WHAT IS THIS?? I CANNOT CONTROL HIS WILL! IT IS ALMOST AS IF HIS FRAME OF MIND IS...TOO LAZY TO RESPOND! MUST CONCENTRATE HARDER...
AND SO, AS VAN DERMEULEN FOCUSES HIS PSYCHIC ATTENTION ON THE SLOTHFUL WILL OF JUGHEAD P. JONES, IT DRAINS SPELLS THE SORCERER HELD ON OTHERS ...WHETHER THE SUBJECT WAS A MILE AWAY...
HUH? WHERE AM I? I DON'T REMEMBER GETTING INTO MY CAR--!
...OR RIGHT IN THE HOUSE!
OH...
JUGGIE! WHAT ARE YOU DOING HERE?
HEY, I ASKED YOU FIRST--ONLY YOU AND BETTY WERE TOO BUSY NAPPING WITH YOUR EYES OPEN!
MY SPELL'S BEEN BROKEN?!
THIS CALLS FOR DRASTIC MEASURES!

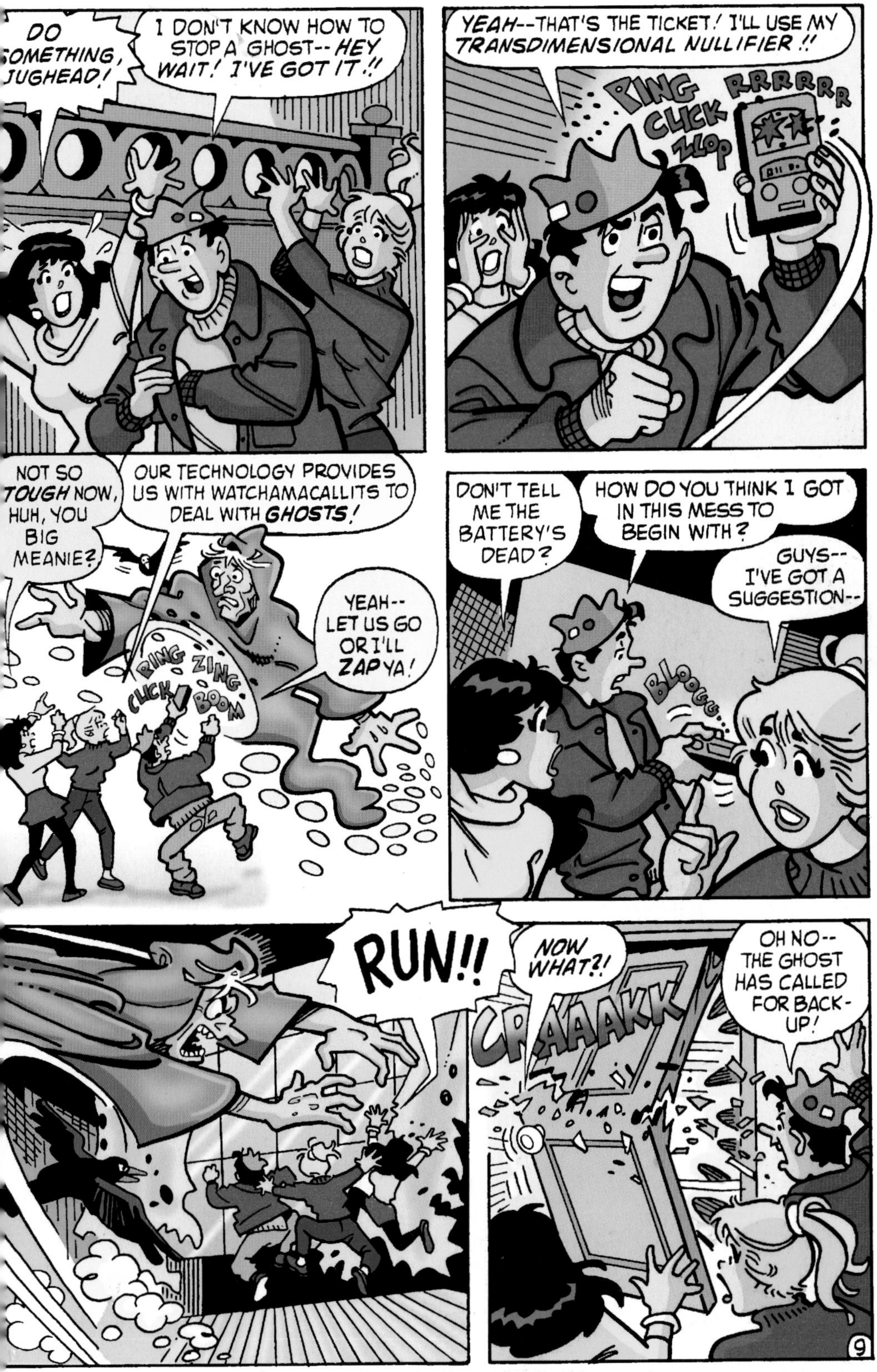
DO SOMETHING, JUGHEAD!
I DON'T KNOW HOW TO STOP A GHOST-- HEY WAIT! I'VE GOT IT!!
YEAH--THAT'S THE TICKET! I'LL USE MY TRANSDIMENSIONAL NULLIFIER!!
RING
CLICK
ZLOP
RRRRRRR
NOT SO TOUGH NOW, HUH, YOU BIG MEANIE?
OUR TECHNOLOGY PROVIDES US WITH WATCHAMACALLITS TO DEAL WITH GHOSTS!
YEAH-- LET US GO OR I'LL ZAP YA!
RING
ZING
CLICK
BOOM
DON'T TELL ME THE BATTERY'S DEAD?
HOW DO YOU THINK I GOT IN THIS MESS TO BEGIN WITH?
GUYS-- I'VE GOT A SUGGESTION--
BLOOGG
RUN!!
NOW WHAT?!
CRAAAKK
OH NO-- THE GHOST HAS CALLED FOR BACK-UP!
9

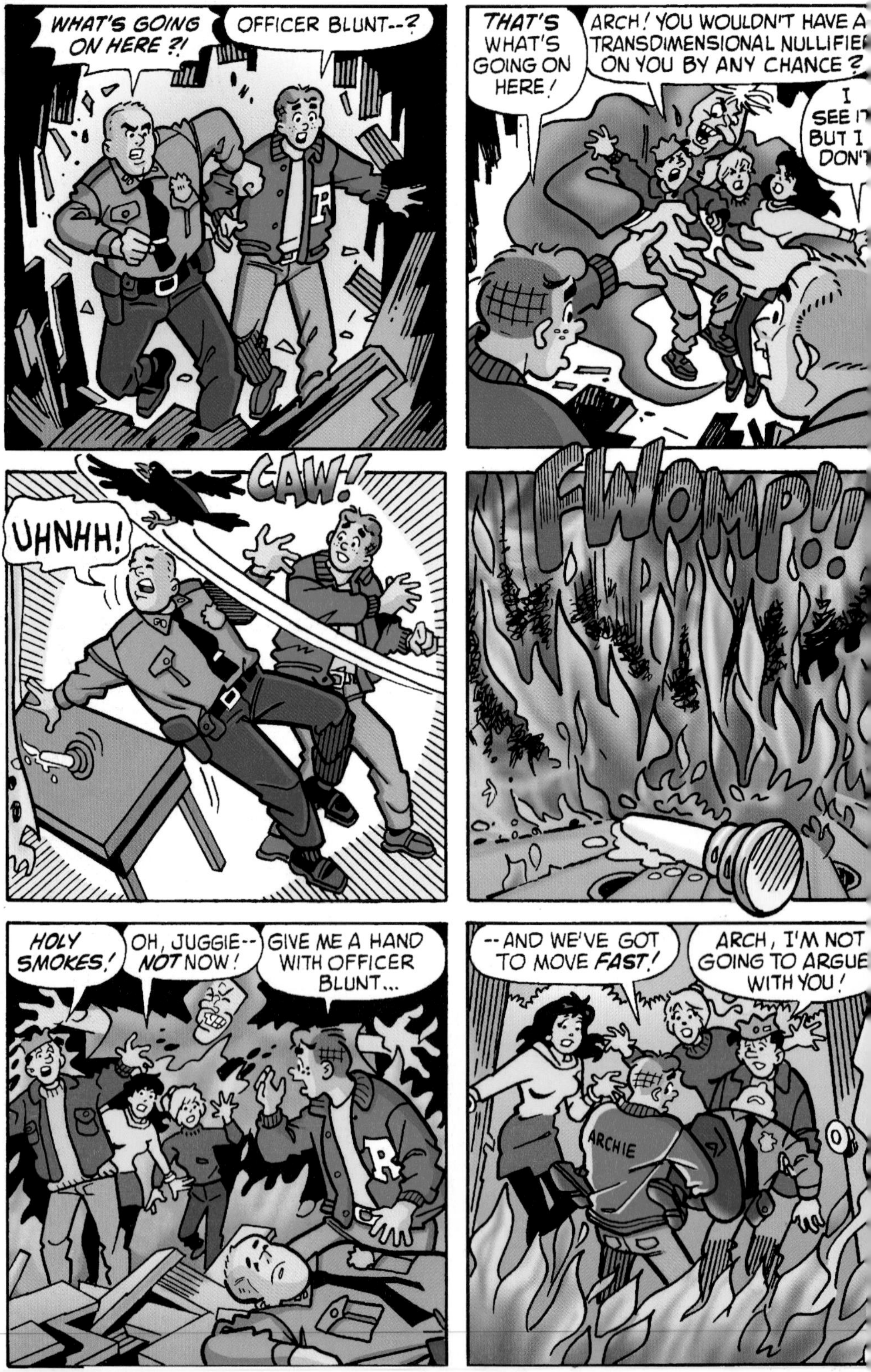
WHAT'S GOING ON HERE ?!
OFFICER BLUNT--?
THAT'S WHAT'S GOING ON HERE!
ARCH! YOU WOULDN'T HAVE A TRANSDIMENSIONAL NULLIFIE ON YOU BY ANY CHANCE?
I SEE I BUT I DON'
CAW!
UHNHH!
FWOMP!!
HOLY SMOKES!
OH, JUGGIE-- NOT NOW!
GIVE ME A HAND WITH OFFICER BLUNT...
--AND WE'VE GOT TO MOVE FAST!
ARCH, I'M NOT GOING TO ARGUE WITH YOU!
ARCHIE

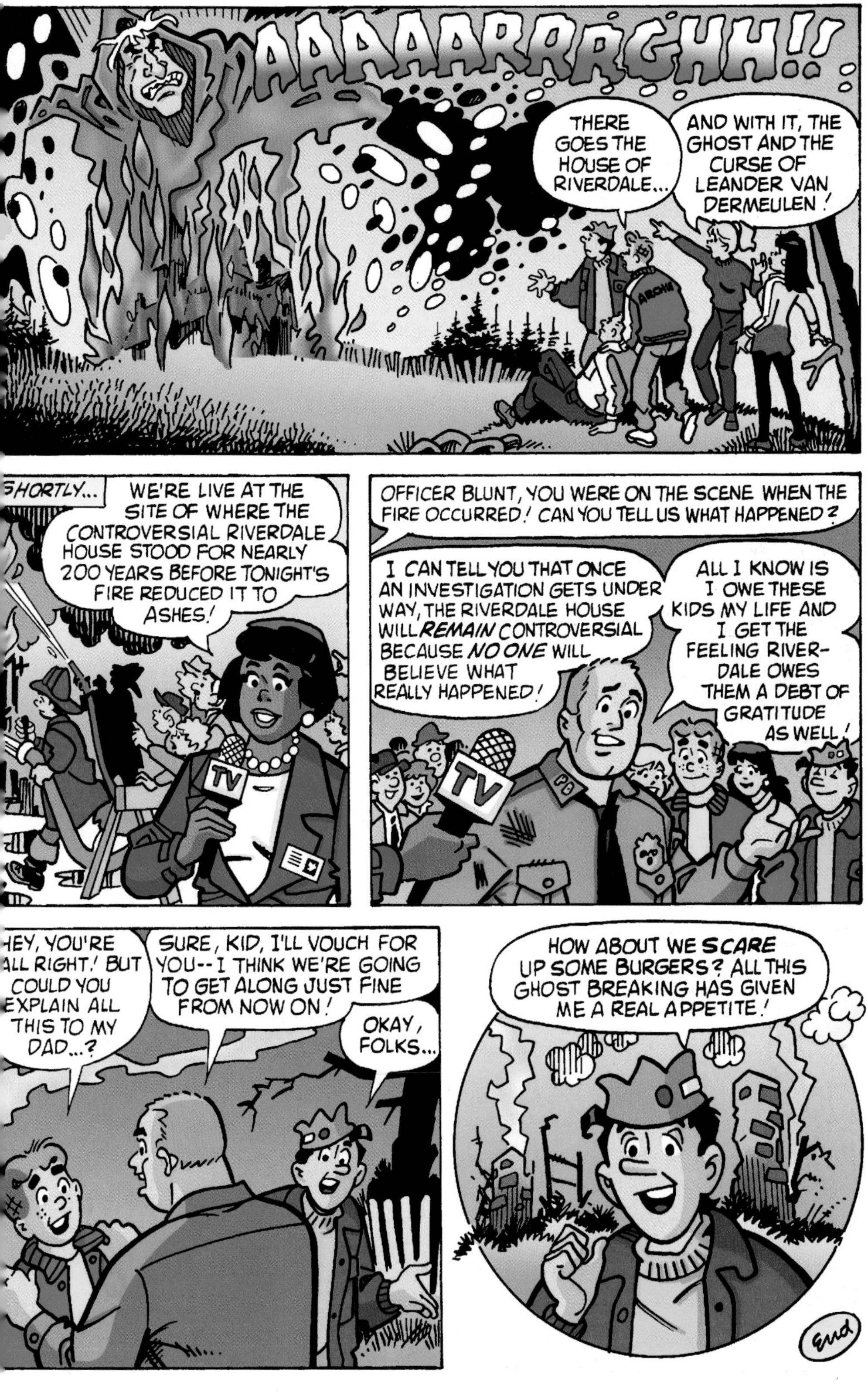
AAAAARRRGHH!!
THERE GOES THE HOUSE OF RIVERDALE...
AND WITH IT, THE GHOST AND THE CURSE OF LEANDER VAN DERMEULEN!
SHORTLY...
WE'RE LIVE AT THE SITE OF WHERE THE CONTROVERSIAL RIVERDALE HOUSE STOOD FOR NEARLY 200 YEARS BEFORE TONIGHT'S FIRE REDUCED IT TO ASHES!
TV
OFFICER BLUNT, YOU WERE ON THE SCENE WHEN THE FIRE OCCURRED! CAN YOU TELL US WHAT HAPPENED?
I CAN TELL YOU THAT ONCE AN INVESTIGATION GETS UNDER WAY, THE RIVERDALE HOUSE WILL *REMAIN* CONTROVERSIAL BECAUSE *NO ONE* WILL BELIEVE WHAT REALLY HAPPENED!
ALL I KNOW IS I OWE THESE KIDS MY LIFE AND I GET THE FEELING RIVER-DALE OWES THEM A DEBT OF GRATITUDE AS WELL!
TV
EY, YOU'RE LL RIGHT! BUT COULD YOU XPLAIN ALL THIS TO MY DAD...?
SURE, KID, I'LL VOUCH FOR YOU-- I THINK WE'RE GOING TO GET ALONG JUST FINE FROM NOW ON!
OKAY, FOLKS...
HOW ABOUT WE ***SCARE*** UP SOME BURGERS? ALL THIS GHOST BREAKING HAS GIVEN ME A REAL APPETITE!
End

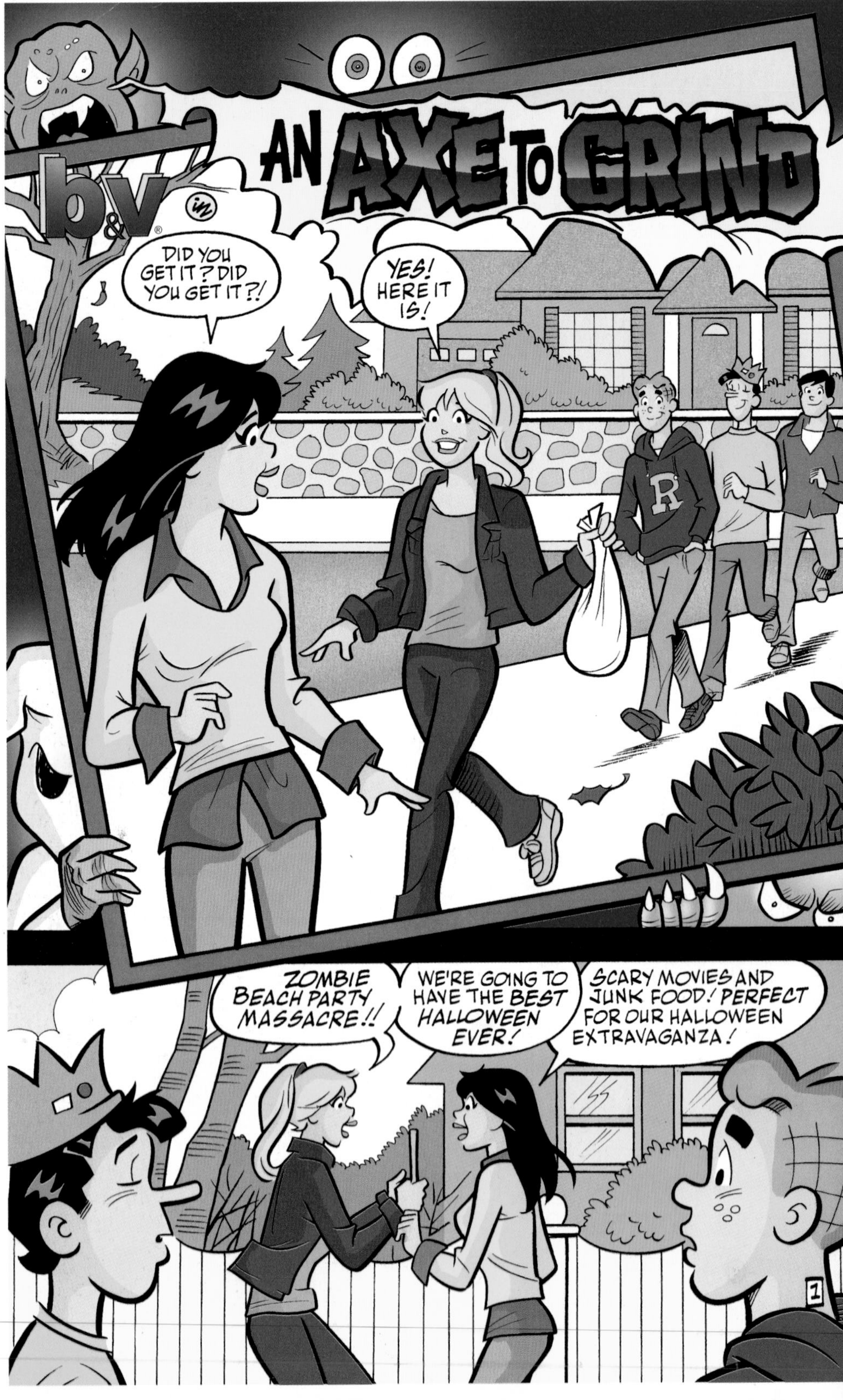
b&v in
AN AXE TO GRIND
DID YOU GET IT? DID YOU GET IT?!
YES! HERE IT IS!
ZOMBIE BEACH PARTY MASSACRE!!
WE'RE GOING TO HAVE THE BEST HALLOWEEN EVER!
SCARY MOVIES AND JUNK FOOD! PERFECT FOR OUR HALLOWEEN EXTRAVAGANZA!
1

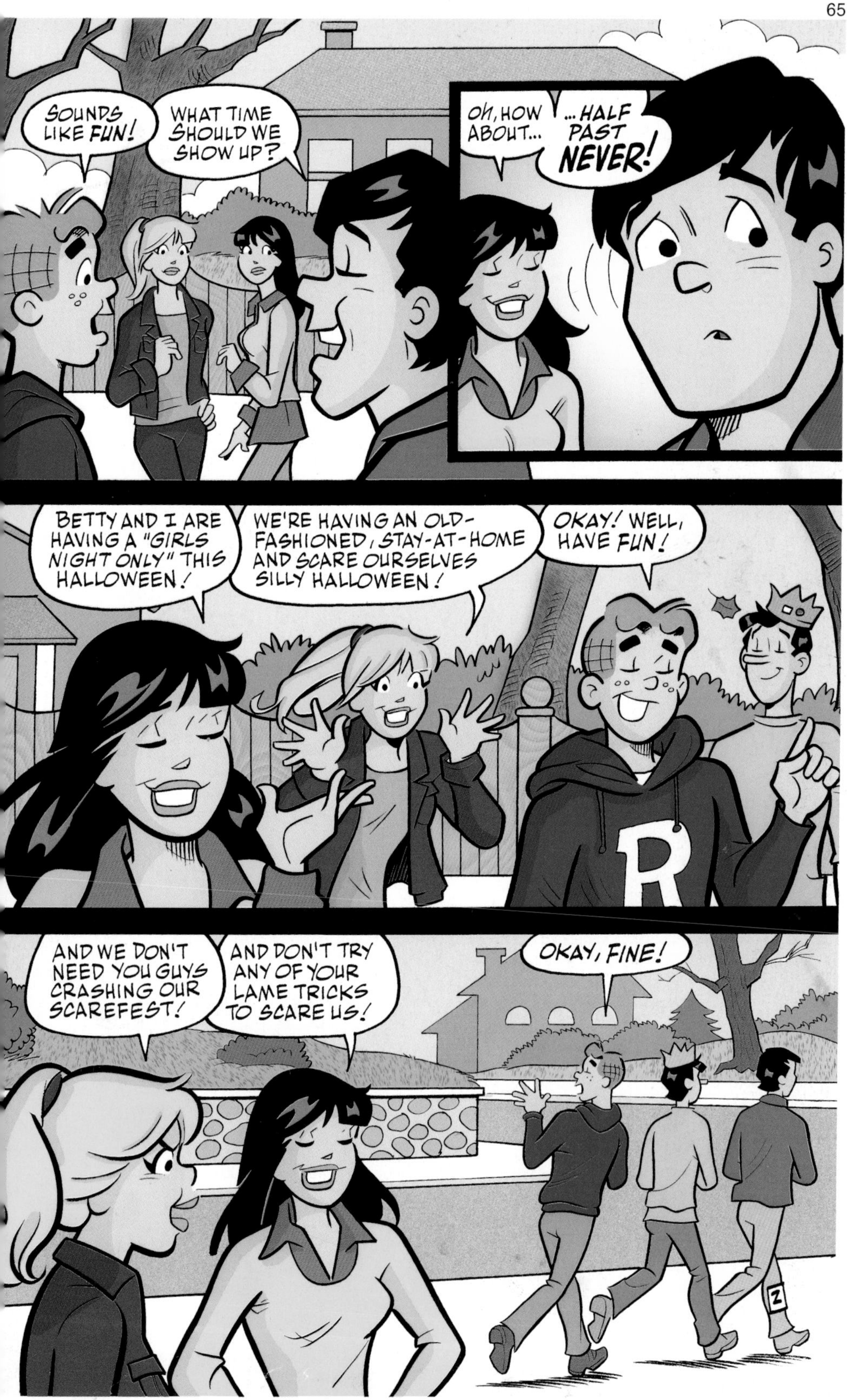
SOUNDS LIKE FUN!
WHAT TIME SHOULD WE SHOW UP?
OH, HOW ABOUT...
...HALF PAST NEVER!
BETTY AND I ARE HAVING A "GIRLS NIGHT ONLY" THIS HALLOWEEN!
WE'RE HAVING AN OLD-FASHIONED, STAY-AT-HOME AND SCARE OURSELVES SILLY HALLOWEEN!
OKAY! WELL, HAVE FUN!
AND WE DON'T NEED YOU GUYS CRASHING OUR SCAREFEST!
AND DON'T TRY ANY OF YOUR LAME TRICKS TO SCARE US!
OKAY, FINE!

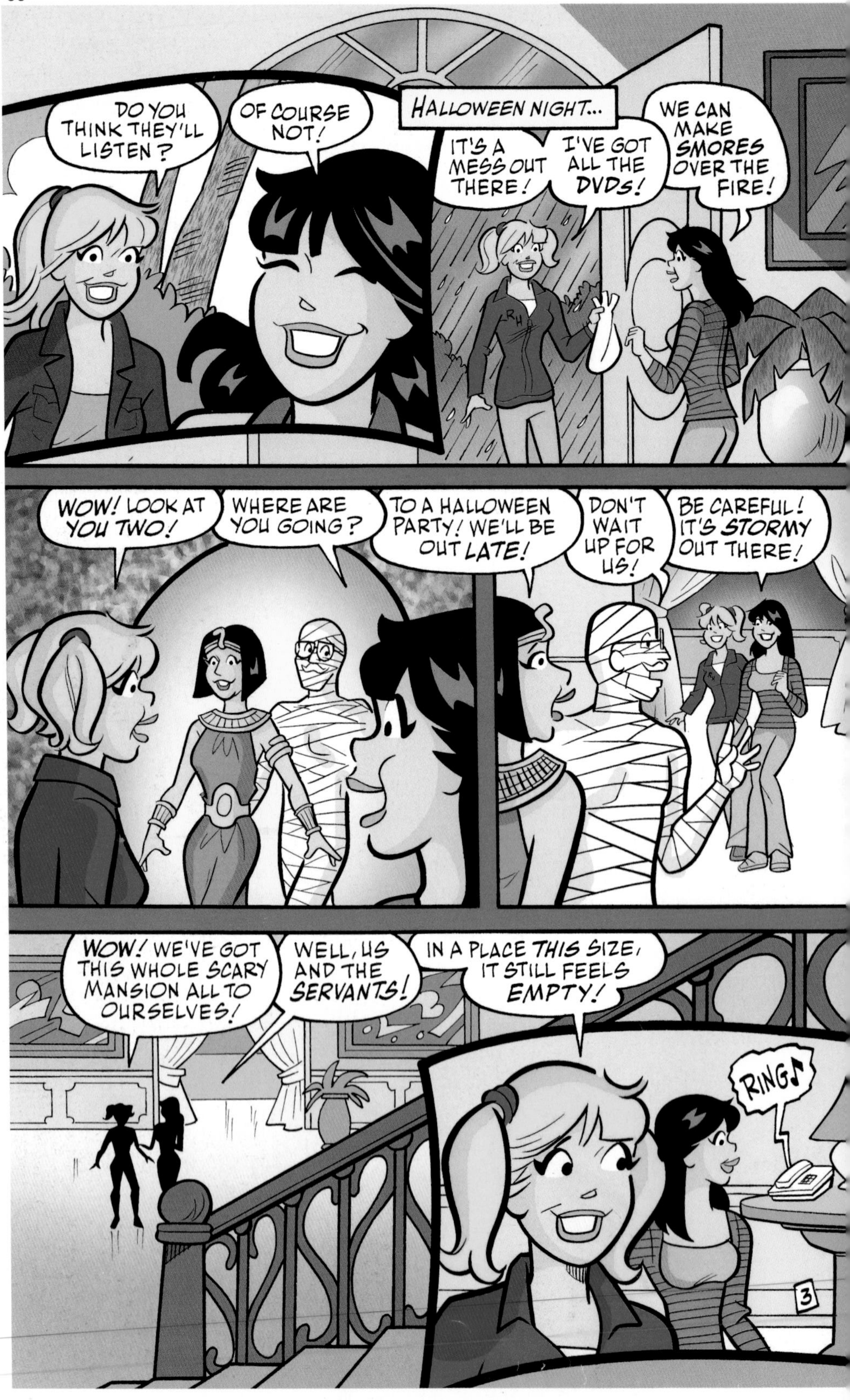
DO YOU THINK THEY'LL LISTEN?
OF COURSE NOT!
HALLOWEEN NIGHT...
IT'S A MESS OUT THERE!
I'VE GOT ALL THE DVDS!
WE CAN MAKE SMORES OVER THE FIRE!
WOW! LOOK AT YOU TWO!
WHERE ARE YOU GOING?
TO A HALLOWEEN PARTY! WE'LL BE OUT LATE!
DON'T WAIT UP FOR US!
BE CAREFUL! IT'S STORMY OUT THERE!
WOW! WE'VE GOT THIS WHOLE SCARY MANSION ALL TO OURSELVES!
WELL, US AND THE SERVANTS!
IN A PLACE THIS SIZE, IT STILL FEELS EMPTY!
RING♪
3

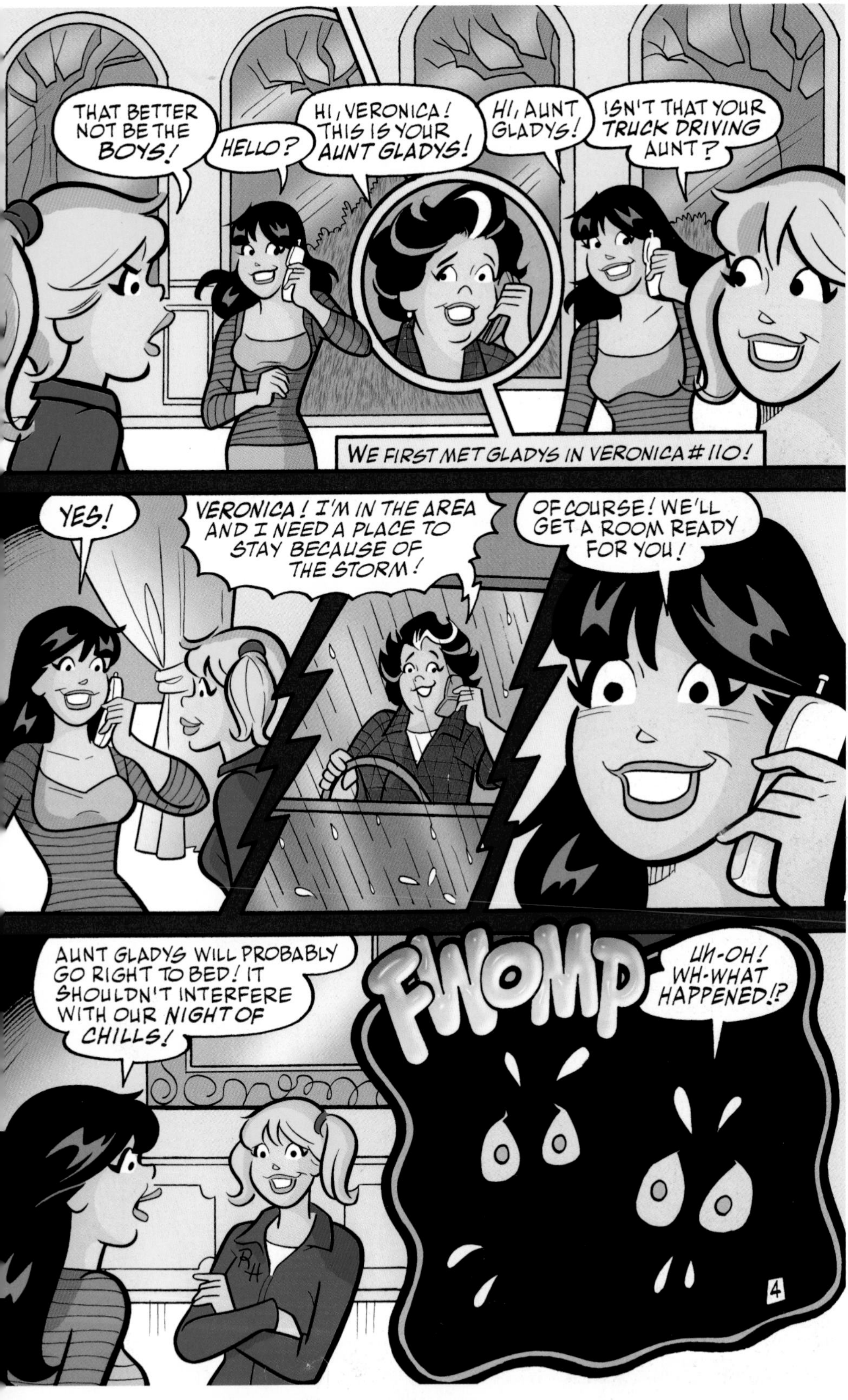
THAT BETTER NOT BE THE BOYS!
HELLO?
HI, VERONICA! THIS IS YOUR AUNT GLADYS!
HI, AUNT GLADYS!
ISN'T THAT YOUR TRUCK DRIVING AUNT?
WE FIRST MET GLADYS IN VERONICA #110!
YES!
VERONICA! I'M IN THE AREA AND I NEED A PLACE TO STAY BECAUSE OF THE STORM!
OF COURSE! WE'LL GET A ROOM READY FOR YOU!
AUNT GLADYS WILL PROBABLY GO RIGHT TO BED! IT SHOULDN'T INTERFERE WITH OUR NIGHT OF CHILLS!
FWOMP
UH-OH! WH-WHAT HAPPENED!?
4

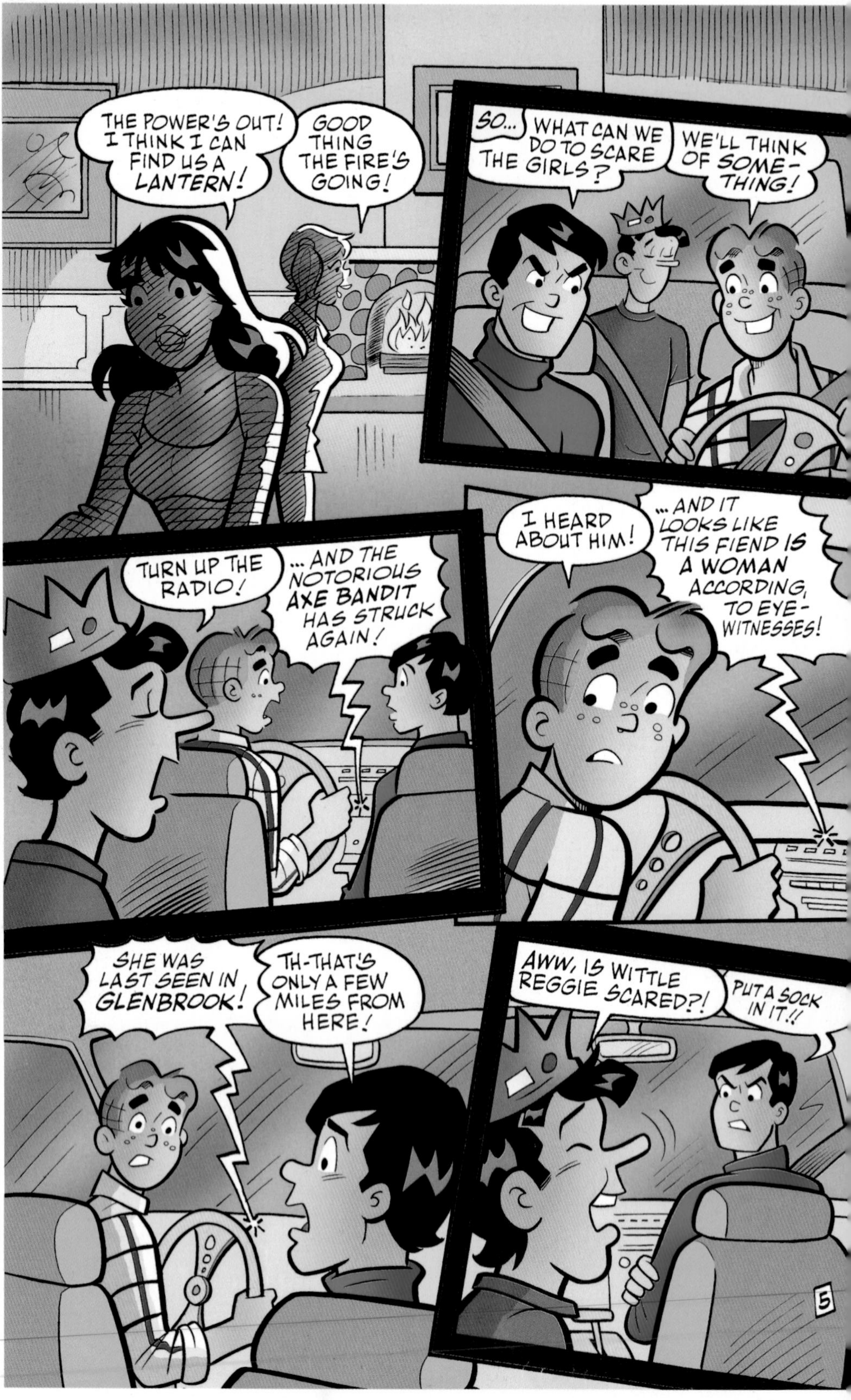
THE POWER'S OUT! I THINK I CAN FIND US A LANTERN!
GOOD THING THE FIRE'S GOING!
SO...
WHAT CAN WE DO TO SCARE THE GIRLS?
WE'LL THINK OF SOME-THING!
TURN UP THE RADIO!
...AND THE NOTORIOUS AXE BANDIT HAS STRUCK AGAIN!
I HEARD ABOUT HIM!
...AND IT LOOKS LIKE THIS FIEND IS A WOMAN ACCORDING TO EYE-WITNESSES!
SHE WAS LAST SEEN IN GLENBROOK!
TH-THAT'S ONLY A FEW MILES FROM HERE!
AWW, IS WITTLE REGGIE SCARED?!
PUT A SOCK IN IT!!
5

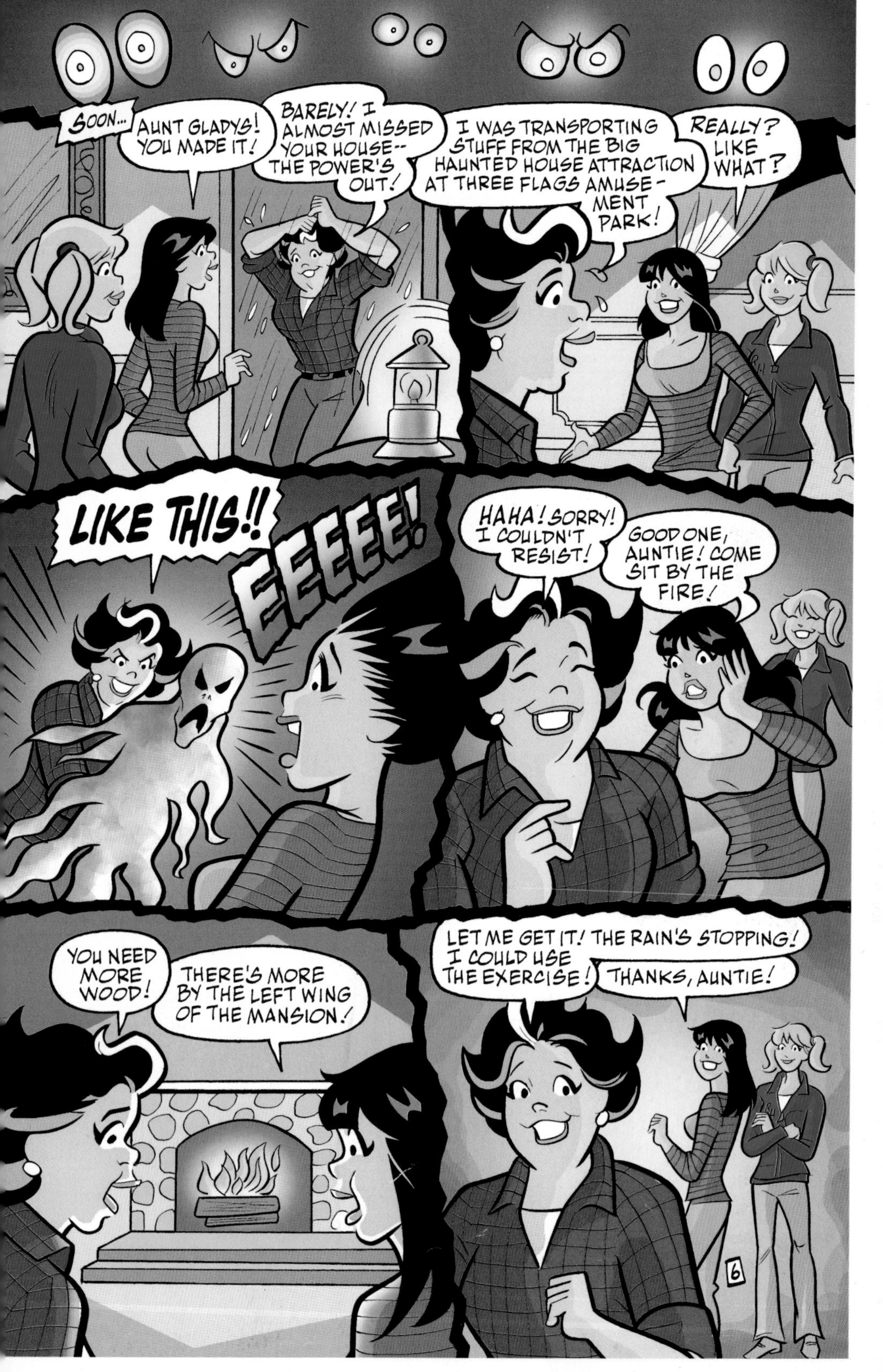
SOON...
AUNT GLADYS! YOU MADE IT!
BARELY! I ALMOST MISSED YOUR HOUSE-- THE POWER'S OUT!
I WAS TRANSPORTING STUFF FROM THE BIG HAUNTED HOUSE ATTRACTION AT THREE FLAGS AMUSE-MENT PARK!
REALLY? LIKE WHAT?
LIKE THIS!!
EEEEE!
HAHA! SORRY! I COULDN'T RESIST!
GOOD ONE, AUNTIE! COME SIT BY THE FIRE!
YOU NEED MORE WOOD!
THERE'S MORE BY THE LEFT WING OF THE MANSION!
LET ME GET IT! THE RAIN'S STOPPING! I COULD USE THE EXERCISE!
THANKS, AUNTIE!
6

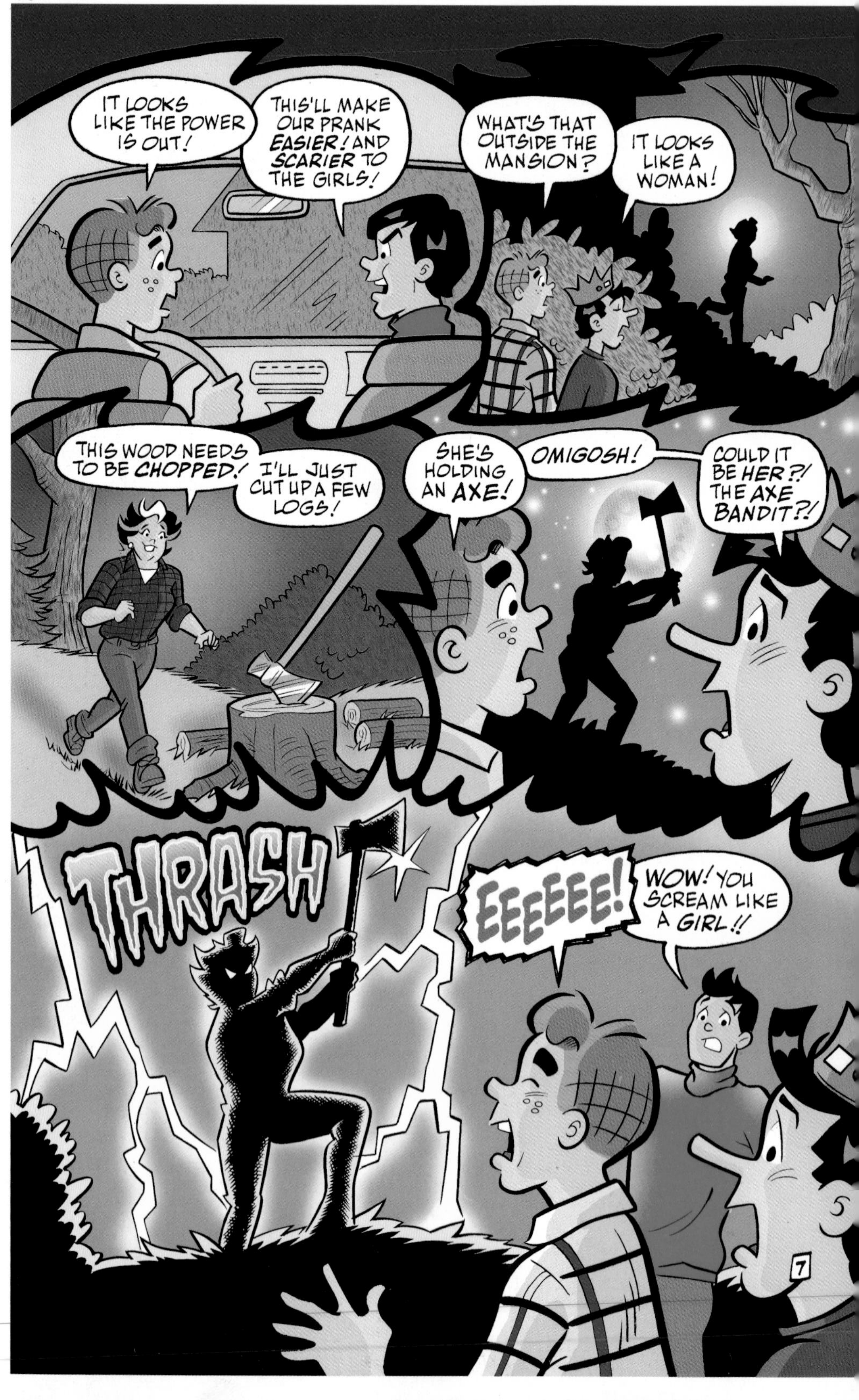
IT LOOKS LIKE THE POWER IS OUT!
THIS'LL MAKE OUR PRANK EASIER! AND SCARIER TO THE GIRLS!
WHAT'S THAT OUTSIDE THE MANSION?
IT LOOKS LIKE A WOMAN!
THIS WOOD NEEDS TO BE CHOPPED!
I'LL JUST CUT UP A FEW LOGS!
SHE'S HOLDING AN AXE!
OMIGOSH!
COULD IT BE HER?! THE AXE BANDIT?!
THRASH
EEEEEE!
WOW! YOU SCREAM LIKE A GIRL!!
7

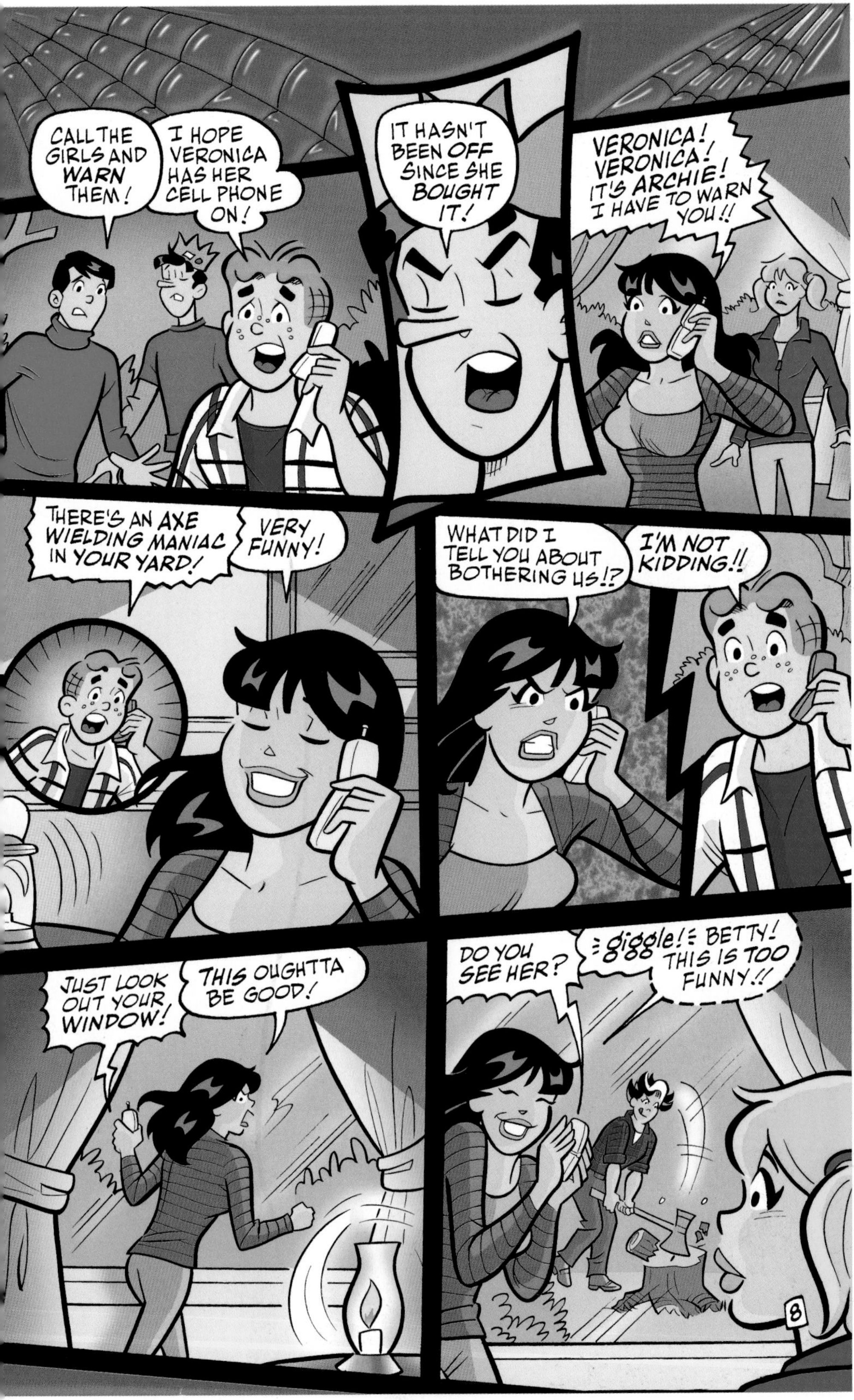
CALL THE GIRLS AND WARN THEM!
I HOPE VERONICA HAS HER CELL PHONE ON!
IT HASN'T BEEN OFF SINCE SHE BOUGHT IT!
VERONICA! VERONICA! IT'S ARCHIE! I HAVE TO WARN YOU!!
THERE'S AN AXE WIELDING MANIAC IN YOUR YARD!
VERY FUNNY!
WHAT DID I TELL YOU ABOUT BOTHERING US!?
I'M NOT KIDDING!!
JUST LOOK OUT YOUR WINDOW!
THIS OUGHTTA BE GOOD!
DO YOU SEE HER?
giggle! BETTY! THIS IS TOO FUNNY!!
8

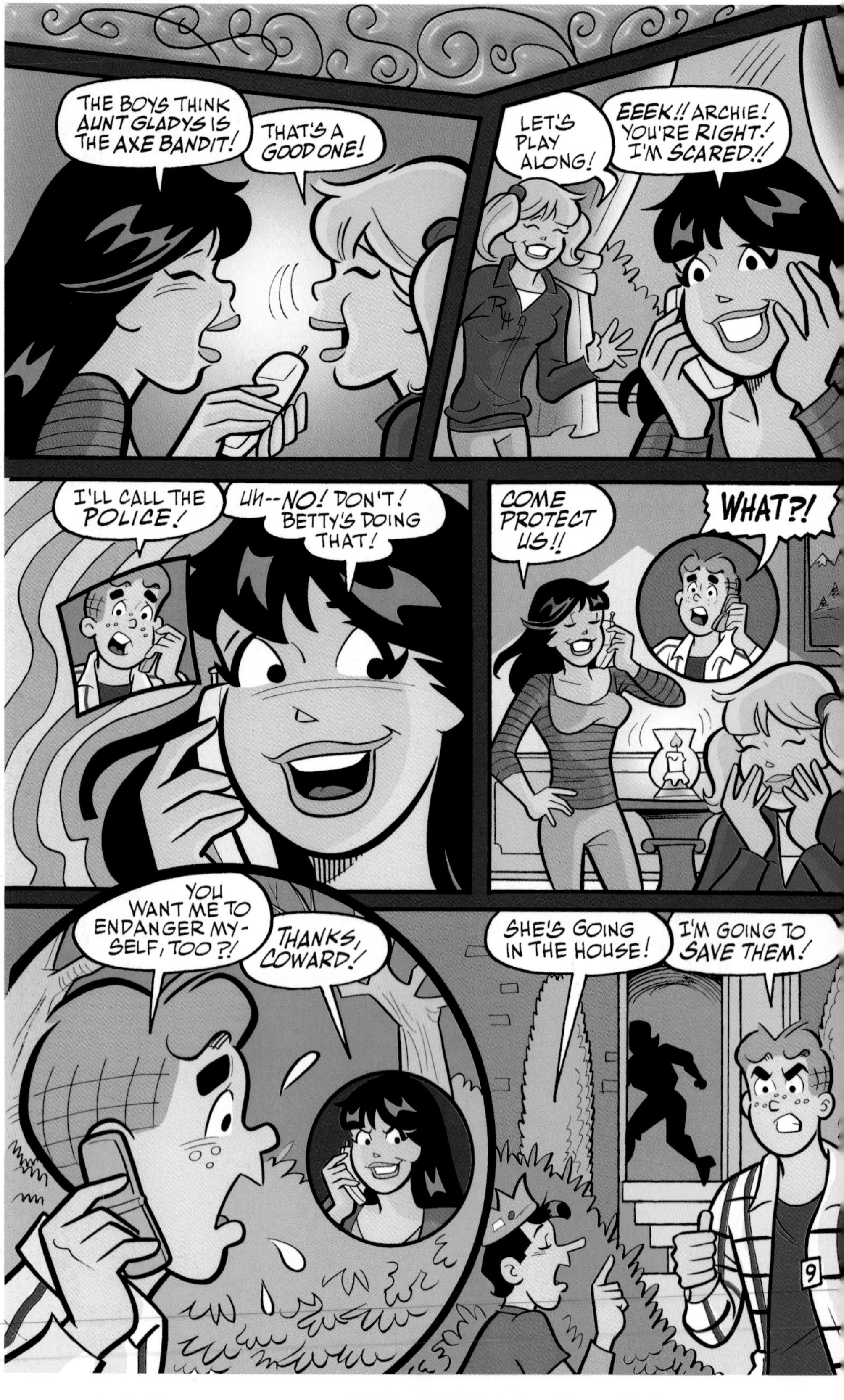
THE BOYS THINK AUNT GLADYS IS THE AXE BANDIT!
THAT'S A GOOD ONE!
LET'S PLAY ALONG!
EEEK!! ARCHIE! YOU'RE RIGHT! I'M SCARED!!
I'LL CALL THE POLICE!
UH--NO! DON'T! BETTY'S DOING THAT!
COME PROTECT US!!
WHAT?!
YOU WANT ME TO ENDANGER MY-SELF, TOO?!
THANKS, COWARD!
SHE'S GOING IN THE HOUSE!
I'M GOING TO SAVE THEM!
9

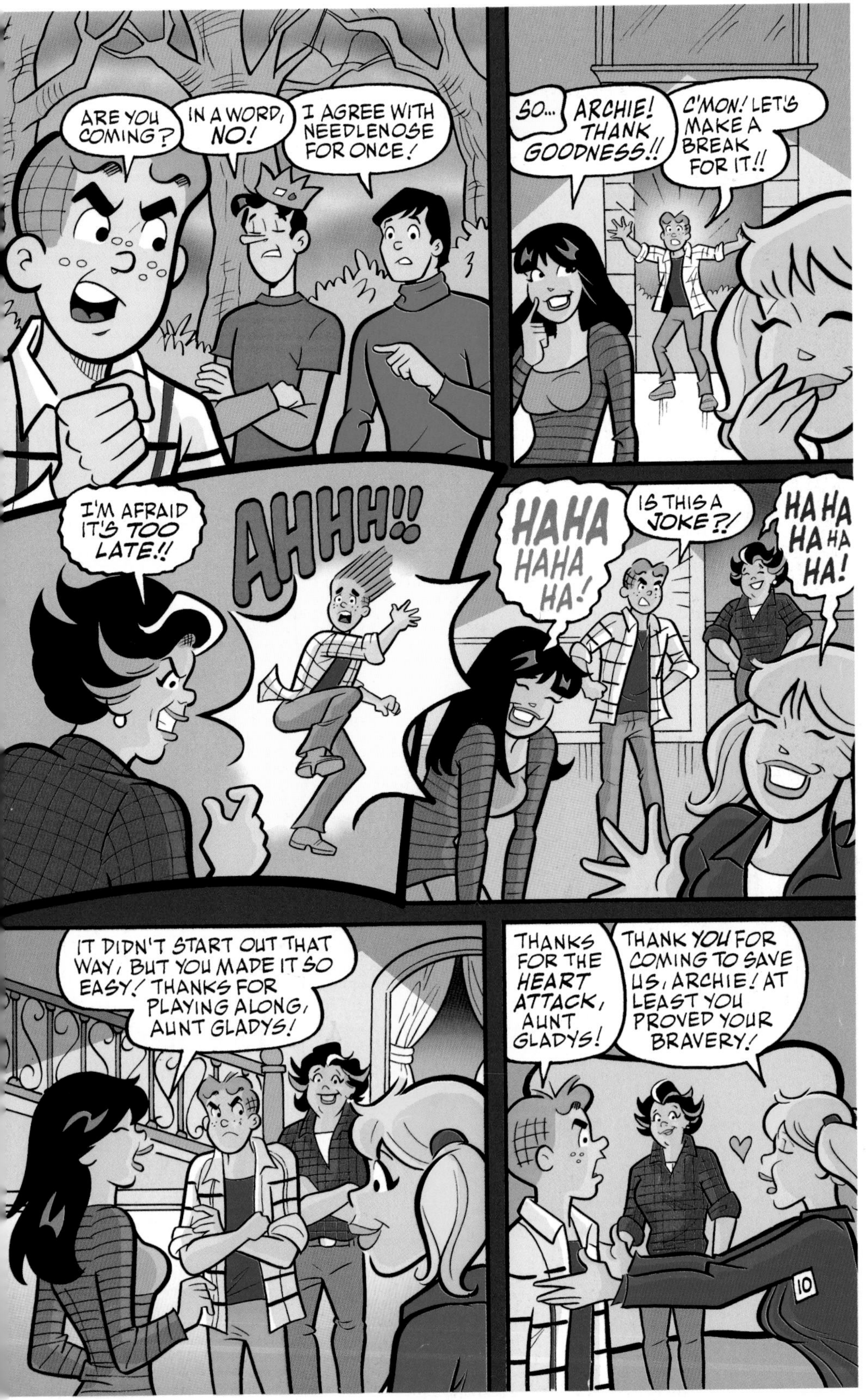
ARE YOU COMING?
IN A WORD, NO!
I AGREE WITH NEEDLENOSE FOR ONCE!
SO...
ARCHIE! THANK GOODNESS!!
C'MON! LET'S MAKE A BREAK FOR IT!!
I'M AFRAID IT'S TOO LATE!!
AHHH!!
HAHA HAHA HA!
IS THIS A JOKE?!
HA HA HA HA HA!
IT DIDN'T START OUT THAT WAY, BUT YOU MADE IT SO EASY! THANKS FOR PLAYING ALONG, AUNT GLADYS!
THANKS FOR THE HEART ATTACK, AUNT GLADYS!
THANK YOU FOR COMING TO SAVE US, ARCHIE! AT LEAST YOU PROVED YOUR BRAVERY!
10

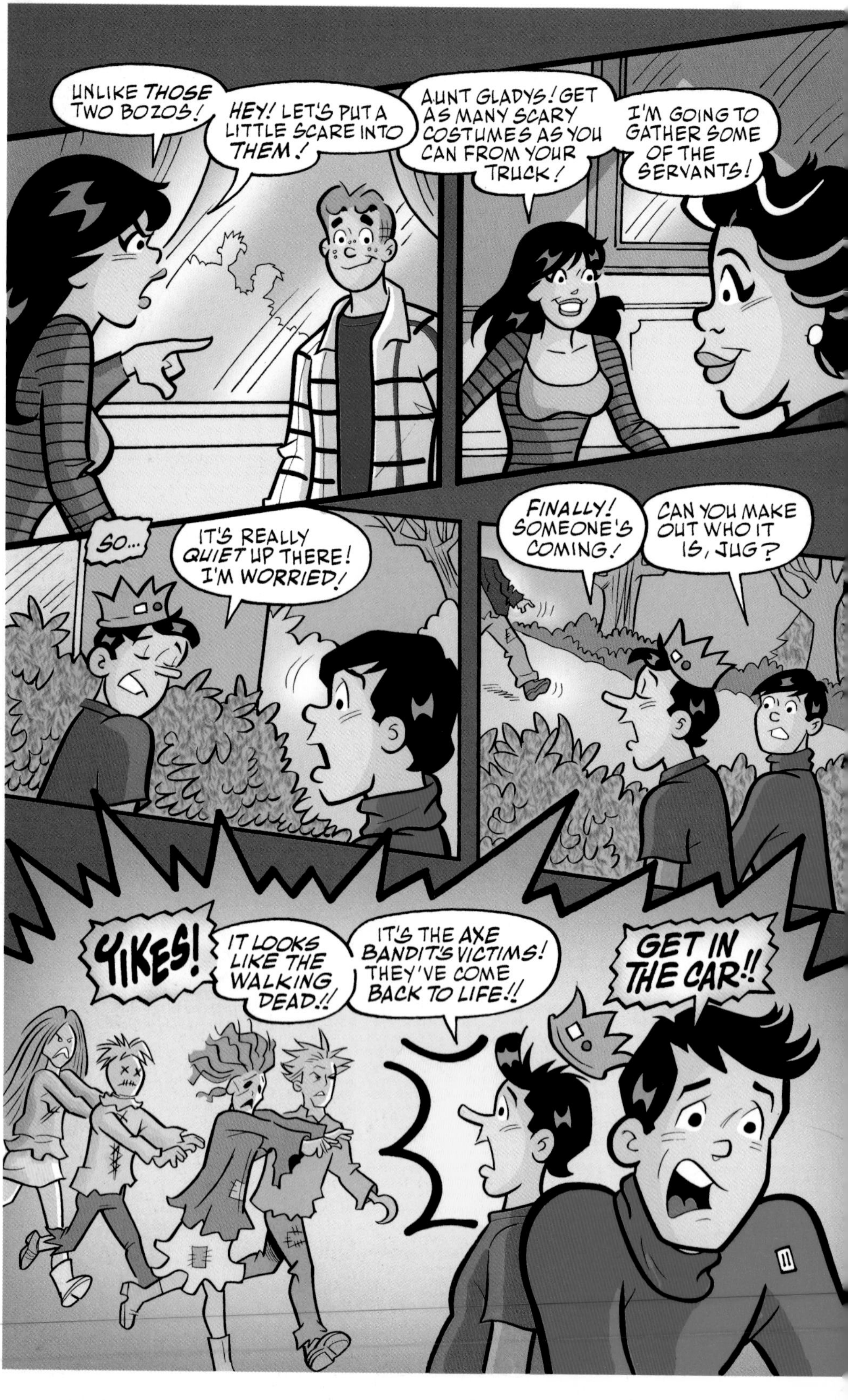
UNLIKE THOSE TWO BOZOS!
HEY! LET'S PUT A LITTLE SCARE INTO THEM!
AUNT GLADYS! GET AS MANY SCARY COSTUMES AS YOU CAN FROM YOUR TRUCK!
I'M GOING TO GATHER SOME OF THE SERVANTS!
SO...
IT'S REALLY QUIET UP THERE! I'M WORRIED!
FINALLY! SOMEONE'S COMING!
CAN YOU MAKE OUT WHO IT IS, JUG?
YIKES!
IT LOOKS LIKE THE WALKING DEAD!!
IT'S THE AXE BANDIT'S VICTIMS! THEY'VE COME BACK TO LIFE!!
GET IN THE CAR!!

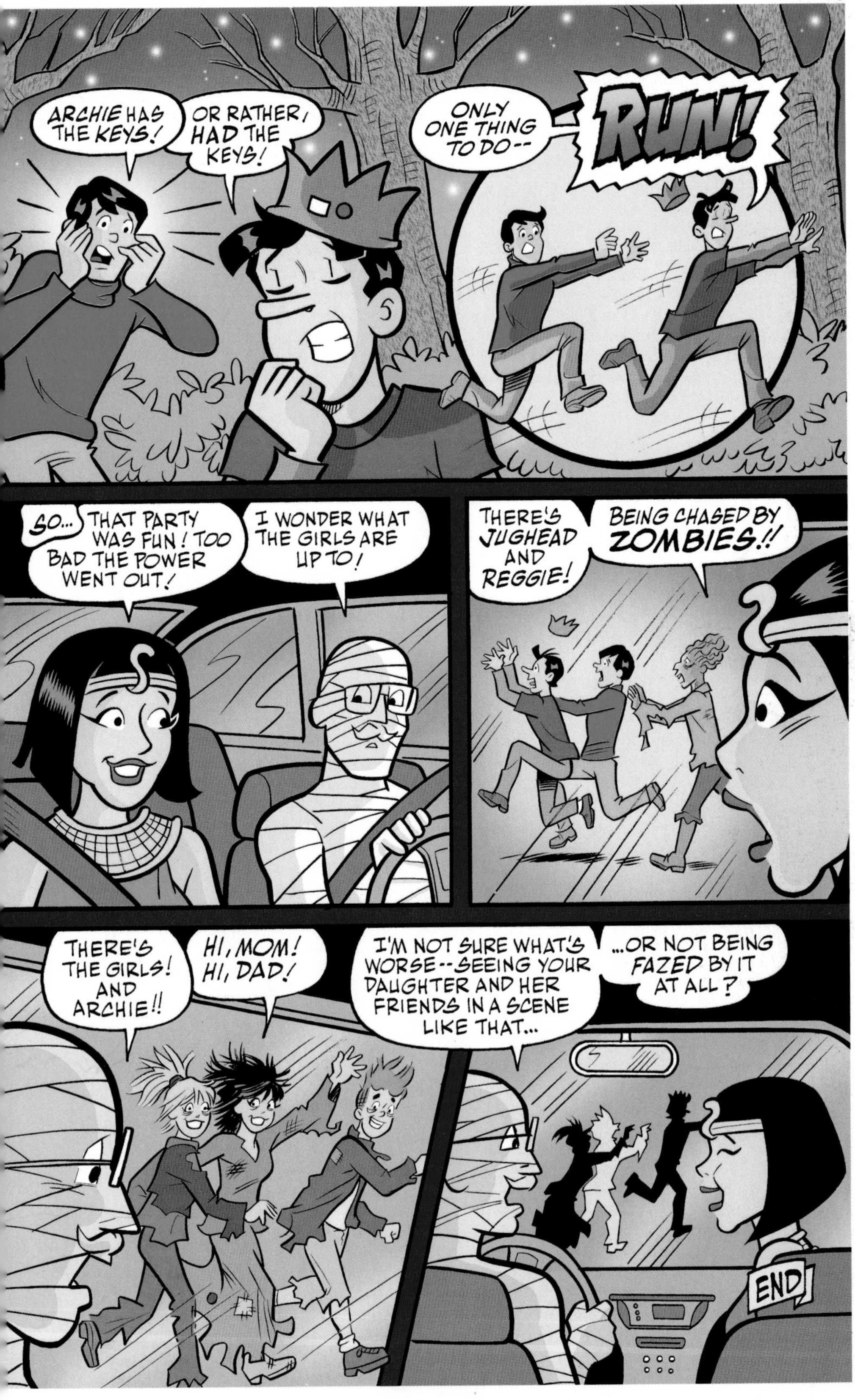
ARCHIE HAS THE KEYS!
OR RATHER, HAD THE KEYS!
ONLY ONE THING TO DO--
RUN!
SO...
THAT PARTY WAS FUN! TOO BAD THE POWER WENT OUT!
I WONDER WHAT THE GIRLS ARE UP TO!
THERE'S JUGHEAD AND REGGIE!
BEING CHASED BY ZOMBIES!!
THERE'S THE GIRLS! AND ARCHIE!!
HI, MOM! HI, DAD!
I'M NOT SURE WHAT'S WORSE--SEEING YOUR DAUGHTER AND HER FRIENDS IN A SCENE LIKE THAT...
...OR NOT BEING FAZED BY IT AT ALL?
END

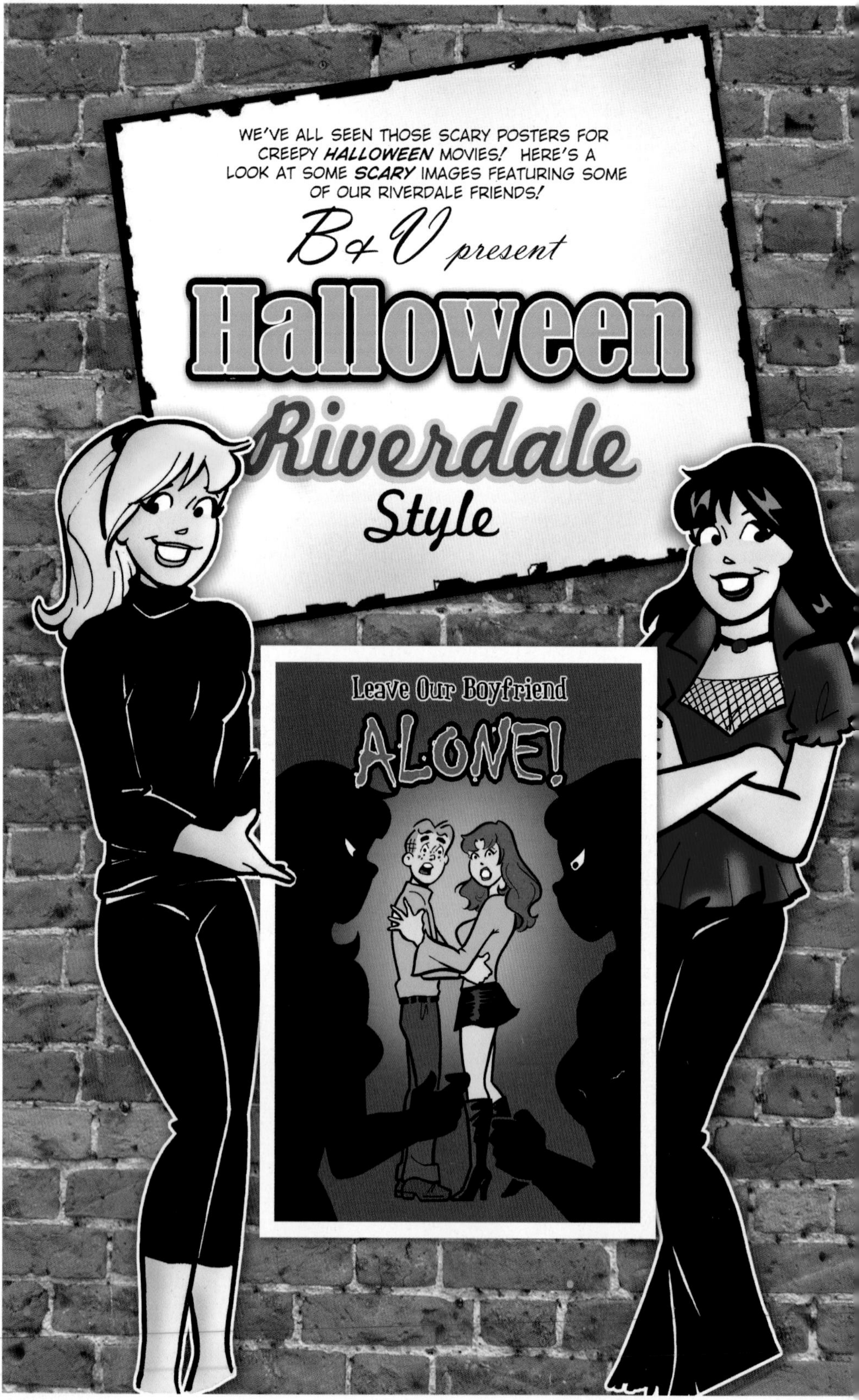
WE'VE ALL SEEN THOSE SCARY POSTERS FOR CREEPY HALLOWEEN MOVIES! HERE'S A LOOK AT SOME SCARY IMAGES FEATURING SOME OF OUR RIVERDALE FRIENDS!
B&V present
Halloween
Riverdale
Style
Leave Our Boyfriend
ALONE!

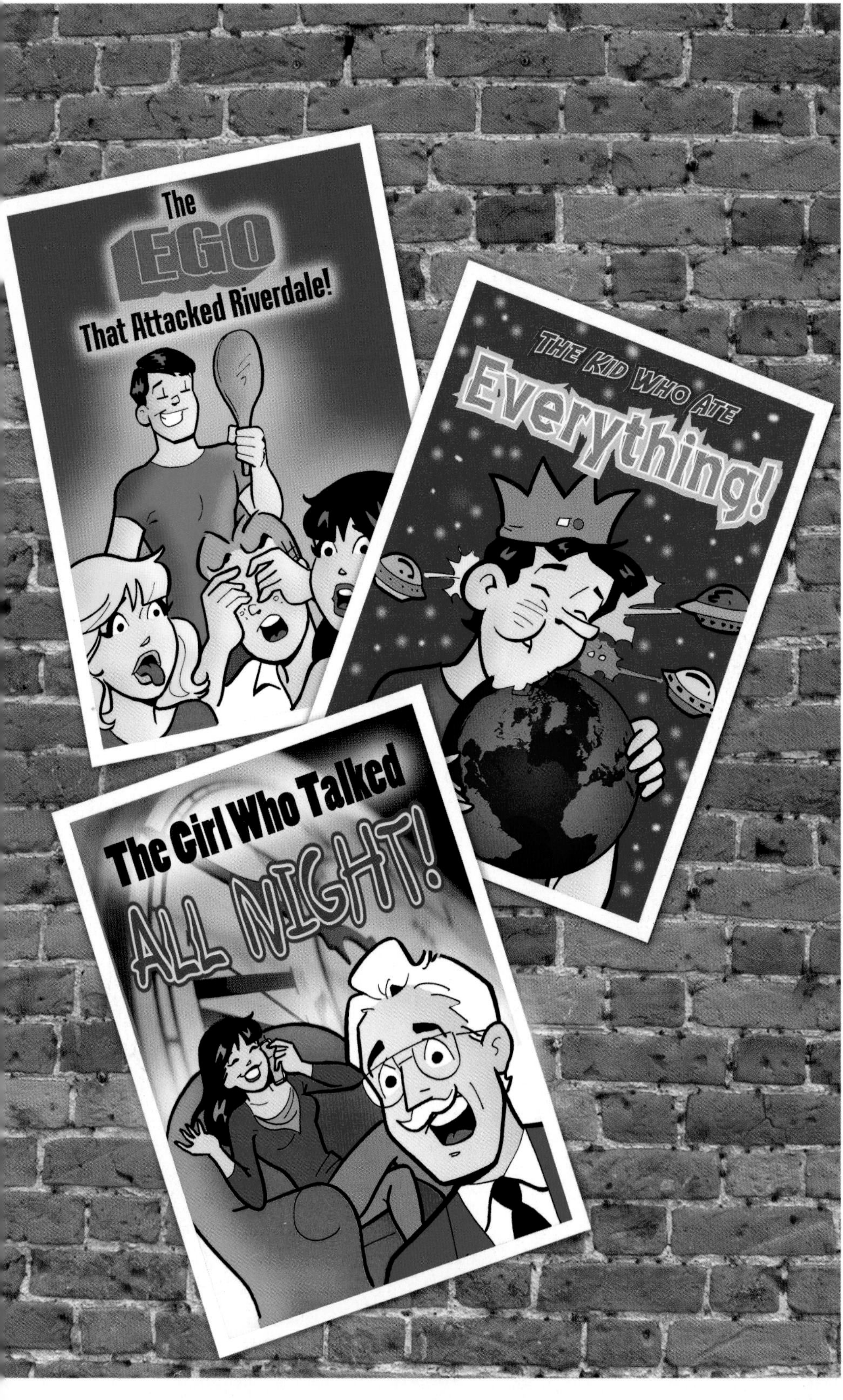
The EGO That Attacked Riverdale!
THE KID WHO ATE Everything!
The Girl Who Talked ALL NIGHT!

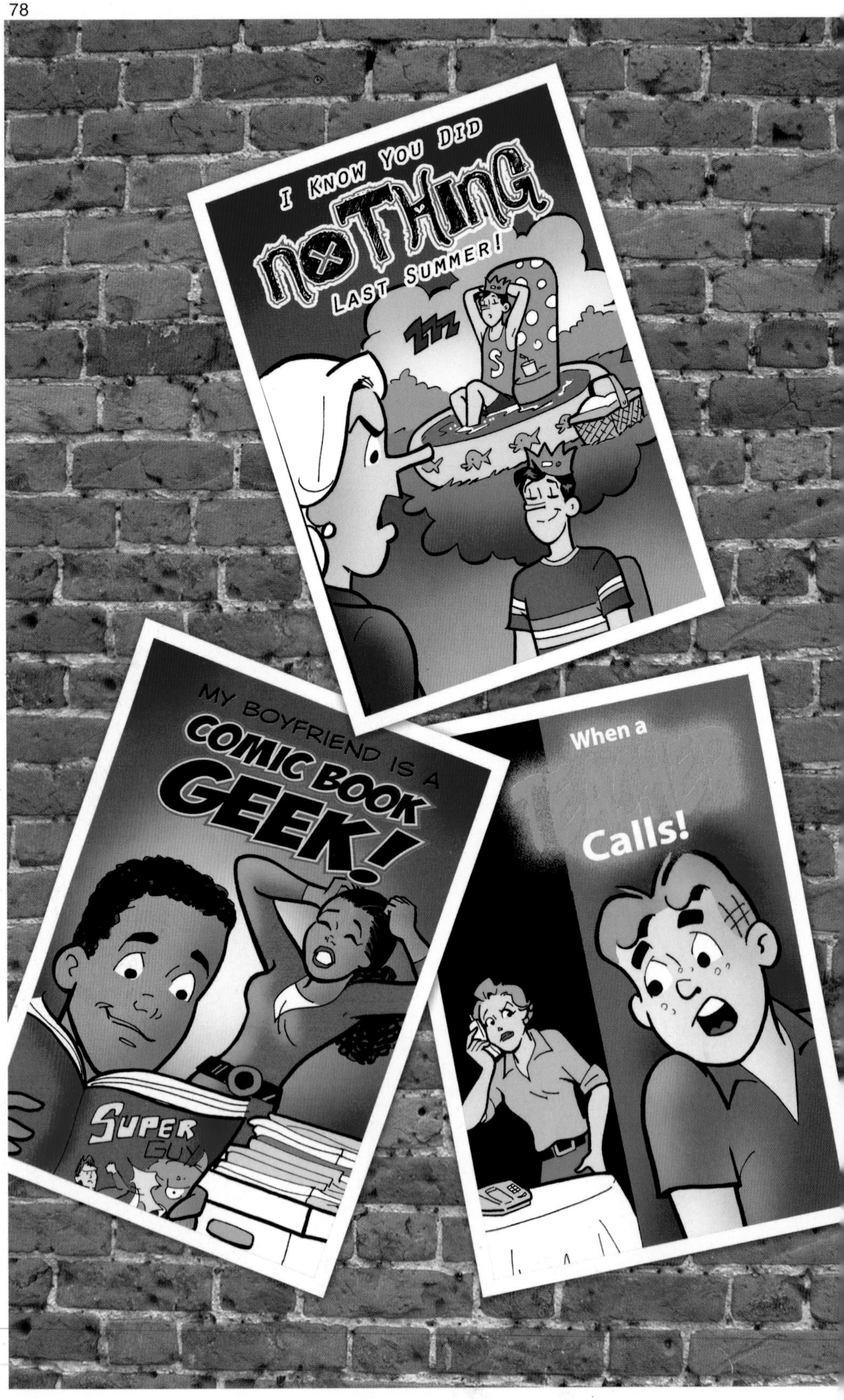
I Know You Did
NOTHING
Last Summer!
zzz
S
My Boyfriend is a
Comic Book
Geek!
Super
Guy
When a
Calls!

The Creature
Who Couldn't
CHOOSE!
THIS ONE IS THE *SCARIEST* ONE OF ALL!
ONE WE LIVE THROUGH EVERYDAY!
END

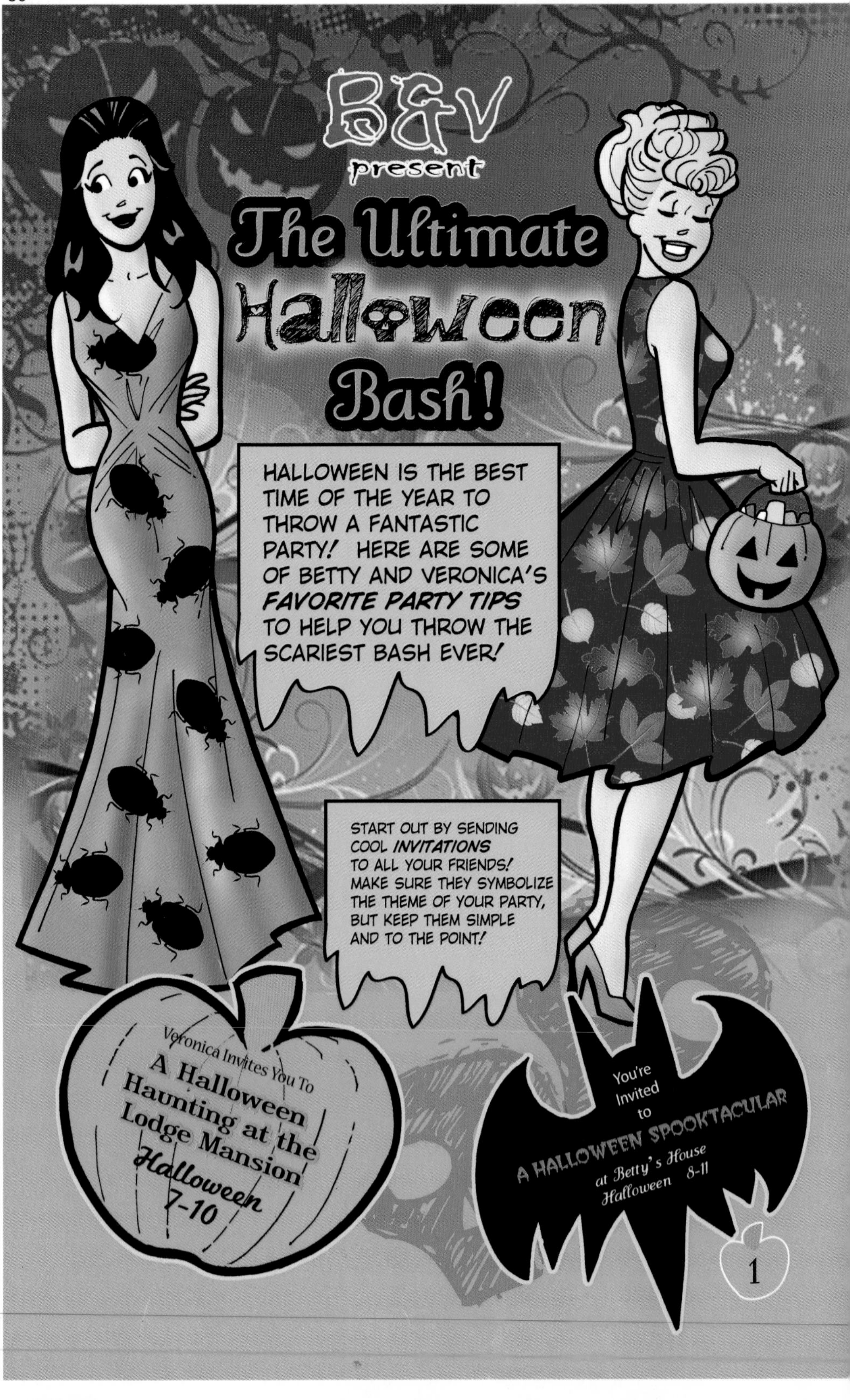
B&V
present
The Ultimate Halloween Bash!
HALLOWEEN IS THE BEST TIME OF THE YEAR TO THROW A FANTASTIC PARTY! HERE ARE SOME OF BETTY AND VERONICA'S FAVORITE PARTY TIPS TO HELP YOU THROW THE SCARIEST BASH EVER!
START OUT BY SENDING COOL INVITATIONS TO ALL YOUR FRIENDS! MAKE SURE THEY SYMBOLIZE THE THEME OF YOUR PARTY, BUT KEEP THEM SIMPLE AND TO THE POINT!
Veronica Invites You To
A Halloween Haunting at the Lodge Mansion
Halloween
7-10
You're Invited to
A HALLOWEEN SPOOKTACULAR
at Betty's House
Halloween 8-11
1

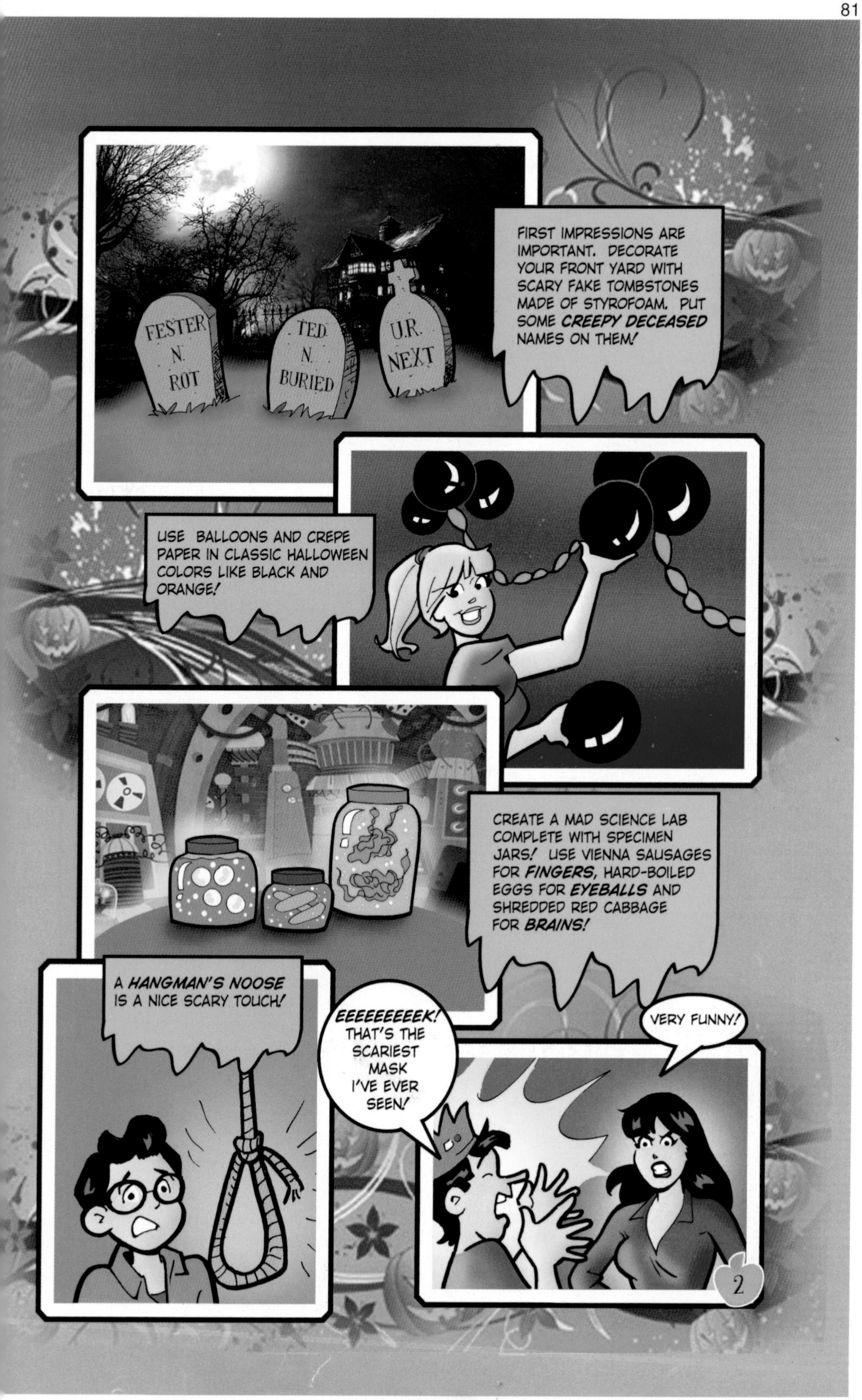
FESTER N. ROT
TED N. BURIED
U.R. NEXT
FIRST IMPRESSIONS ARE IMPORTANT. DECORATE YOUR FRONT YARD WITH SCARY FAKE TOMBSTONES MADE OF STYROFOAM. PUT SOME CREEPY DECEASED NAMES ON THEM!
USE BALLOONS AND CREPE PAPER IN CLASSIC HALLOWEEN COLORS LIKE BLACK AND ORANGE!
CREATE A MAD SCIENCE LAB COMPLETE WITH SPECIMEN JARS! USE VIENNA SAUSAGES FOR FINGERS, HARD-BOILED EGGS FOR EYEBALLS AND SHREDDED RED CABBAGE FOR BRAINS!
A HANGMAN'S NOOSE IS A NICE SCARY TOUCH!
EEEEEEEEEK! THAT'S THE SCARIEST MASK I'VE EVER SEEN!
VERY FUNNY!
2

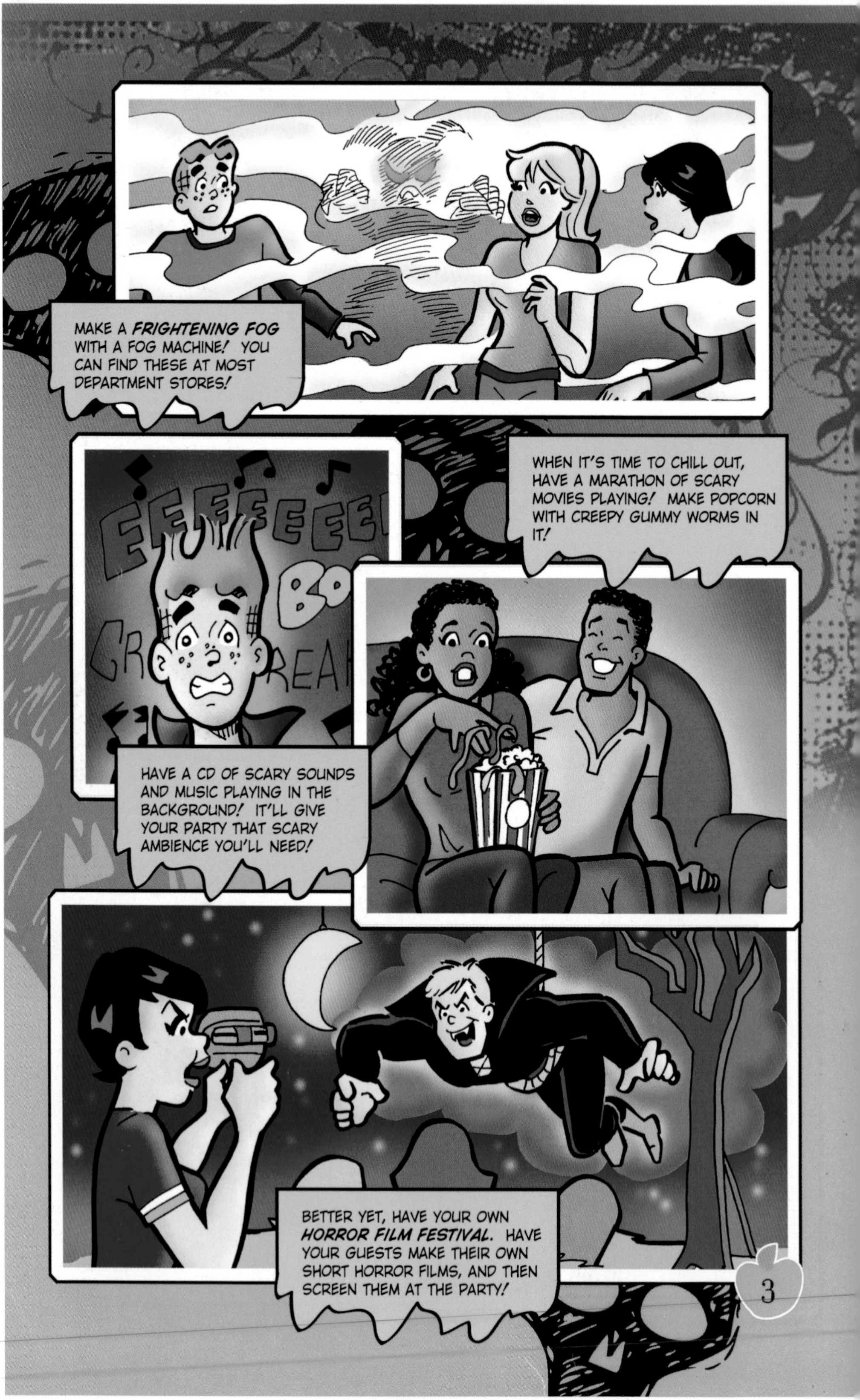
MAKE A ***FRIGHTENING FOG*** WITH A FOG MACHINE! YOU CAN FIND THESE AT MOST DEPARTMENT STORES!
HAVE A CD OF SCARY SOUNDS AND MUSIC PLAYING IN THE BACKGROUND! IT'LL GIVE YOUR PARTY THAT SCARY AMBIENCE YOU'LL NEED!
WHEN IT'S TIME TO CHILL OUT, HAVE A MARATHON OF SCARY MOVIES PLAYING! MAKE POPCORN WITH CREEPY GUMMY WORMS IN IT!
BETTER YET, HAVE YOUR OWN ***HORROR FILM FESTIVAL.*** HAVE YOUR GUESTS MAKE THEIR OWN SHORT HORROR FILMS, AND THEN SCREEN THEM AT THE PARTY!
3

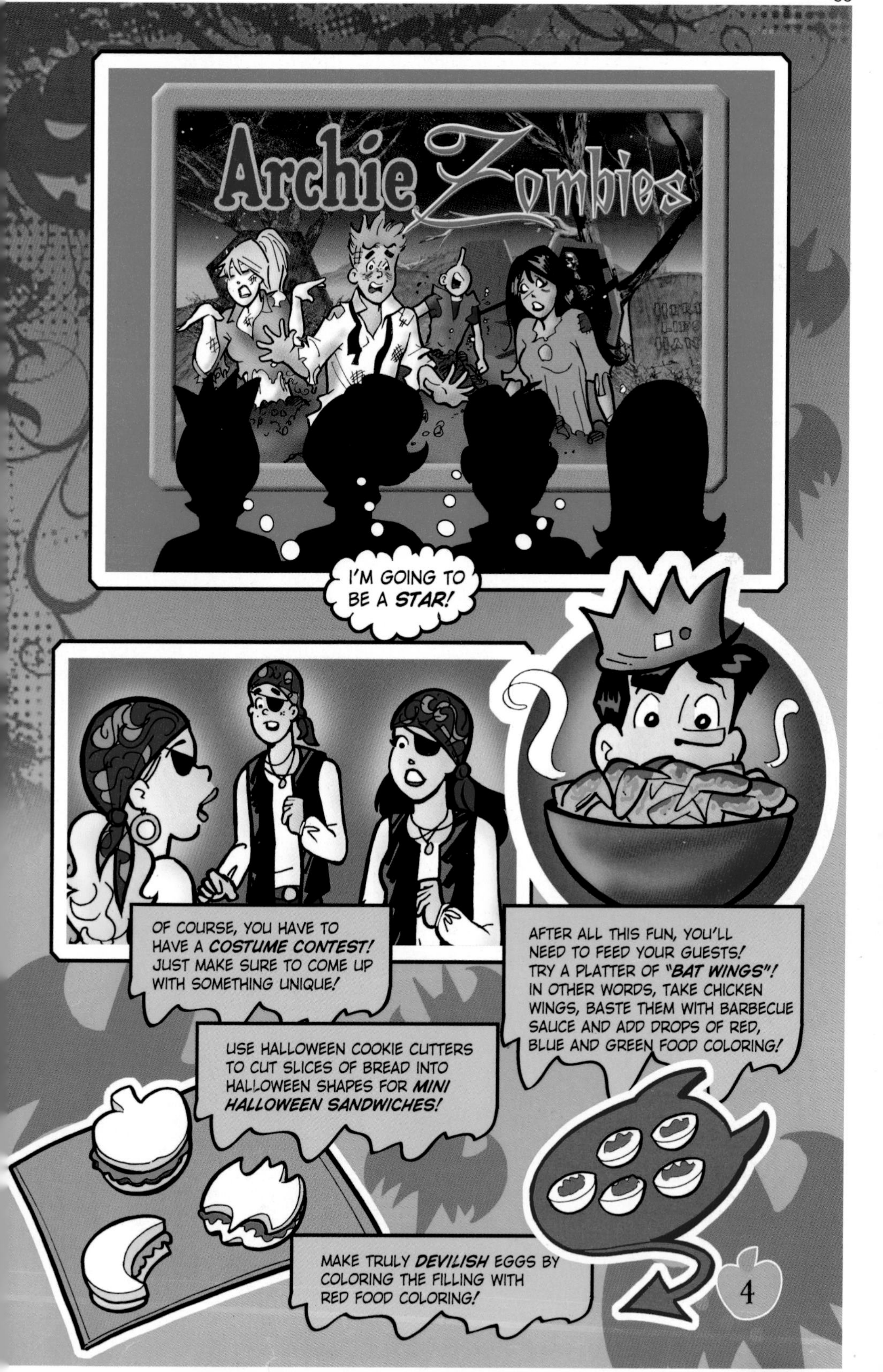
Archie Zombies
I'M GOING TO BE A STAR!
OF COURSE, YOU HAVE TO HAVE A COSTUME CONTEST! JUST MAKE SURE TO COME UP WITH SOMETHING UNIQUE!
AFTER ALL THIS FUN, YOU'LL NEED TO FEED YOUR GUESTS! TRY A PLATTER OF "BAT WINGS"! IN OTHER WORDS, TAKE CHICKEN WINGS, BASTE THEM WITH BARBECUE SAUCE AND ADD DROPS OF RED, BLUE AND GREEN FOOD COLORING!
USE HALLOWEEN COOKIE CUTTERS TO CUT SLICES OF BREAD INTO HALLOWEEN SHAPES FOR MINI HALLOWEEN SANDWICHES!
MAKE TRULY DEVILISH EGGS BY COLORING THE FILLING WITH RED FOOD COLORING!
4

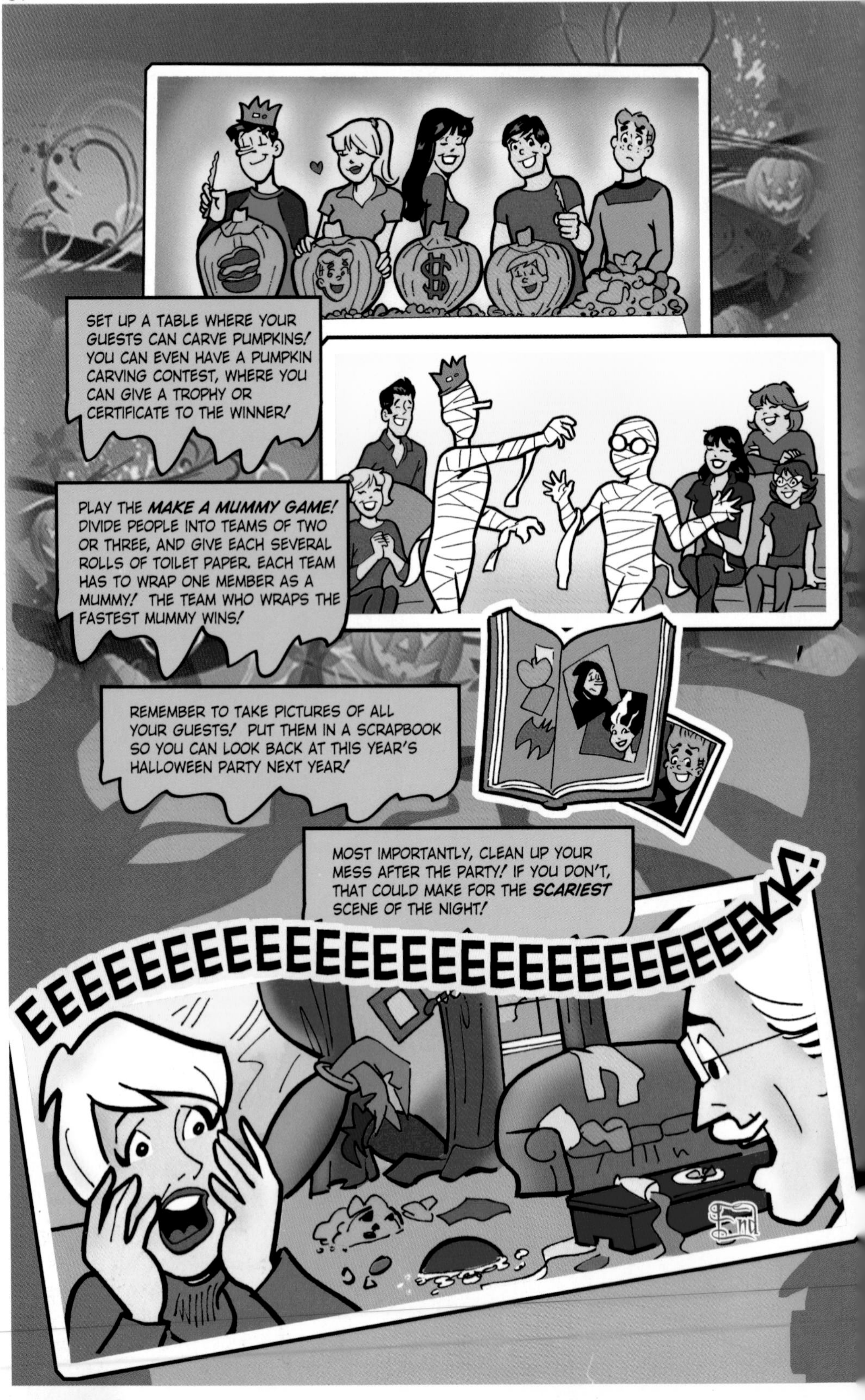
SET UP A TABLE WHERE YOUR GUESTS CAN CARVE PUMPKINS! YOU CAN EVEN HAVE A PUMPKIN CARVING CONTEST, WHERE YOU CAN GIVE A TROPHY OR CERTIFICATE TO THE WINNER!
PLAY THE *MAKE A MUMMY GAME!* DIVIDE PEOPLE INTO TEAMS OF TWO OR THREE, AND GIVE EACH SEVERAL ROLLS OF TOILET PAPER. EACH TEAM HAS TO WRAP ONE MEMBER AS A MUMMY! THE TEAM WHO WRAPS THE FASTEST MUMMY WINS!
REMEMBER TO TAKE PICTURES OF ALL YOUR GUESTS! PUT THEM IN A SCRAPBOOK SO YOU CAN LOOK BACK AT THIS YEAR'S HALLOWEEN PARTY NEXT YEAR!
MOST IMPORTANTLY, CLEAN UP YOUR MESS AFTER THE PARTY! IF YOU DON'T, THAT COULD MAKE FOR THE *SCARIEST* SCENE OF THE NIGHT!
EEEEEEEEEEEEEEEEEEEEEEEEEKK!

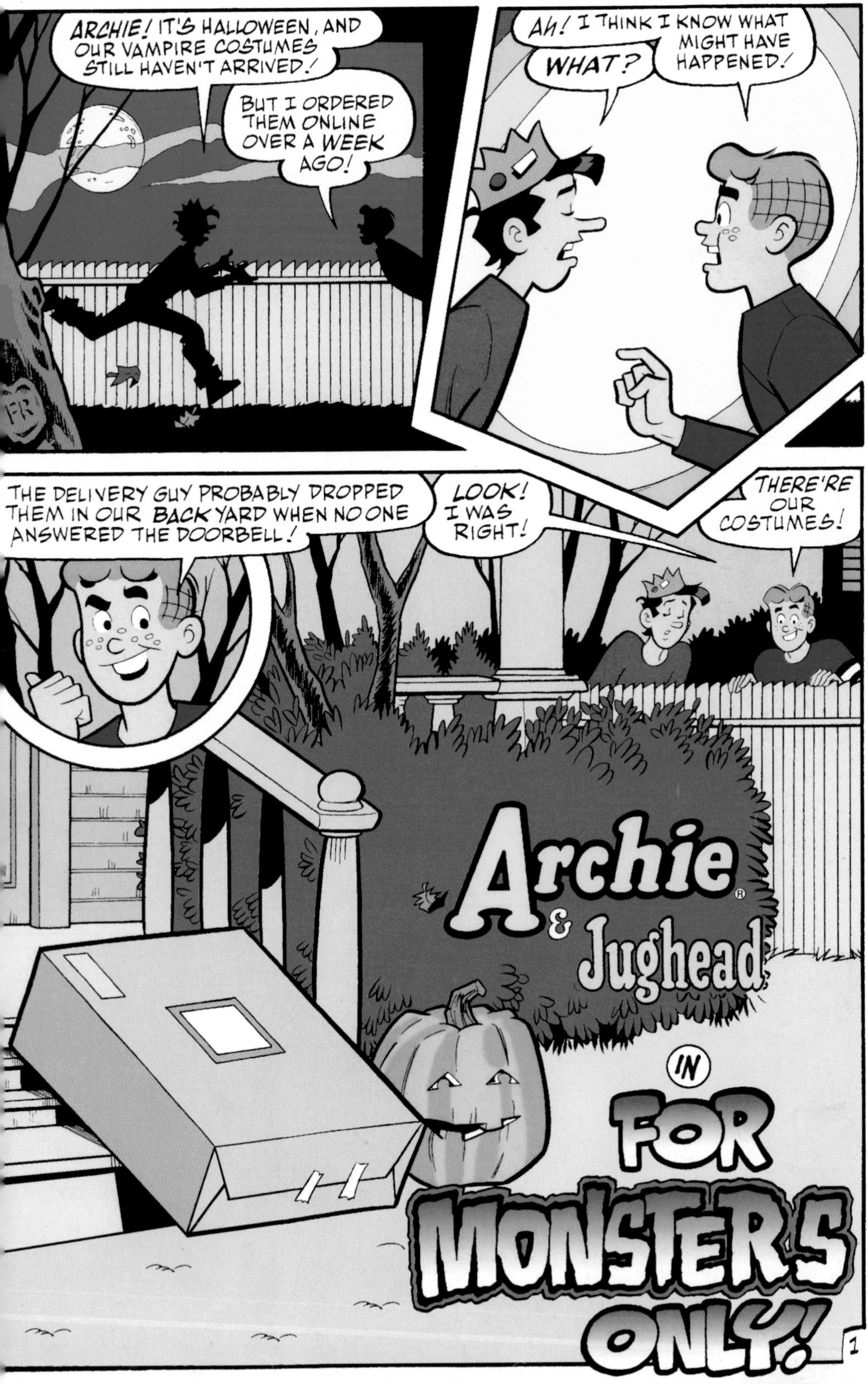
ARCHIE! IT'S HALLOWEEN, AND OUR VAMPIRE COSTUMES STILL HAVEN'T ARRIVED!
BUT I ORDERED THEM ONLINE OVER A WEEK AGO!
AH! I THINK I KNOW WHAT MIGHT HAVE HAPPENED!
WHAT?
THE DELIVERY GUY PROBABLY DROPPED THEM IN OUR BACK YARD WHEN NO ONE ANSWERED THE DOORBELL!
LOOK! I WAS RIGHT!
THERE'RE OUR COSTUMES!
Archie & Jughead
IN
FOR MONSTERS ONLY!
1

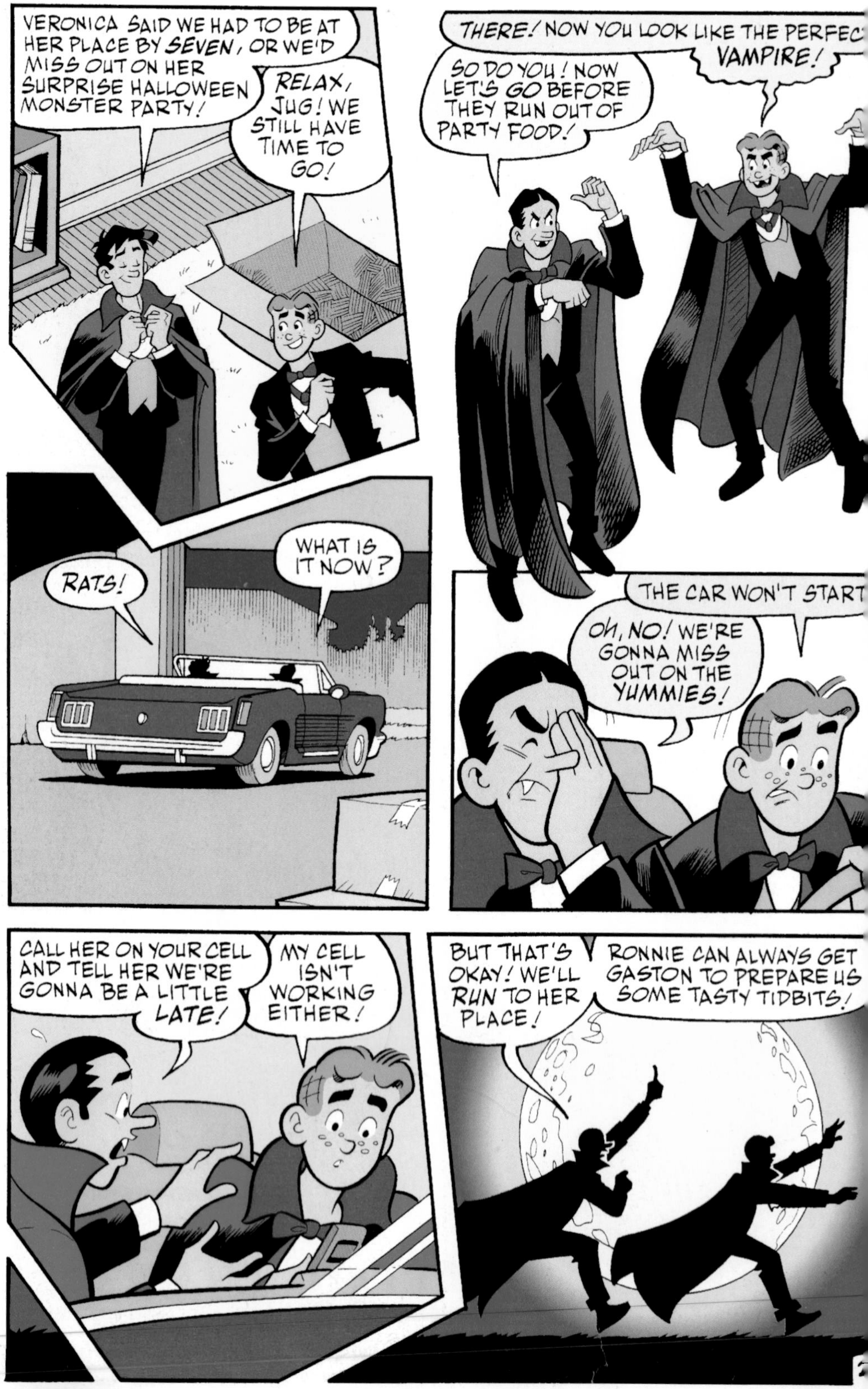
VERONICA SAID WE HAD TO BE AT HER PLACE BY SEVEN, OR WE'D MISS OUT ON HER SURPRISE HALLOWEEN MONSTER PARTY!
RELAX, JUG! WE STILL HAVE TIME TO GO!
THERE! NOW YOU LOOK LIKE THE PERFECT VAMPIRE!
SO DO YOU! NOW LET'S GO BEFORE THEY RUN OUT OF PARTY FOOD!
RATS!
WHAT IS IT NOW?
THE CAR WON'T START
OH, NO! WE'RE GONNA MISS OUT ON THE YUMMIES!
CALL HER ON YOUR CELL AND TELL HER WE'RE GONNA BE A LITTLE LATE!
MY CELL ISN'T WORKING EITHER!
BUT THAT'S OKAY! WE'LL RUN TO HER PLACE!
RONNIE CAN ALWAYS GET GASTON TO PREPARE US SOME TASTY TIDBITS!

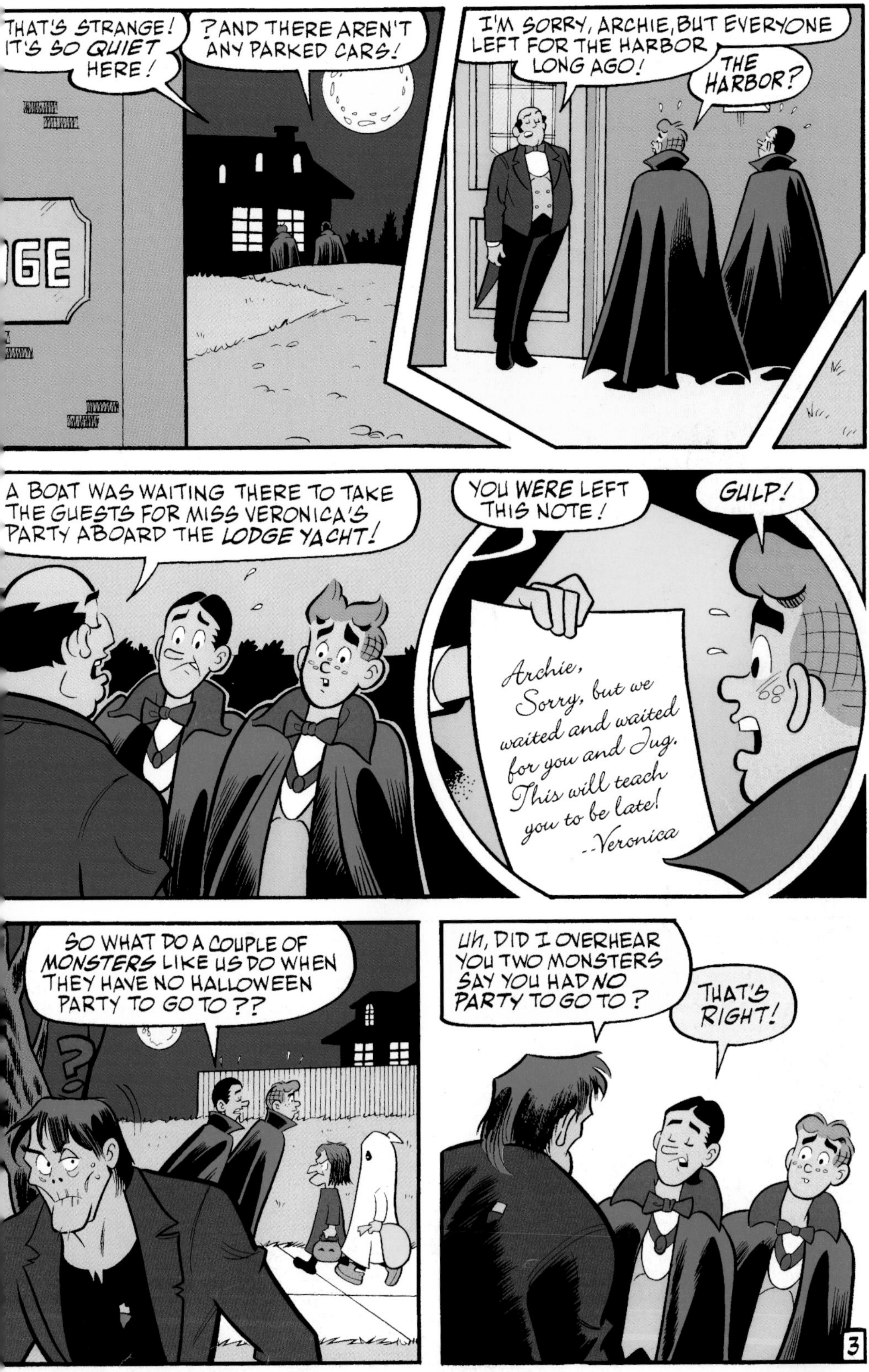
THAT'S STRANGE! IT'S SO QUIET HERE!
? AND THERE AREN'T ANY PARKED CARS!
I'M SORRY, ARCHIE, BUT EVERYONE LEFT FOR THE HARBOR LONG AGO!
THE HARBOR?
A BOAT WAS WAITING THERE TO TAKE THE GUESTS FOR MISS VERONICA'S PARTY ABOARD THE LODGE YACHT!
YOU WERE LEFT THIS NOTE!
GULP!
Archie,
Sorry, but we waited and waited for you and Jug. This will teach you to be late!
--Veronica
SO WHAT DO A COUPLE OF MONSTERS LIKE US DO WHEN THEY HAVE NO HALLOWEEN PARTY TO GO TO??
UH, DID I OVERHEAR YOU TWO MONSTERS SAY YOU HAD NO PARTY TO GO TO?
THAT'S RIGHT!
3

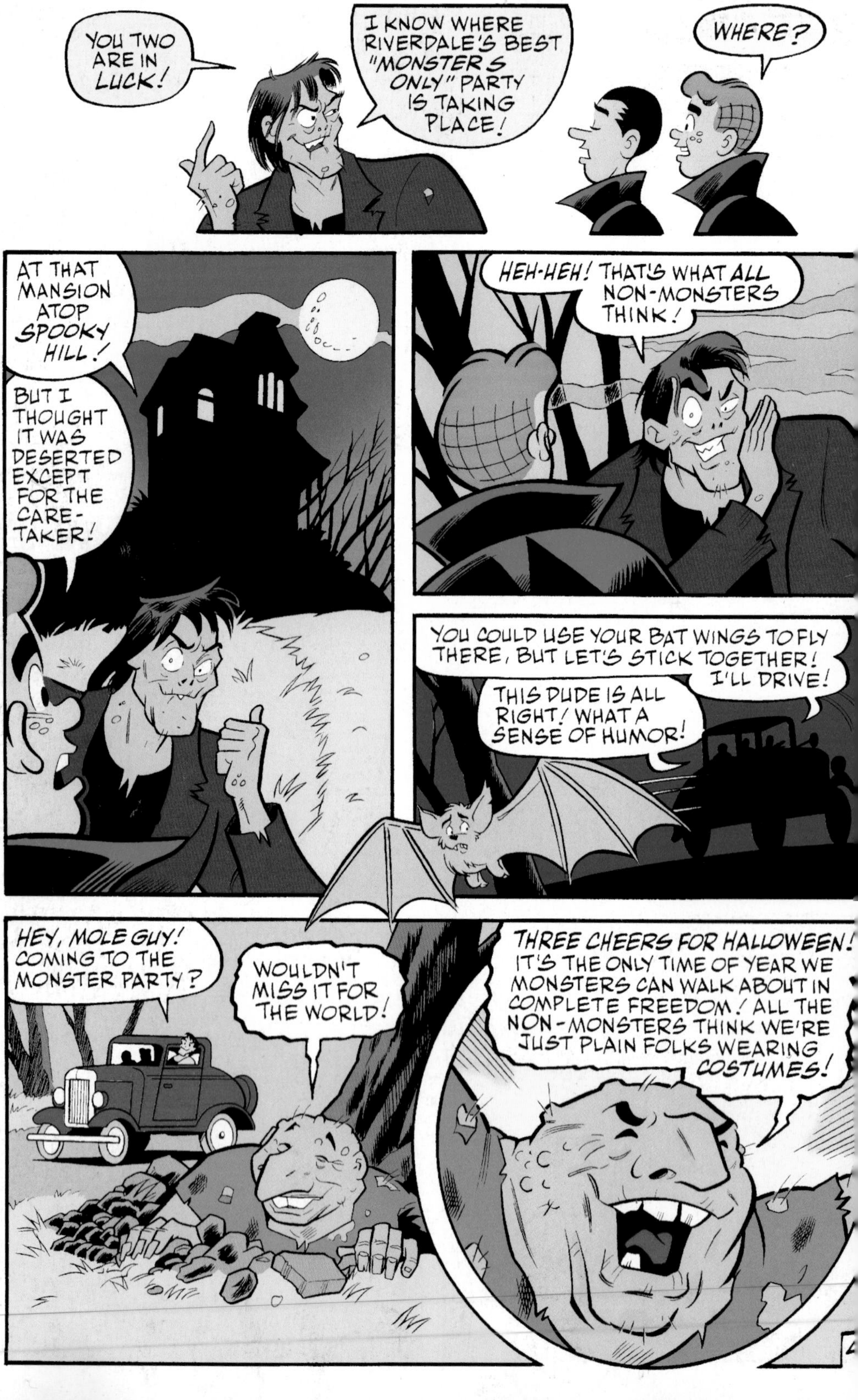
YOU TWO ARE IN LUCK!
I KNOW WHERE RIVERDALE'S BEST "MONSTERS ONLY" PARTY IS TAKING PLACE!
WHERE?
AT THAT MANSION ATOP SPOOKY HILL!
BUT I THOUGHT IT WAS DESERTED EXCEPT FOR THE CARE-TAKER!
HEH-HEH! THAT'S WHAT ALL NON-MONSTERS THINK!
YOU COULD USE YOUR BAT WINGS TO FLY THERE, BUT LET'S STICK TOGETHER! I'LL DRIVE!
THIS DUDE IS ALL RIGHT! WHAT A SENSE OF HUMOR!
HEY, MOLE GUY! COMING TO THE MONSTER PARTY?
WOULDN'T MISS IT FOR THE WORLD!
THREE CHEERS FOR HALLOWEEN! IT'S THE ONLY TIME OF YEAR WE MONSTERS CAN WALK ABOUT IN COMPLETE FREEDOM! ALL THE NON-MONSTERS THINK WE'RE JUST PLAIN FOLKS WEARING COSTUMES!

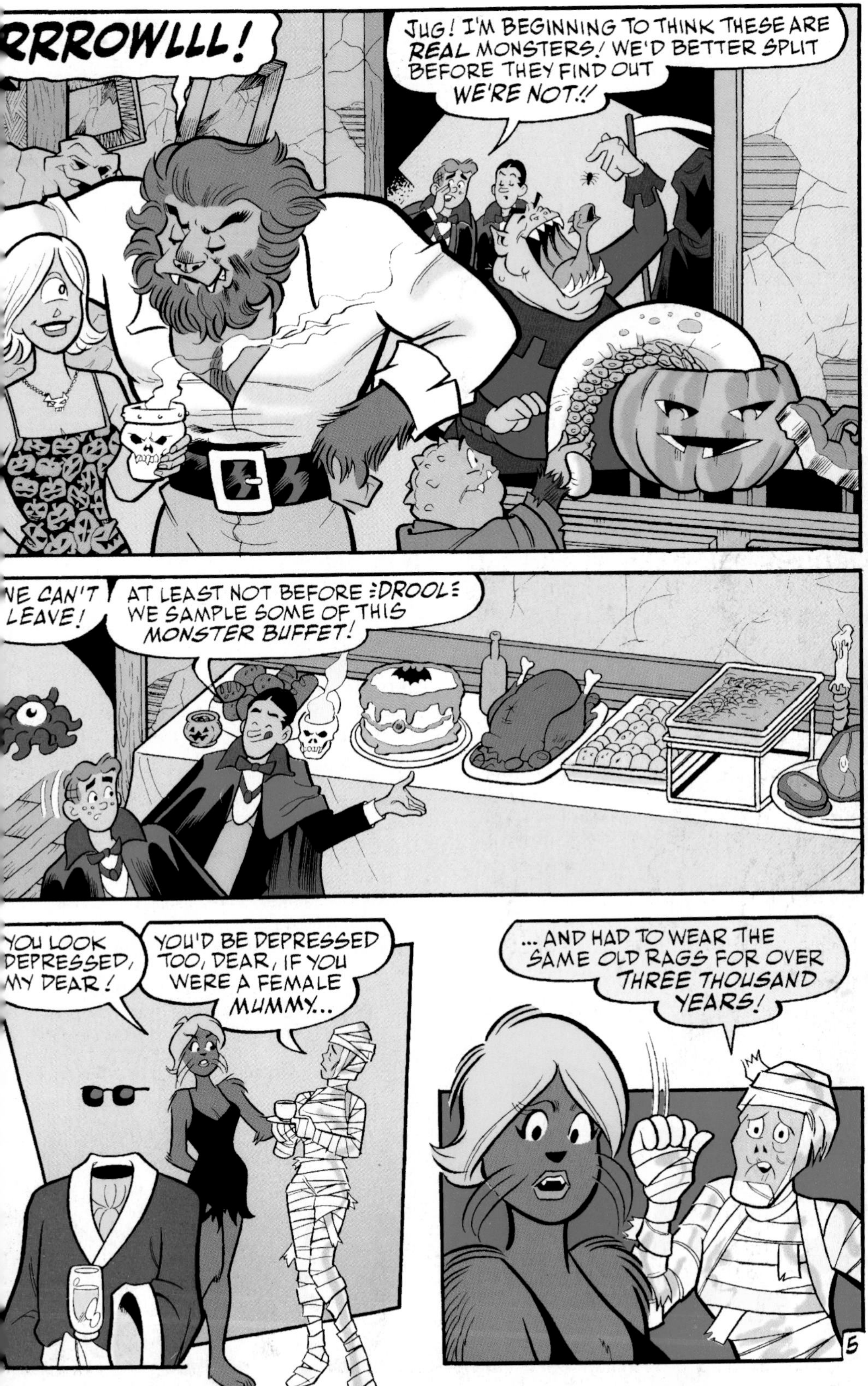
RRROWLLL!
JUG! I'M BEGINNING TO THINK THESE ARE REAL MONSTERS! WE'D BETTER SPLIT BEFORE THEY FIND OUT WE'RE NOT!!
WE CAN'T LEAVE!
AT LEAST NOT BEFORE =DROOL= WE SAMPLE SOME OF THIS MONSTER BUFFET!
YOU LOOK DEPRESSED, MY DEAR!
YOU'D BE DEPRESSED TOO, DEAR, IF YOU WERE A FEMALE MUMMY...
... AND HAD TO WEAR THE SAME OLD RAGS FOR OVER THREE THOUSAND YEARS!
5

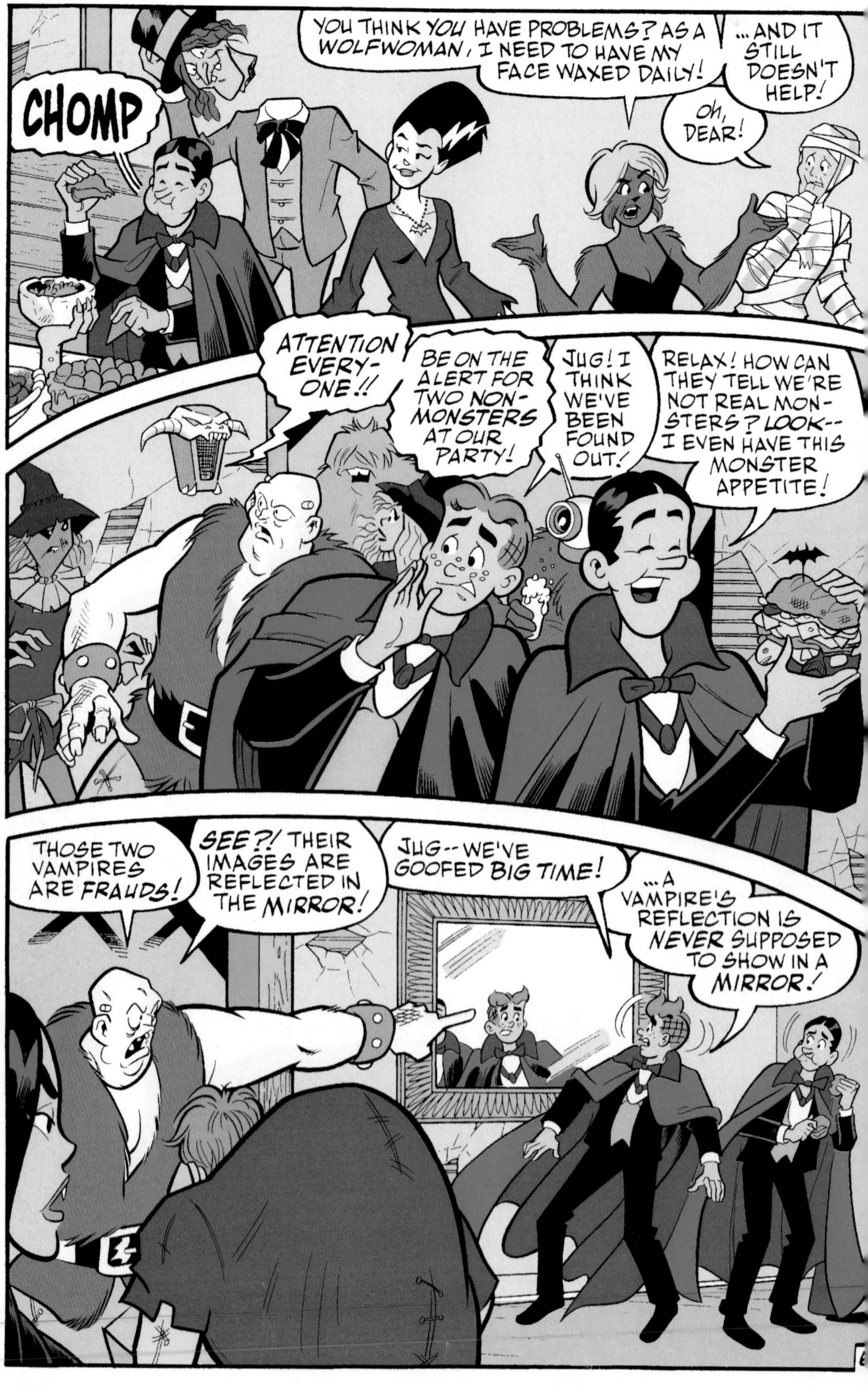
CHOMP
YOU THINK YOU HAVE PROBLEMS? AS A WOLFWOMAN, I NEED TO HAVE MY FACE WAXED DAILY!
...AND IT STILL DOESN'T HELP!
OH, DEAR!
ATTENTION EVERY-ONE!!
BE ON THE ALERT FOR TWO NON-MONSTERS AT OUR PARTY!
JUG! I THINK WE'VE BEEN FOUND OUT!
RELAX! HOW CAN THEY TELL WE'RE NOT REAL MON-STERS? LOOK-- I EVEN HAVE THIS MONSTER APPETITE!
THOSE TWO VAMPIRES ARE FRAUDS!
SEE?! THEIR IMAGES ARE REFLECTED IN THE MIRROR!
JUG-- WE'VE GOOFED BIG TIME!
...A VAMPIRE'S REFLECTION IS NEVER SUPPOSED TO SHOW IN A MIRROR!

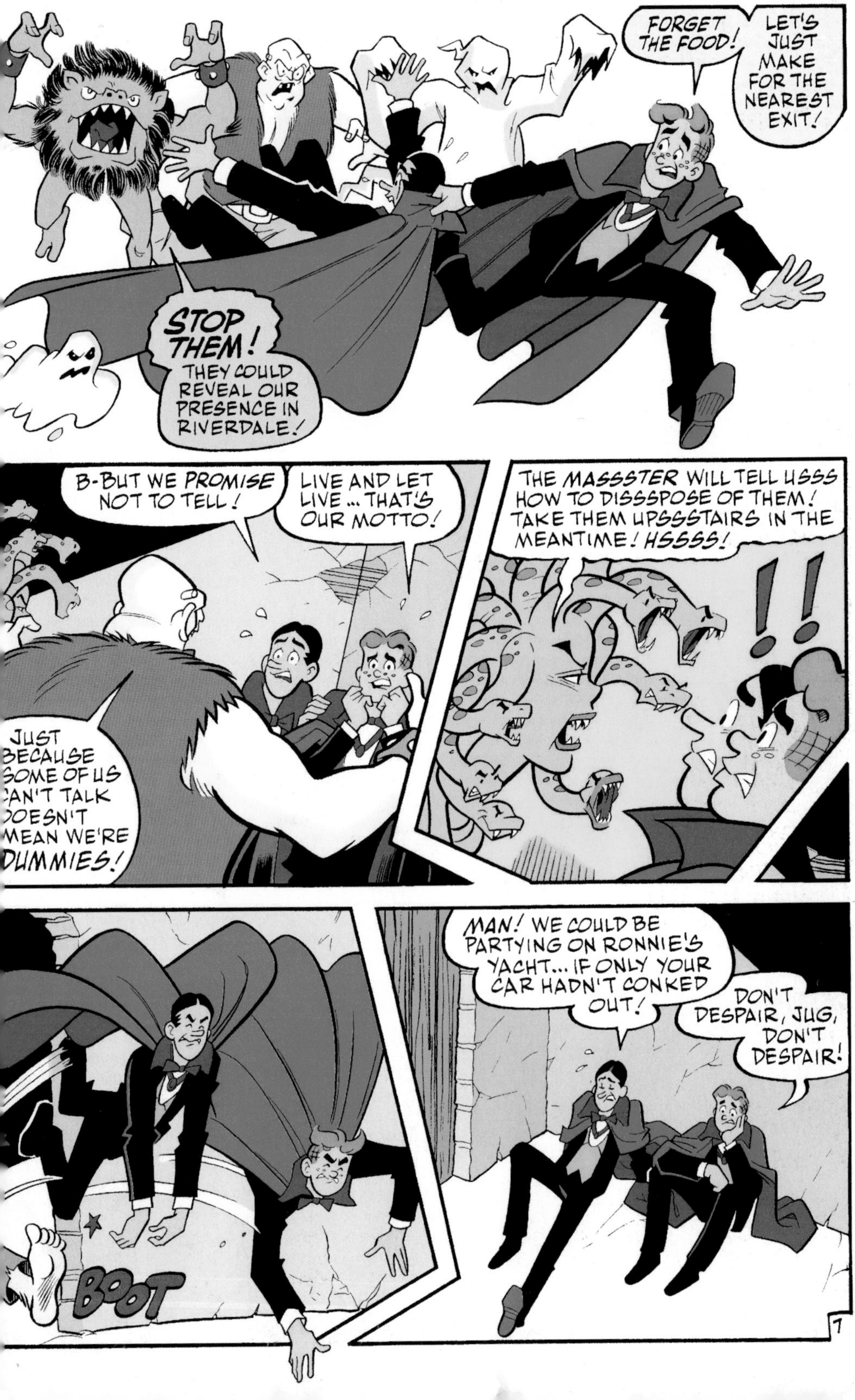
FORGET THE FOOD!
LET'S JUST MAKE FOR THE NEAREST EXIT!
STOP THEM! THEY COULD REVEAL OUR PRESENCE IN RIVERDALE!
B-BUT WE PROMISE NOT TO TELL!
LIVE AND LET LIVE ... THAT'S OUR MOTTO!
JUST BECAUSE SOME OF US CAN'T TALK DOESN'T MEAN WE'RE DUMMIES!
THE MASSSTER WILL TELL USSS HOW TO DISSSPOSE OF THEM! TAKE THEM UPSSSTAIRS IN THE MEANTIME! HSSSS!
!!
BOOT
MAN! WE COULD BE PARTYING ON RONNIE'S YACHT... IF ONLY YOUR CAR HADN'T CONKED OUT!
DON'T DESPAIR, JUG, DON'T DESPAIR!
7

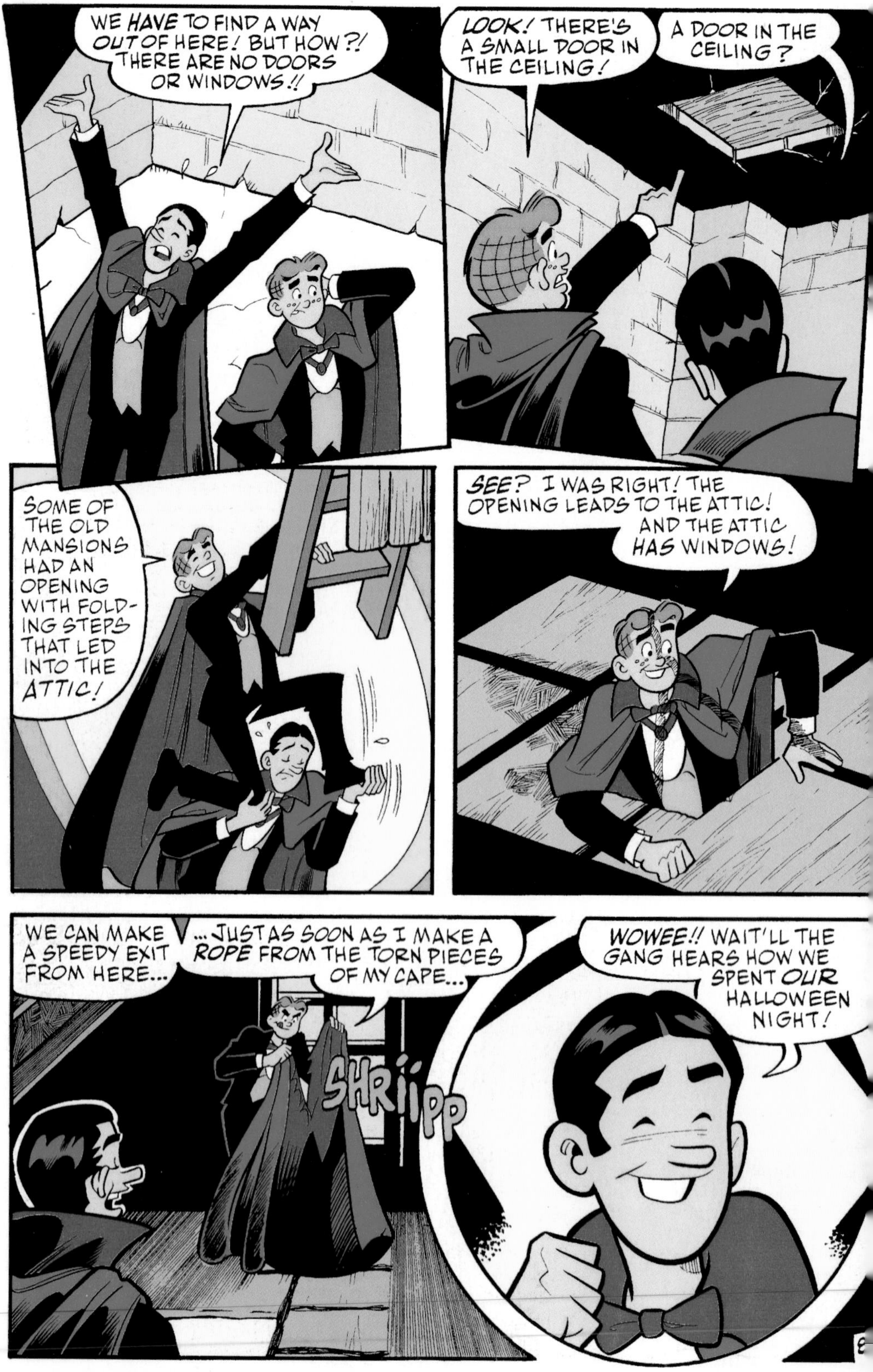
WE HAVE TO FIND A WAY OUT OF HERE! BUT HOW?! THERE ARE NO DOORS OR WINDOWS!!
LOOK! THERE'S A SMALL DOOR IN THE CEILING!
A DOOR IN THE CEILING?
SOME OF THE OLD MANSIONS HAD AN OPENING WITH FOLD-ING STEPS THAT LED INTO THE ATTIC!
SEE? I WAS RIGHT! THE OPENING LEADS TO THE ATTIC! AND THE ATTIC HAS WINDOWS!
WE CAN MAKE A SPEEDY EXIT FROM HERE...
...JUST AS SOON AS I MAKE A ROPE FROM THE TORN PIECES OF MY CAPE...
SHRIIPP
WOWEE!! WAIT'LL THE GANG HEARS HOW WE SPENT OUR HALLOWEEN NIGHT!

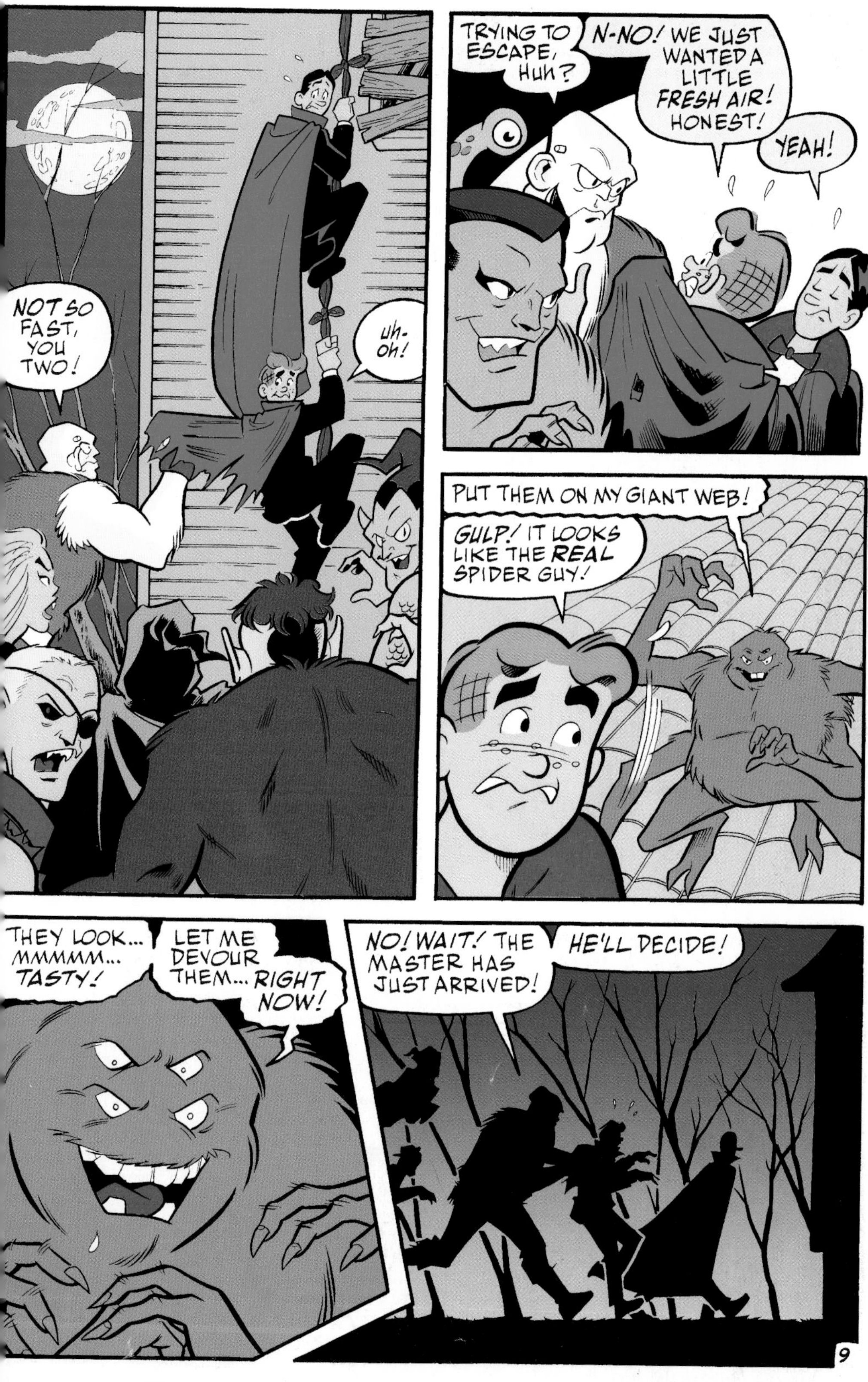
NOT SO FAST, YOU TWO!
uh-oh!
TRYING TO ESCAPE, HUH?
N-NO! WE JUST WANTED A LITTLE FRESH AIR! HONEST!
YEAH!
PUT THEM ON MY GIANT WEB!
GULP! IT LOOKS LIKE THE REAL SPIDER GUY!
THEY LOOK... MMMMM... TASTY!
LET ME DEVOUR THEM... RIGHT NOW!
NO! WAIT! THE MASTER HAS JUST ARRIVED!
HE'LL DECIDE!
9

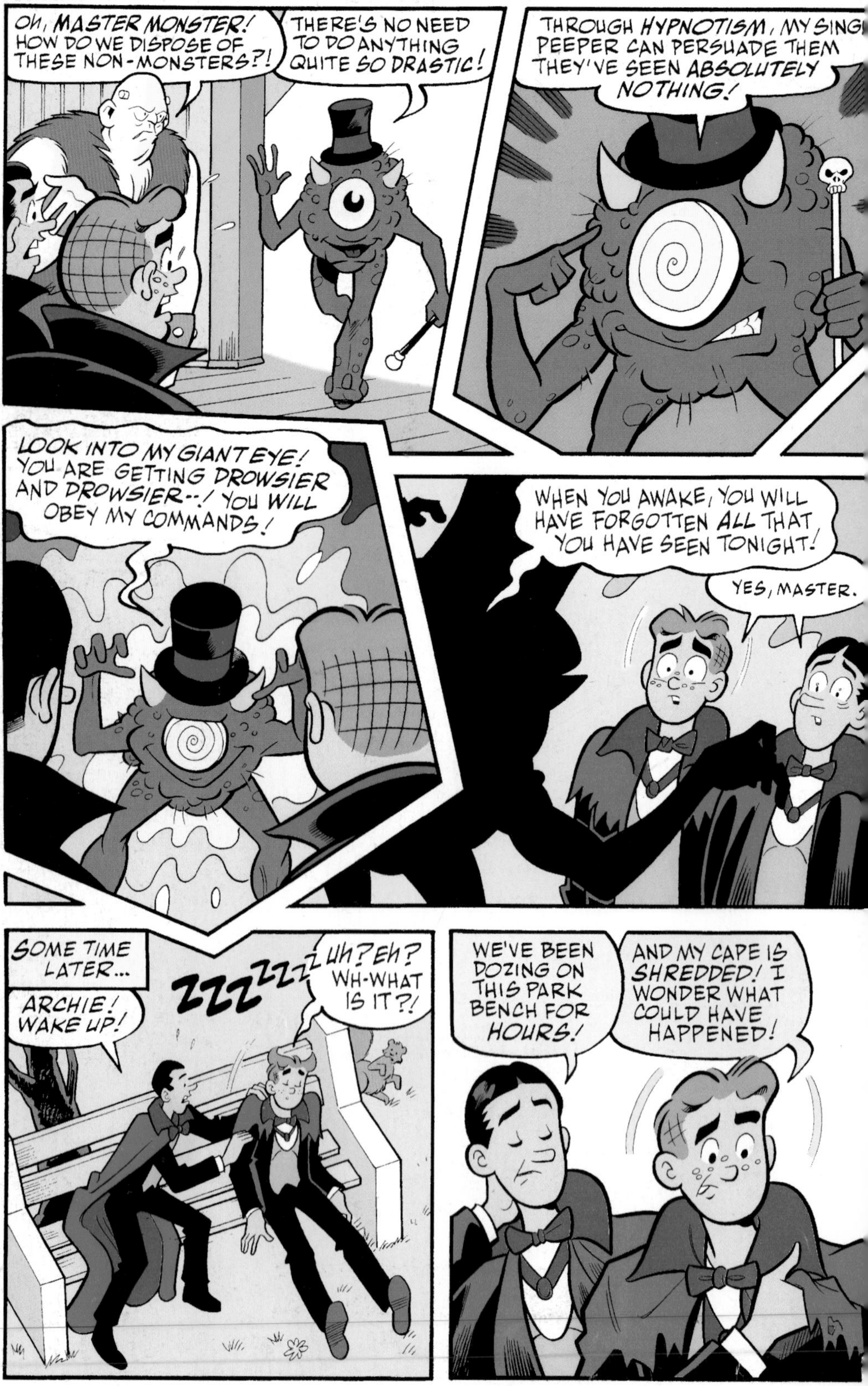
OH, MASTER MONSTER! HOW DO WE DISPOSE OF THESE NON-MONSTERS?!
THERE'S NO NEED TO DO ANYTHING QUITE SO DRASTIC!
THROUGH HYPNOTISM, MY SING PEEPER CAN PERSUADE THEM THEY'VE SEEN ABSOLUTELY NOTHING!
LOOK INTO MY GIANT EYE! YOU ARE GETTING DROWSIER AND DROWSIER--! YOU WILL OBEY MY COMMANDS!
WHEN YOU AWAKE, YOU WILL HAVE FORGOTTEN ALL THAT YOU HAVE SEEN TONIGHT!
YES, MASTER.
SOME TIME LATER...
ARCHIE! WAKE UP!
ZZZZZZZ
UH? EH? WH-WHAT IS IT?!
WE'VE BEEN DOZING ON THIS PARK BENCH FOR HOURS!
AND MY CAPE IS SHREDDED! I WONDER WHAT COULD HAVE HAPPENED!

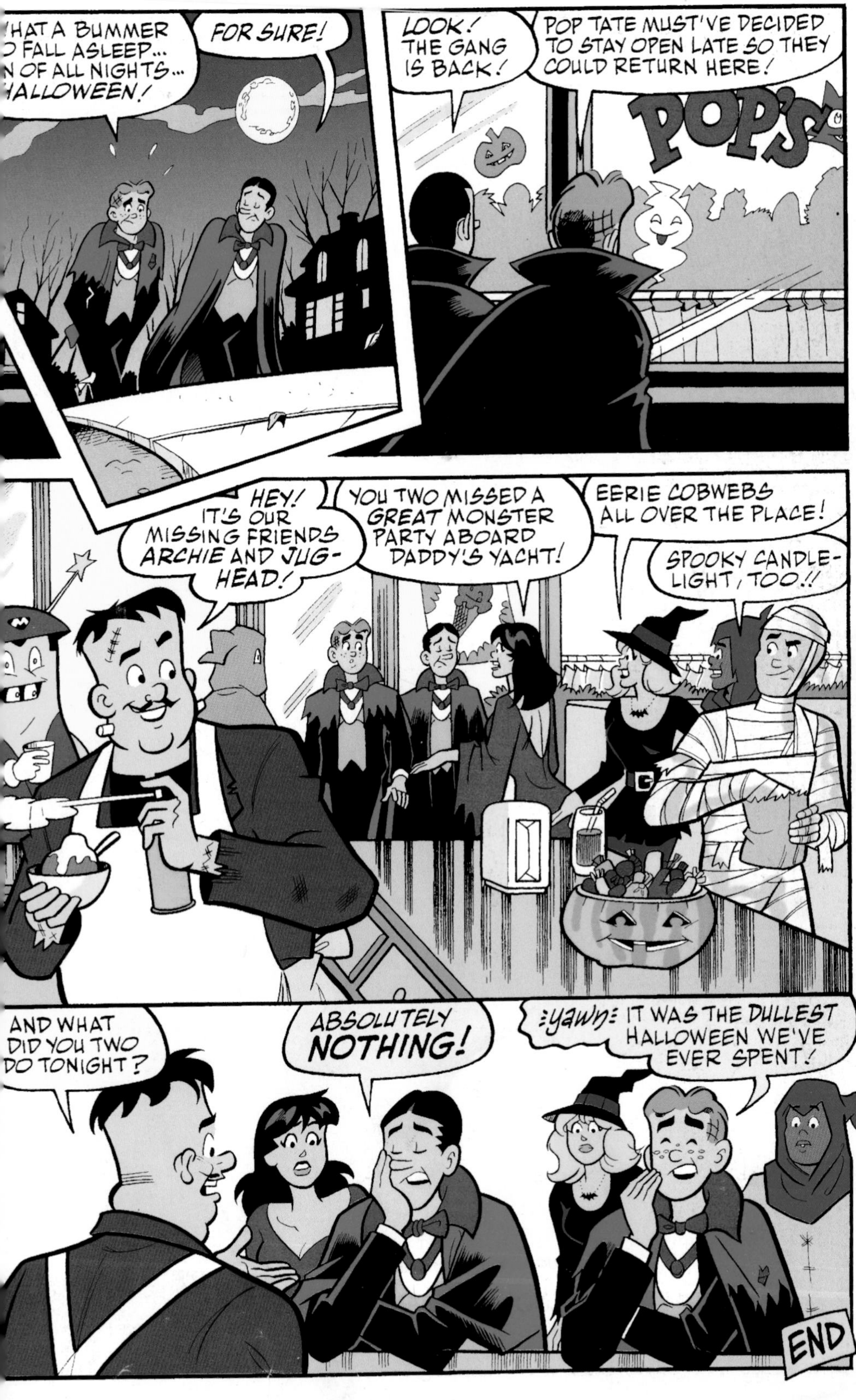
HAT A BUMMER
FALL ASLEEP...
N OF ALL NIGHTS...
HALLOWEEN!
FOR SURE!
LOOK! THE GANG IS BACK!
POP TATE MUST'VE DECIDED TO STAY OPEN LATE SO THEY COULD RETURN HERE!
POP'S
HEY! IT'S OUR MISSING FRIENDS ARCHIE AND JUG-HEAD!
YOU TWO MISSED A GREAT MONSTER PARTY ABOARD DADDY'S YACHT!
EERIE COBWEBS ALL OVER THE PLACE!
SPOOKY CANDLE-LIGHT, TOO!!
AND WHAT DID YOU TWO DO TONIGHT?
ABSOLUTELY NOTHING!
yawn IT WAS THE DULLEST HALLOWEEN WE'VE EVER SPENT!
END

There's nothing scary about thes
great Archie Comics graphic novels

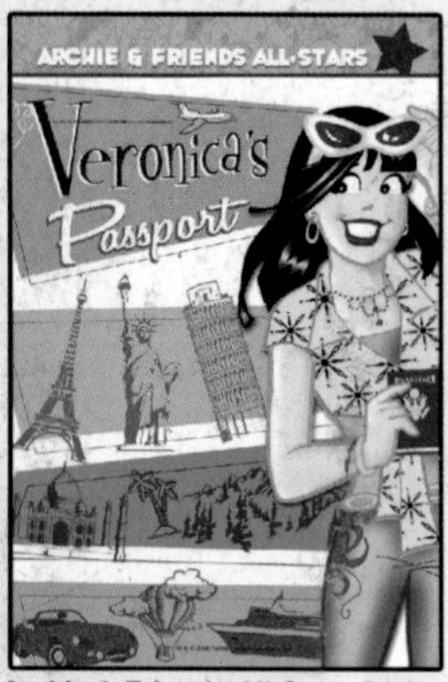
ARCHIE & FRIENDS ALL-STARS
Veronica's
Passport

Archie & Friends All Stars Series: Veronica's Passport

Pack your bags and take a trip across the globe with the trendiest traveller around, Veronica Lodge.

ISBN: 978-1-879794-43-6

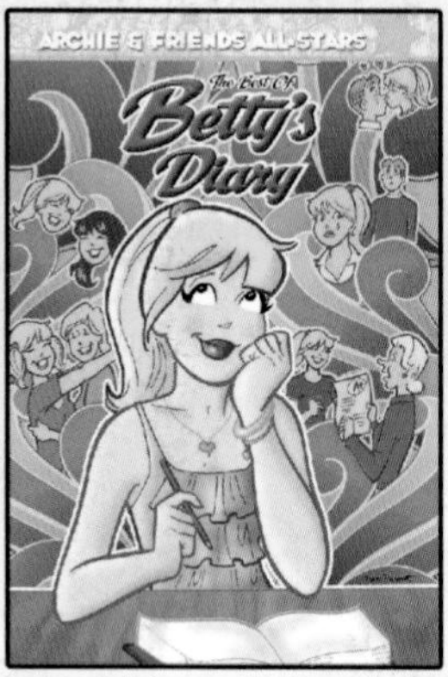
ARCHIE & FRIENDS ALL-STARS
The Best Of
Betty's
Diary

Archie & Friends All Stars Series: The Best of Betty's Diary

Everyone thinks they know Betty Cooper, but even the girl next door has some secrets of her own.

ISBN: 978-1-879794-46-7

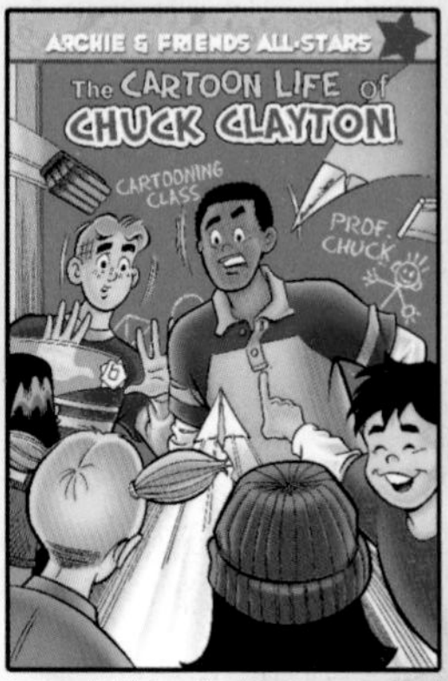
ARCHIE & FRIENDS ALL-STARS
The CARTOON LIFE of
CHUCK CLAYTON
CARTOONING CLASS
PROF. CHUCK

Archie & Friends All Stars Series: The Cartoon Life of Chuck Clayto

Go on a wild ride where life imitates art, and the other way around with Riverdale's own Chuck Clayton!

ISBN: 978-1-879794-48-1

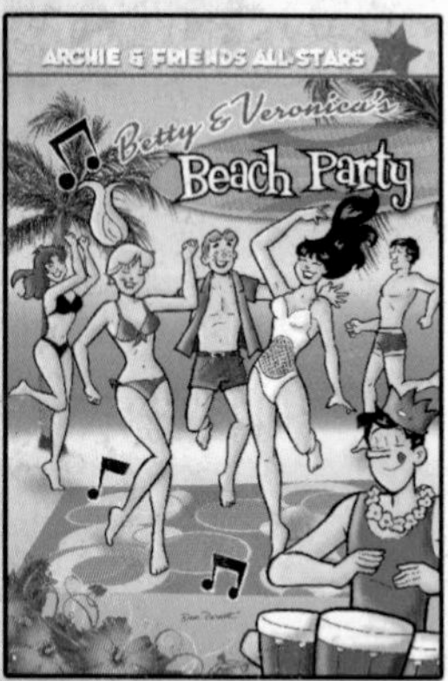
ARCHIE & FRIENDS ALL-STARS
Betty & Veronica's
Beach Party

Archie & Friends All Stars Series: Betty & Veronica's Beach Party

Grab your surfboard and put on your swimsuit because the girls of summer are back and ready to party!

ISBN: 978-1-879794-50-4

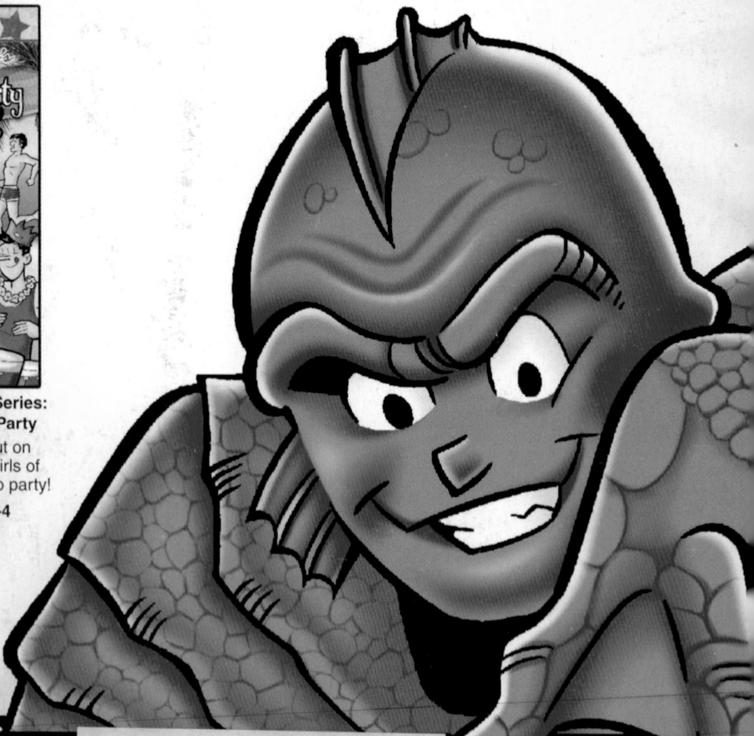

AVAILABLE AT YOUR LOCAL
COMICS SHOP OR BOOKSTORE!
ALSO AVAILABLE ONLINE AT ARCHIECOMICS.COM

ARCHIECOMICS.COM